# No Fooling Around

Talia Hunter

# Chapter One

## Asher

My new neighbor was a big problem.

And it wasn't because she was the most beautiful woman I'd ever seen.

My problem with her had nothing to do with how spectacular she looked in an emerald-green swimsuit that made her bronze skin glow. It wasn't that I found the freckles on her long, bare legs alluring, or that I enjoyed watching her sleek black hair swing across her shoulders as she walked. And it wasn't anything to do with the stupendously ugly dog by her side.

My problem was that she was there at all, strolling gracefully along the deck of the house next door. I had big plans for that house, and it was supposed to be empty.

So what was she doing there?

"Who's that, Asher?" asked my twin brother Kade, walking out of the house to join me on my back deck.

Then he jerked to a halt, noticing the animal next to her. "Whoa. Is that a dog?"

"It's a Neopolitan Mastiff." I shifted on my chair, a little hot even though my outdoor table and chairs were positioned under the overhang of the roof and I was sitting in the shade.

My brother was wearing board shorts and had a towel slung over his shoulder, clearly about to head onto the beach for a swim. Kade and his girlfriend Natalie had arrived late last night, and were staying in my spare bedroom for a few days before they headed back to LA. But this morning, there was no sign of Natalie. She was either still tucked up in bed or busy working on the novel she was writing.

Kade lifted a hand to shade his eyes before squinting at the dog next door. "Its skin is too big for its body. What do you think it weighs?"

"Around a hundred and eighty."

He let out a low whistle. "Its jowls must weigh fifty pounds on their own."

The dog in question plodded heavily along, accompanying my new neighbor as she headed toward the steps at the back of her deck that provided access to the white sand of San Dante beach. Though we could see her, she couldn't see us. Her deck was lower than ours, and there was a small privacy screen that shielded us. We could look all we liked, and she wouldn't know we were there.

"Seems she and I have the same idea," said Kade. "She's going for a swim too." He started to move, and I put up a hand to stop him.

"Wait. Don't follow her onto the beach yet. I don't want you to run into her."

Kade's eyebrows shot up. "Why not? Who is she?"

"I haven't been able to find out, but she's been living there for eighteen days. She has to be connected to the house's previous occupant."

His eyes widened. "You think she could be a friend of Santino's?" He sounded shocked. Probably because my old neighbor, Santino Martin, was a scum-sucking drug dealer, and a year ago we'd watched with satisfaction as the police charged into his house to arrest him. We'd helped put Santino behind bars where he belonged, and I hoped he'd rot in jail forever.

I nodded. "She must know him. Why else would she be staying in his house?"

My new neighbor said something to her dog, presumably telling it to stay put, then went out her back gate and started down the steps to the beach, her hips gently swaying as she descended. Her body was an awe-inspiringly perfect combination of rounded curves and long limbs, and I was mesmerized by the motion of her buttocks and legs. She glided like an ice skater, and despite my annoyance at her unwelcome presence, I couldn't have dragged my gaze from her movements if there were a gun to my head.

Kade seemed to be struck equally dumb. Even the woman's dog stared mournfully after her, its broad shoulders sagging as she vanished from view.

"I'm going for my swim now." Kade started toward

my back stairs, sounding far too eager for my liking, as though the woman was a drawcard instead of a danger.

"If you see her on the beach, stay away," I warned.

"But don't you want to know how she's connected to Santino? If I strike up a conversation, I could ask her." My prankster brother shot me a mischievous look over his shoulder that made my heart sink.

Kade didn't know the whole truth.

When he and I were sixteen, Mom had died from a drug overdose. A man called Four-Finger-Frankie had been her drug dealer, and Santino was Frankie's supplier. I blamed them both for her death. So when they'd turned up in San Dante, I'd figured out a way to bring them down. Thanks to me, they were both sitting in jail, awaiting trial.

Kade knew I'd bought this house because it was next to Santino's. And he knew I'd asked Mason to arrange for a police surveillance team to watch Santino from my spare bedroom so they could get the evidence they needed to arrest him. But he didn't know the rest of my plan—that I planned to make enough money from Santino's house that none of us would ever have to worry about our finances again.

My scheme was both devious and top secret. It was also precarious. I couldn't afford for anything to go wrong. Which was why I used a sharp tone with Kade now.

"There are plenty of other women on the beach you can talk to. Any friend of Santino's is no friend of ours."

"But you're single, and she's very attractive. There's no way you're not curious to find out more about her."

"Kade, don't do anything..." I broke off with a frustrated sound, because my brother was already hurrying down the steps, heading toward the sand.

Frowning, I watched him go. We were fraternal twins, not identical. We had a similar build, but his hair was lighter than mine, a mid-brown that was hard to keep track of as he walked through the groups of sunbathers and people exercising on the beach.

If only Kade were more predictable. He had his own TV show, and not only was he a celebrity, he had a silver tongue and could talk anyone into anything. Now that he was happily dating the woman he'd been in love with for years, he *should* be less of a wild card. But if he decided to use his considerable charm on my new neighbor, who knew what could happen?

I was considering going after him and tackling him to the ground, when a lithe black shape appeared from the side of the deck and slunk through the shadows, making her way toward me. It was a black cat. *My* black cat. And she had something dangling from her mouth.

It didn't take great powers of deduction to guess she was bringing me a pair of women's panties.

Nemesis was a compulsive kleptomaniac and talented cat burglar. In the three years since I'd adopted her, she'd been breaking into people's houses and bringing home trophies—mostly socks, stuffed toys, and slippers. Once she'd proudly dropped a pair of pink fluffy handcuffs at my feet.

But in the eighteen days since my new neighbor had moved into the house next door, her panties had become my cat's favorite prey. The pair Nemesis dropped in front of me this time were black silk with delicate lace detailing. And after presenting them, Nemesis let out a loud, deep purr and wove herself around my legs, her tail held high.

"What did I tell you about staying out of the house next door?" I said, refusing to pet her. Receiving regular stolen panty deliveries wasn't my idea of keeping a low profile and limiting contact with my mysterious neighbor. Nemesis seemed determined to be as difficult as Kade, and I couldn't afford to let either of them mess up my scheme.

Sighing, I scooped the panties up.

They rustled.

There was a piece of paper pinned inside them. A note, written in perfect cursive handwriting that was just as beautiful as the panties themselves.

In even, curved letters, the note said: *Stop stealing my panties, you perv.*

My first reaction was to laugh. Until it hit me that my beautiful neighbor must actually think I was a creep who got off on panty pilfering. She clearly hadn't seen Nemesis in action and was picturing a weirdo who was stealing her panties for his own sexual gratification, presumably to do something repugnant that involved tossing his egg salad onto them.

Unacceptable.

Though I didn't want to have anything to do with my

new neighbor, how could I let her go on thinking I was a pervert?

Taking the panties inside, I added them into the box of Nemesis's trophies I kept in the hall closet. I'd given up looking for the owners of my cat's stolen goods, but didn't throw the items away because people occasionally came looking for them.

I didn't put my neighbor's handwritten note into the box with her panties. Instead, I took it into my office, where I found a graphite pencil. On the note's blank side, I drew a sketch of Nemesis carrying a pair of panties. Then I switched to a regular ballpoint to write a short explanation under the drawing.

*'Nemesis by name, nemesis by nature'.*

Before I could think better of it, I went outside to drop the anonymous note into my neighbor's mailbox. When she saw it, she'd know a cat was the thief. Hopefully she'd secure her house to stop Nemesis from sneaking in and stealing from her, so I wouldn't have any more panties to deal with.

When I went back inside, I found Natalie, Kade's girlfriend, in the kitchen making herself a coffee. She was wearing sweatpants, a t-shirt, and bare feet, and her long brown hair was messy. When she picked up the mug to take a sip of coffee, steam fogged her thick glasses for a moment.

"Morning, Asher." She blinked sleepy blue eyes at me from behind the fog.

"Morning." I gave her a friendly nod. Natalie was a nice person, and my brother was noticeably happier when he was with her, his ever-present smile becoming more genuine. I'd given their relationship my seal of approval.

"Has Kade gone for a swim?" she asked. "I was still dozing when he got up. He told me what he was doing, but I was too sleepy to listen."

I nodded. "He hasn't been gone long. It's not too late to join him. In fact, I think you should. It's a pleasant morning. Perfect for swimming." I had an ulterior motive for coaxing her. If Natalie joined Kade on the beach, it'd distract him from searching for my neighbor and making trouble.

"Sounds lovely, but I'd better get some work done while Kade's not here. I promised myself I'd write an entire chapter today." Coffee in hand, and apparently immune to my persuasion, she padded back to the bedroom.

The aroma of fresh coffee that went with her made me decide to make myself a second cup. Then I took it into my home office to drink it at my desk, in front of my computer, while I adjusted the calculations in my business's latest financial spreadsheets.

But I'd barely started tweaking the figures when my phone rang with an unknown number. When I answered it, a woman's voice came over the line.

"Asher Lennox? This is Ying Lee from the U.S. Attorney's Office. We're prosecuting the Santino Martin case. We have you listed as a possible witness, and I'm calling to follow up. Are you still available to testify?"

I recognized her voice. I'd spoken to her after Santino's arraignment to let her know I'd seen some of his illegal actions from my window before the surveillance team had arrived to take over.

"We probably won't need your testimony," Ms. Lee went on. "But we'd like to know we can call on you if we do."

"Of course." I liked the idea of staring Santino in the eye while I helped send him to jail. The only thing more satisfying would be if I could do the same thing to Four-Finger-Frankie. Frankie's trial would be a few weeks after Santino's, but seeing as I hadn't been able to spy on him the way I'd watched Santino, I'd have to trust the surveillance team had all the evidence they needed to send him away without any more help from me.

"The trial will start on the twenty-ninth," Ms. Lee said, unnecessarily. It was two weeks away, and I'd been counting down the days. "I'll be in touch with further information before then," she added.

"Wait," I said, before she could hang up. "A forfeiture notice has been registered against Santino's house. Can you tell me when the confiscation hearing will be scheduled?"

"Just a moment." In the pause before she spoke again, I heard her tapping on her keyboard as she looked it up on her computer. "Okay, I see the notice. If the defendant is found guilty, the confiscation hearing will be part of his sentencing and that's when his house will be seized."

Just as I'd expected. And according to my research, Santino had paid cash for his house and had no mortgage or other complications. It would be a straightforward seizure, so things should move quickly after his trial. The house was likely to be auctioned within a few weeks.

"Someone's living there," I said. "They moved into the house eighteen days ago. Is that legal?"

"Hmm," she said after a moment, clearly reading the information in front of her. "The defendant petitioned the court for access to the property. It was granted a month ago."

I thanked her and hung up, feeling dissatisfied. My contact in the Justice Department hadn't informed me, and I still didn't know who the stranger was, or why she was living next door. Not that it'd matter once the house was seized and the mystery woman was evicted.

Returning to my spreadsheets, I was fiddling with the figures and trying to work out how to improve them when I heard Kade coming back from the beach. Natalie was still in their bedroom, presumably hard at work on her novel, so I went to meet Kade in the kitchen. My brother's wet hair was sticking up in spikes, and he flashed me his charming, lazy grin. The grin made him look utterly unlike me, as though he was my opposite instead of my twin. It had won him millions of female fans and made his cooking show into a hit.

His fans had no idea what a trickster my brother could be, but I knew him well enough that the hint of smug satisfaction in his grin made me cross my arms and glower.

"What have you done?" I asked.

He took a glass out of the cupboard, deliberately taking his time. "Remember we talked about me making friends with your new neighbor, and you agreed it would be a good way to discover her connection to Santino?" He moved to the faucet to fill up the glass.

Sinking onto one of the kitchen stools, I dropped my head to rub the part of my forehead that was suddenly starting to ache. "Don't tell me you spoke to her." I groaned.

"Her name's Iola. She seems nice, and you're having dinner with her tomorrow night."

I jerked my face up. "What? *I'm* having dinner with her?"

"You're single, and she was open to a blind date. Luckily, she happened to be free tomorrow. There's no point in wasting time, right, Ash?" Though he was still at the sink, facing away from me, I could hear suppressed laughter in his voice.

My headache intensified. "Kade, I said to stay away from her."

"Huh. Did you?" He turned with his glass of water, his eyes wide and innocent. "Sometimes your instructions just fly out of my head. It's a character flaw, actually. Something I really need to work on." His mischievous grin crept back. Lifting the glass, he brandished it as though offering a toast. "Aren't you happy? I've scored you a hot date."

# Chapter Two

## Iola

Nemesis, huh? I studied the clever little drawing of a cat on the note I'd just brought inside from my mailbox, taking a few moments to admire it before I shook my head.

I didn't believe it for a second.

A cat couldn't be the underwear thief who'd been stealing panties from my washing line and the dresser in my bedroom. No cat could climb that high. No cat could break into my house. And no cat with any sense would go anywhere near Ruff.

My dog was lying on the floor next to my painting easel, chewing on a toy that used to be a giraffe. Though it was supposedly indestructible, Ruff had already chewed off its head and legs. Now it had just a long neck and body, and it was disturbing how much Ruff looked like she was chewing on a spotted vibrator.

Ruff was incredibly solid and her size was intimidating, even if her sagging skin gave her the air of a mournful monk. She might have slowed down a lot in the last few years, but she was still an excellent guard dog. No thieving cat could possibly get past her.

"Did you let a cat wander around?" I asked Ruff, just to make sure.

Ruff dropped the giraffe and lifted her giant head. Her eyes always drooped in the corners, and her floppy eyebrows formed a worried frown. But somehow she managed to give me a look that was even more sorrowful than usual, as though she was heartbroken I doubted her.

"Don't worry, I don't believe the thief could be feline," I told her. "No kitty would dare disrespect you like that."

Placated, Ruff dropped her head onto her paws, her jowls splaying so she looked like she was melting into the floor.

I moved to my easel to start mixing paints. It was time to concentrate on the painting I was trying to finish. I'd been working day and night, and this was the final painting in the series that would hopefully cover my bills that so badly needed paying. It just needed highlights and lowlights added to increase the contrast. Oh, and maybe a light wash over some of the deeper colors to make them more translucent.

I squeezed some white paint onto my palette, then hesitated. It was hard to focus on the colors I was supposed to be mixing when I kept glancing at the note I'd left on the little table that held my paints.

The person who'd sketched the cat had known what they were doing. The drawing was simple but beautiful, the cat's form captured in quick, efficient lines. Could Kade have drawn it? He was the only neighbor I'd met, but he was a chef, not an artist.

I still couldn't believe a famous TV star had introduced himself on the beach, then set me up with his brother. I wasn't nearly ready to go on a date, and if I hadn't been so star-struck and tongue-tied, I would have turned down the offer. But Kade had stunned me with his celebrity smile and overwhelming charm when he'd strode over to introduce himself and tell me he was staying next door. I'd barely managed to stutter my own name, and when he'd asked if I'd have dinner with his brother, somehow I'd found myself nodding.

In retrospect, it was a terrible idea. The last few weeks had been difficult enough without adding a blind date to the mix.

Still, after seven years trapped in a joyless marriage, I was trying to convince myself it would be okay. After all, Benedict had spent seven years whittling away at my confidence. This could be a chance to rebuild it, and to spread my wings a little. Going on a date with a mystery man was scary, and a risk, but it was just dinner. And if I let him know I wasn't interested in anything more than a meal, surely he'd have to accept that. Not all men were like Benedict.

I realized I was still staring at the note instead of mixing paints, and gave myself an impatient mental shake. But to be able to forget about it, I'd have to send the thief a reply.

Grabbing a fresh piece of paper, I drew Ruff in cartoon style, exaggerating the solid squareness of her head and shoulders, and giving her a mean stare. I drew her snarling, with drool dripping from her huge jowls and a pair of panties under one paw.

Underneath the drawing, I wrote:
*Bite wounds are red,*
*Bruises are blue,*
*I swallow kitties whole,*
*But thieving perverts get chewed.*

Okay, I wasn't Doctor Seuss. Not even close. But hopefully the message was clear enough, even if my rhyming was awful.

There was only one way I could think of to deliver the note. Going into my bedroom, I opened my panty drawer and selected a pair to sacrifice. There weren't many to choose from. I was running low. Again. I had to keep buying more panties from the local lingerie store, and I'd shopped there so often the woman who owned it must have thought I had a crush on her.

Grabbing my pen, I added one more line to the note I'd written:

*P.S. I want my panties back, pervert!*

I pinned the note into my sacrificial pair, then took them out to the washing line and pegged them up, ready for the panty thief to steal.

Once back in my painting room, I went back to

mixing paint to get the right highlight color, then started adding touches of light to the painting. It was starting to look good. I'd been nervous about going from painting landscapes to surreal portraits, but the series I'd been working on had burst from my hand onto the canvas, like I was purging the terrible years of my marriage through explosions of color.

This house was perfect for painting, with its big windows that weren't so good for privacy, but let the Californian sunlight flood in. When my father's lawyer had called me in London to say Dad was in jail, it had been a shock. But then he'd told me Dad wanted me to move into his house, and I'd jumped at the chance to leave Benedict months earlier than I thought I'd be able to. I'd taken Ruff and flown halfway across the world with no idea what exactly I was fleeing to. All I'd hoped for was a bed to sleep in while I created enough paintings to start selling them.

What I'd found was a beach house with stunning ocean views, direct access to the sand, and even a swimming pool. There was a photograph of Dad on the mantel, the first glimpse of him I'd had for years. Looking at it made me yearn for the father I'd always wished I could be closer to. Not just that, but the house was full of Dad's furniture and in spite of the mess the police had left behind when they'd searched the place, his clothes were still hanging in the closet. I could even detect a faint whiff of his cologne on them.

Being in Dad's house almost made me feel like I was

getting to know him again. Like he could step through the door at any moment and we'd be able to talk things through, find a way to reconcile. If only he wasn't in jail, awaiting trial. In two weeks, he'd either be found innocent and freed, or he'd be convicted and have to stay where he was for a long time. In the meantime, I'd filled in the visitation forms and I was waiting for them to be processed and approved so I could finally get to see him.

My phone rang as I was putting some last touches on the painting. Though the screen read *Unknown Number*, I figured it must be Gloria, the woman who ran the community center where I was about to hold my exhibition, so I put down my brush to answer it.

"Hello?"

"Hello Iola," said a male voice I'd hoped never to hear again.

"Benedict?" The word came out as a yelp that made Ruff lift her head and whine.

I stepped closer to Ruff, as much to reassure myself as her. But surely Benedict had to still be thousands of miles away, in London?

"How did you get this number?" I squeaked.

"As your husband, it's my right to have your phone number. Until death do us part, darling." His rounded, upper-class British vowels rolled through the phone's speaker like expensive grenades.

Dragging in a deep breath, I forced myself to sound angry instead of afraid. "If you have something to tell me, call my lawyer. He's dealing with your crap so I don't have to."

He made a tsking sound. "A few weeks on your own, and you're already developing disgusting habits. Don't use foul language, Iola."

"Sign the crap-shit-fuck divorce papers, Benedict, and get the crap-shit-fuck out of my life."

His voice hardened. "I'm not signing any papers, darling. Members of the aristocracy don't get divorced. How would it look?"

"I don't *care* how it looks. Besides, if Princess Diana can get divorced, so can I."

"And what happened to our beloved Princess Di? Killed in a tunnel. Such a terrible shame."

"Are you threatening me?" I crouched next to Ruff to run my free hand over her back, taking comfort from the feel of her muscles under my hand.

"I'm merely concerned for your welfare. And for Lady Ruffington's. How is my dog, by the way? Still in good condition, I trust?"

"Bad news. Ruff died. She's gone, Benedict." I patted Ruff's head by way of apology.

"A big dog like Lady Ruffington is expensive to keep fed, and I know you don't have any money. Enough is enough. I've indulged your little vacation, but now it's time for you to come home."

"Never."

"Then I'll come to California and get you."

My stomach turned over. How had Benedict discovered I'd left England, let alone where I'd gone? When I swallowed, there was a bitter taste in the back of my throat. The taste of fear.

"I've already organized my trip," he added when I didn't answer. "I hear the coast is lovely at this time of year."

"California's a big state. You'll never find me."

"I know exactly where you are. San Dante looks delightful. I'm even willing to do a little sightseeing before taking you home, so we can use the time to discuss your behavior."

My stomach was churning so violently I felt like throwing up. With my British bank accounts frozen, I couldn't afford to skip town, not unless Ruff and I slept in my car. Besides, I wanted to see Dad as soon as my visit was approved, and to support him during his trial. I hadn't come all this way to be forced away now.

"If you come here, I'll call the police," I said as forcefully as I could manage. "And when my lawyer gets me access to our bank accounts, I'll—"

"Your cut-rate, bargain-bin lawyer?" Benedict chuckled. "My lawyer runs the best firm in London, and you know what a good friend he is. Not to mention that I can afford to pay him, because unlike you, I have other funds to draw on. I'm afraid your access to our bank accounts will be frozen for a very long time."

Straightening, I paced to the windows with long, agitated strides. "I'll make you a deal. All I want is the money I earned from my paintings, and for you to leave me and Ruff alone. You can have everything else. I'll sign away my half of the house, just give me my money back."

"I won't give you a thing. Either come back to England or get used to being poor."

"Better to be poor than go back to you, Benedict." I hissed the words through clenched teeth, my rage surging so high it swamped my fear. "I'd rather starve to death in a ditch and let Ruff eat my corpse."

"You know I'd never let that happen to my obedient wife, or my prize-winning dog. What would people say?"

"I don't care what—"

"Must run, darling, I have a flight to catch. But I'll see you and Lady Ruffington soon."

"You're not—" It was too late, he'd already hung up. I snarled the rest of the sentence anyway. "You're not just a prick, Benedict, you're the whole damn cactus!"

He was right about one thing. I'd spoken to my lawyer that morning, and the courts apparently didn't care that the small amount of money I'd been able to take with me was almost gone. If Benedict kept me cut off from our bank accounts, I'd better sell my paintings quickly or I'd be forced to beg for coins on street corners.

Ruff lifted her head, dragging her heavy jowls off the floor. Her eyes reflected my worry back at me.

"It'll be okay," I reassured her. "Benedict's title and connections won't carry any weight once he leaves England. He'll lose some of his power as soon as he gets on a plane. Besides, if he turns up here, you can bite him, okay?"

Only I knew she wouldn't. Ruff had been well trained by professionals. She'd never harm anyone she knew, even Benedict.

Ruff dropped her head back onto her paws with a weary sigh, which I matched with a sigh of my own.

"I'm going to double-check all the doors and windows are locked," I said. "Just in case."

Ruff closed her eyes.

## Chapter Three

### Asher

I spent the next day reviewing progress at my construction site and having meetings in the project office, which was a converted shipping container that would be moved to the next site once the work on this one was completed. It held a cheap wooden desk, a few chairs, and a filing cabinet with all the site documentation and plans, so they were on hand when needed. Basic, but functional.

The project office always had a distinctive smell—coffee, wet boots, solvent, and the aroma of sandwiches. That afternoon, the office also held a small-but-forceful Texan. Namely, my forewoman, Brenda. She was forty-something, and short enough that her high-vis jacket had been made especially for her, along with her tiny steel-capped boots. She was highly experienced in the construction industry, and the way she took no nonsense from anyone was beautiful to watch. It was a male-dominated industry, and Brenda's slight stature, blue eyes, and long blonde hair made strangers underestimate her. The smart ones only did it once.

Brenda had worked for me for years. She oversaw the day-to-day running of the site, handling the demands of both customers and employees. Without her my business wouldn't have been nearly as successful.

Lately, I'd been feeling pangs of guilt whenever I spent time with her. As an employer, my primary responsibility was to keep my staff working. When I'd taken out the loan to buy my house and Santino's, I'd used my business as collateral. If things went wrong, I'd put her job at risk.

"Work is starting to wind up here," Brenda said, oblivious to my guilty thoughts. She took her hard hat off and set it on the floor before settling onto the chair on the other side of the desk. "I'll be able to start moving people to the next project soon, only you still haven't told me what's next on the schedule."

She was right. With Santino's trial coming up, it was time to get the next project started.

I took some blueprints out of my briefcase, but before spreading them on the desk, I met her gaze. "What I'm about to show you is confidential. I need your word you won't share any of these details."

"Ooo, mysterious." With a little smile, she leaned in. "Need me to swear a blood oath, boss?"

If we hadn't worked together for so long, I might have been tempted to say yes. But as Brenda was one of the only people outside my immediate family I trusted, I just put the blueprints on the desk for her to examine.

She stood up to get a better look at them. "We'll be building apartments next? Who's the client?"

"I am. This is my project, and I'm funding it myself."

Her face jerked up, her eyes wide. "You're fooling me, right?"

Instead of answering, I stayed silent and allowed her to take in my serious expression. After a moment, she frowned back down at the blueprints. "This can't be beachfront? I didn't know there were any building sites that size left on the beachfront. Not around here."

"There will be when I buy the house next to mine."

"Then you'll own two lots next to each other," she said slowly. "And doubling the land size changes the council restrictions on what you can build."

"That's right. On their own, they're single-dwelling lots. Joining them together will rewrite the rules."

Because a big site was worth far more than two smaller ones, their value would skyrocket, and the huge financial risk I'd taken—including paying way over market value to buy the house next to Santino's so the police surveillance team could watch him from there—would be well rewarded. I'd known they'd have to catch him using his house for drug trafficking for it to be seized and sold. So I'd arranged it.

"With that much land, you'll be able to build up to, what? Six floors?"

I nodded. "Twelve luxury apartments, each with two carparks and wide sea views."

Brenda gave a low whistle. "They're going to be worth a fortune."

Twenty-five million dollars, to be precise. Not that she needed to know the exact figure.

Seeing as Santino and his associates had killed our mother, I figured my father and brothers deserved a twenty-five-million-dollar payday to keep them safe for the rest of their lives.

"We need to set up our supply lines for the construction materials," I said. "But I don't want the project becoming public knowledge until I've bought my neighbor's house. Start sourcing everything we'll need, but do it quietly."

"Sure, boss." Brenda grinned. "Can I tell you I'm impressed, or should that stay a secret too?"

I checked my watch, feeling another pang of guilt for the financial risks I'd taken that I had no intention of telling her about. "I need to go. I'll email you the materials list so you can get started."

"On it, boss." As I folded the blueprints, she added, "One last thing before you go. With this build about to wrap up, I'd like to book in our next shindig."

"Of course." Every time we finished a big project, she liked to throw a party to celebrate. It was a way to thank the team for their hard work and help them feel good about what they'd achieved. Brenda organized it, and I paid the bill. It had become an established tradition and even if funds were tight, I couldn't ask her to skip it.

She put her hands on her hips. "Call me stubborn for

always asking, but will you think about turning up to the party this time?"

"No thanks."

"You want to give me a reason why not?" She tilted her head down to give me a disapproving frown. "And don't try to spin me that nonsense about it being better to keep your distance."

"It isn't nonsense." I shut the blueprints safely back in my briefcase.

"That's all you're going to say? I guess one of these days I'll learn to stop wasting my breath."

I nodded at her, starting for the door. "Good. See you tomorrow."

Brenda looked a little disappointed, which was surprising. I had no idea why she still asked me to attend parties when my answer never changed.

When I was sixteen—toward the end of the two years my brothers and I had spent in Mexico—Mom had been spiraling into the depths of her drug addiction. She'd spent most nights out with her dealer and wouldn't come home until the early hours of the morning, if she came home at all. One night in particular stuck out in my mind, though I wasn't sure why, when it had been like so many others. I'd been lying awake listening to Kade's gentle snores coming from the other side of our tiny bedroom when I'd heard the familiar scratching and thumping sounds of Mom struggling to unlock the front door. After a few minutes, she'd finally managed to get the door open and stumble inside. Her heeled shoes had clattered across the floor as she'd either kicked them off or fallen out of them. The living room's bright light had flicked on, and a few moments later Mom was silhouetted in the doorway of our bedroom. She'd lost weight over the previous months and was shockingly thin. Her jutting hip bones were the only things holding up her jeans, and her small, low-cut top displayed the sharpness of her clavicle bones. Her hair was lank, and her skin mottled. She had sores on her arms and one on her neck.

Her gaze met mine. She stared at me for several long moments, while her substance-impaired brain processed the fact I was awake. I kept my face impassive, always careful not to show my dismay at the way her body was deteriorating.

Mom's gaze swung from me to Kade and she lurched over to his bed, almost collapsing on top of him. "Wake up, darling." Her voice was slurred. "Wake up, my little prince. Mommy's home."

Kade woke reluctantly, his face crumpled as he tried to hold onto sleep. But he let Mom drag him out of bed and into the living room. He let her put on music and swayed with her as she tried to dance. And when she asked Kade to tell her he loved her, he repeated it patiently, as many times as she needed to hear it.

I lay still, as I had so many nights before, saying nothing until Mom eventually passed out on the couch and Kade could go back to bed. Though I'd do anything for my brother, bitter experience had already taught me there was no way to help him. His natural charm drew people in, Mom included. She wanted him—and only him—to comfort her.

And if there was a small place somewhere deep inside me that ached at her dismissal, it was easily quietened. After all, it wasn't a rational or logical feeling to have. Nobody would *want* to be pulled out of bed at three in the morning to humor their stoned, needy mother. And sure enough, when Kade came back into our bedroom, he was pale and rigid with the force of his emotions. Once in bed, he turned to face the wall, and his breaths stayed shallow and tight for a long time.

I never let Kade see how wretched I felt to be unable to help him. It was easier for him if I showed nothing. Better if I pretended not to know how much he hated being the sole focus of Mom's cloying attention.

Instead, I'd thought up other ways to try to improve our situation. I'd left AA and NA pamphlets in Mom's bedroom, and when she woke up feeling hungover and remorseful, I'd tried to talk her into going to meetings. I'd made friends with potential sobriety coaches and sponsors, all the time trying to figure out a way to make enough money to send her to one of those expensive rehab centers. And I'd done my best to keep Mom from being fired from the restaurant where she worked, cajoling her to turn up on time, and begging her boss to give her chance after chance.

Though I'd tried to make any kind of difference, however small, nothing had helped, and I'd been constantly frustrated. And if I hadn't been able to keep my distance, emotionally speaking, I might not have survived the experience without deep-rooted scars. Kade had let his emotions eat him up, while I'd managed to contain mine. Remaining detached had proved to be the smartest way to handle things, and I'd learned an important lesson, one I was still utilizing in my business life. After all, what good would it do to get to know my employees? What if I had to fire someone, or they let me down? That's why I had Brenda. I was well aware of my responsibilities toward the people I employed, but Brenda kept me from having to interact with them.

"I'll send you the details of the shindig anyway, boss, in case you change your mind," Brenda said as I was opening the door to leave.

I shook my head at her stubbornness. She had my respect—more than anyone outside of my family—and I'd do everything humanely possible to make sure her job was secure. That didn't include attending her parties.

"Don't count on it," I said as I left.

I got back to my house around four o'clock. But with my unwelcome blind date looming, I couldn't concentrate on any of the work I'd come home to do. I was too busy snooping on Iola. If she was related to Santino, I figured they could have the same surname, so I ran a Google search and narrowed down the options until I found her.

I squinted at the picture on the screen. The grainy black-and-white photograph was from a British newspaper and had been taken seven years ago, but it was definitely a younger version of my mysterious neighbor. She was wearing a wedding gown. The camera had captured her looking stunned, and not in a good way. She looked as though she'd accidentally gotten into a rollercoaster car with no safety belt and was staring down at an impossibly steep drop.

Santino was standing on one side of Iola, wearing one of his expensive suits. A quick calculation told me he was fifty-one in the picture, but his hair was still thick and black with no sign of gray. Posed together with Iola, I could see some similarities in their nose and face shape, though Santino looked sharply masculine and very arrogant, with his chin high and his stare hard, while Iola's features were soft and beautiful.

On Iola's other side was a blond man with mean eyes who didn't look much younger than Santino. His arm was wrapped possessively around Iola, and he looked down his nose at the camera, his posture as arrogant as Santino's. The caption under the photo read, *The Honorable Benedict Appleby Junior, son of Viscount Appleby, marries Iola Martin.*

So my neighbor was Santino's daughter. She'd married an older man, but was definitely living alone in the house next door.

Digging further, I managed to find one more news article that mentioned Iola. It was from a small San Diego-based paper, dated fifteen years ago. The article was a brief report of a house fire caused by an electrical fault. Iola had been rescued from the burning house by a neighbor who'd pulled her out of her bedroom window. Her mother had perished in the blaze. There was no mention of her father, so maybe Santino hadn't been living in the house at the time.

Next I searched for 'Iola Appleby', and the results

that came up made me rock back in my chair. Iola was an artist, and she painted beautiful landscapes. Deep red sunsets and green forests that seemed to go on forever. Oceans dappled with light. Her work was for sale in a London gallery, and it was expensive.

"Nat and I are going out." Kade sauntered into my office, freshly shaven and wearing an impeccably tailored shirt and slacks, along with a smug grin. "Why haven't you changed for your date yet, Ash?"

I pretended to peer at my annoying brother. "You have cat hair on your shirt," I lied, choosing not to answer his question. "And where'd you buy that cologne, a dime store?"

Kade leaned his shoulder against the wall, crossing one leg over the other. "What are you going to wear tonight?"

"Those slacks don't go with that shirt," I said. "And do you really think those shoes are a good idea?"

My brother grinned. "My clothes match perfectly. It's yours I'm worried about." He nodded at my black jeans and dark gray t-shirt. "You *are* planning to change, right? I told Iola you'd pick her up from her front door at seven o'clock sharp."

I squinted at his chin. "Is that a pimple? I hope you and Natalie aren't going anywhere fancy."

"Where are you taking Iola?" He seemed undeterred by my attempts at deflection. "It'd better be somewhere nice. Maybe that new French place?"

I blew out a disgruntled breath. "What makes you

think I won't just go next door to cancel the ill-advised date you arranged?"

"You'll go on the date because it'd be rude to pull out now. Besides, you want to know her connection to Santino, and why she's living next door."

"Actually, I'm almost certain she's Santino's daughter."

"His daughter?" Kade's eyebrows lifted. "Really?"

"Really. And now that I know their connection, there's no point in taking her out."

"Other than the fact she's beautiful, and you're intrigued by her. You'll go out with her because you like to know everything about everyone. You can't have a mystery woman living next door and not want to find out more."

I frowned. Most people found me hard to read, but my twin brother didn't seem to have that problem, and it was irritating when he was right.

Kade and I were very different, but we were close in a way that most people would probably find hard to understand. If I was caught on a train track, my brother wouldn't hesitate to jump in front of me, sacrificing his life to give me an extra second to get free.

He also used to fart on my pillow.

"It seems disingenuous to go out with her when I was the one who got her father arrested," I told him.

"But you'll still go."

"You're enjoying this way too much," I accused.

He shrugged. "What can I say? Watching you grind your teeth is fun."

I looked around for something to throw at him, but my desk was too tidy. There wasn't even a pen handy. Only my computer mouse, which was too delicate to risk.

"Ready to go?" asked Natalie, appearing in the doorway of my office. She was wearing a little black dress, and looked very nice.

When Kade turned to her, his smile grew. "You're gorgeous." He moved close to her so he could kiss her neck.

She gave a pleased laugh. "Thanks, so are you." Her gaze went to me. "Not changed yet, Asher? Shouldn't you put on something a little nicer?" From the amusement in her tone, it was clear Kade had told her about the date he'd set up with Iola.

"You can leave now. Both of you." I picked up my mouse, testing its weight. Perhaps it wasn't too delicate to throw.

"Have fun tonight, okay?" Grinning, Natalie hooked her hand through Kade's arm.

"Sure. Now go." I waved a hand irritably, gesturing for them to leave faster.

I'd already made a plan for tonight's date. I'd take Iola to dinner and prompt her to talk about herself, then when I'd satisfied my curiosity, I'd take her home. I'd stay polite but distant. And I definitely wouldn't get so friendly with her that I'd feel bad when I bought Santino's house out from under her.

# Chapter Four

## Iola

Why in the world had I agreed to go on a blind date?

It was seven o'clock, and I'd been getting more and more nervous all afternoon. Now I was pacing up and down my living room while I waited for Kade's brother to arrive. Where was he, anyway? Had he decided not to come? All he had to do was walk over from next door, but if he didn't turn up, I'd be relieved.

I smoothed my sweaty palms over my white dress. It was probably the wrong choice of outfit for tonight. Being short of funds, I still only had the clothes Benedict had thought were suitable, and he'd told me I looked sweet and virginal in white. Yes, wearing the white dress had been a mistake. In fact, now I wished I'd burned it. But it was too late to change.

"Forget about Benedict," I ordered myself. "Don't be

nervous. And when Asher turns up, don't blurt out any bad puns. Just be normal."

Ruff had been asleep on the floor but when I spoke, she lifted her head and blinked at me.

"Don't look at me like that," I told her. "I'm sure I can be like everyone else if I try hard enough."

Problem was, I felt anything but normal. How could I act that way after Benedict's phone call? Even without the pressure of a blind date, I was jittery and on edge.

Ruff dropped her head with a sigh, and I checked the clock again. Two minutes past seven. Maybe Kade's brother had already had other plans for tonight, and hadn't bothered to tell me.

Someone rapped on my front door.

My stomach turned over. I walked down the hallway holding my breath and looked through the peephole to make sure it wasn't Benedict before I opened the door.

On my doorstep was a man so handsome, my stomach fluttered. He was almost too handsome. Like a painting that doesn't look real because the artist didn't add any flaws.

He wore navy trousers and a matching shirt. His hair was dark brown, almost black, and his eyes were gunmetal gray. His jaw looked like it had been built from Lego blocks, and the intelligence in his eyes looked sharp enough to stab a whole lot of hearts. I could picture him collecting them like bills on a spike.

"You're Kade's brother," I said unnecessarily. "Asher, right?"

They looked similar, but this man had darker hair and

eyes, he was slightly leaner, and his face was more angular. If Kade was a watercolor, his brother was a charcoal drawing, in darker tones, with sharper lines.

Asher inclined his head in agreement. "And you're Iola." Stepping forward, he extended his hand. The movement made my eyes go from his muscular shoulders to his slender hips, drinking in the perfect lines of his snug-fitting shirt. He was built like the letter T, and my guess was it stood for *Trouble*.

I took the hand he offered. As his fingers closed around mine, his sharp gray eyes analyzed me like a math puzzle, as though he could calculate exactly who I was in an instant. I don't know if it was that feeling of being assessed or just a static energy discharge, but when our hands met, I was ultra-aware of his touch. Almost as though his skin was sending tiny pulses of electricity into me.

"Are you ready to go?" he asked, motioning to the black Tesla he'd pulled into my driveway. Considerate of him to do that, though he could have just left it next door and asked me to walk over to it.

"Sure." I shot a look back down my hallway. Ruff hadn't barked when Asher had knocked. I could just see her head where she lay on her bed in the living room, and I was pretty sure she'd fallen asleep again. Some guard dog she was.

Locking the door behind me, I walked beside Asher to his car. "Where are we going?"

"An Italian restaurant. Do you like pasta?"

I nodded, not trusting myself to speak, and he opened

his car's passenger door for me. Unlike his brother, he didn't wear a permanent smile, but his serious expression didn't bother me. At least it meant I didn't need to fake a cheerful smile in return.

I got into the car and Asher waited until I'd adjusted my dress before closing the door. It wasn't until he was walking around to the driver's side that I suddenly realized I'd been so focused on Benedict being the primary danger in my life, I'd willingly gotten into a complete stranger's car. How did I know Asher wasn't an admirer of Hannibal Lector or that freaky Buffalo Bill guy from the same movie? He might be planning to take me to a secluded cabin in the woods and sew a dress from my skin. After all Benedict's threats, it'd be an ironic way to go.

Still, what was I going to do, jump back out of his car? That would be too embarrassing to have to explain. Foolish or not, I couldn't make myself move. Seemed something inside me would rather I get stitched up—literally—than look silly. So I sat fidgeting as Asher slid into the driver's seat and started the engine. Being so close to him made me a little dizzy, mostly because of his ridiculous good looks, but also thanks to the very manly musk scent of his cologne.

Before pulling away, Asher reached into the back seat and grabbed a small, soft package, which he handed to me. "This is for you," he said without inflection.

My heart was beating too fast as my mind raced through all the possibilities of what could be inside the plain brown wrapping paper. If it turned out to be a sewing pattern for a human-skin onesie, I could be in real trouble.

"A gift?" I stammered.

"A response to your last note." When I stared blankly at him, he added, "The one pinned to your underwear."

"Oh!" I felt my eyes widen and my stomach drop. "*You're* the panty pervert?" The last thing I would have expected was for a panty thief to be so good looking. Why couldn't weirdoes wear identifying name tags? It would make things so much easier if he had a, *'Hello, I'm a Pervy Panty Sniffer'* sticker on the front of his shirt.

Without waiting for him to reply, I ripped open the parcel. Several pairs of my missing panties tumbled out. There was also a photo of a black cat carrying a pair of panties in its mouth, which was probably supposed to be more convincing than the sketch he'd already given me. On the back of the photo, someone—presumably Asher—had drawn a single upraised cat paw, and written the words 'Cat Peower'.

Cute.

If it wasn't for Ruff, I might have been convinced. But some of the panties had been stolen from the drawer in my bedroom, and no cat would willingly go into a house with a big dog inside. Not if it wanted to come out alive.

"Nemesis is the panty thief, not me," said Asher. His tone was still mild and his attention seemed entirely focused on the road, as though this was his idea of barely-interesting small talk.

I snorted my derision. Maybe not my best idea, seeing as the evidence seemed to be in favor of him being a pervert, which probably meant the odds of him also being a serial killer had also increased. "Are you kitten me?" I asked, not quite managing to keep the conversation completely pun-free. "You're seriously going to keep pretending a cat's the purr-petrator?"

When I was nervous, I made jokes. Bad ones.

But if Asher caught the puns, he didn't react. "I'm not pretending," he said in the same conversational tone. "I included photographic evidence." He pulled his gaze from the road long enough to nod at the parcel. "There's a gift card in there too. Consider it an apology for the inconvenience."

I tugged the card from the brown paper wrapping. It had been purchased from the local lingerie shop, for a very generous amount.

"I can't accept this," I said, putting the card on the dashboard.

I caught a flicker of surprise in his eyes, a momentary crack in his impenetrable armor. "Why not?"

"It's too much, and I don't want to owe you anything." I flushed a little when I heard how blunt it sounded. I should have thought of a more polite way to phrase it.

He turned the car into San Dante's main street. "Please take it. You'll need it for when Nemesis takes more of your underwear."

I blinked at him. "*More* of my underwear?" Was he admitting he wasn't intending to stop stealing from me?

"Once my cat gets an idea in her head, nobody can stop her."

He pulled into a parking space and shut the engine off. Seeing as we were outside an Italian restaurant, I could probably stop worrying about being taken to a remote cabin in the woods and having my skin flayed. Which was lucky, seeing as the delicious aroma of Italian food was already drifting into the car, making my mouth water. As the hours had crept closer to the first date I'd had in years, I'd been too nervous to even think about food. Now my stomach had woken up and was starting to rumble.

I left the pile of panties on the passenger seat when I got out of Asher's car, figuring if he got weird looks from passers-by, he only had himself to blame. He escorted me into the restaurant, which was a cute little bistro with checkered tablecloths, dim lighting, and little candles in jars flickering on every table. The place was almost full—not surprising considering how heavenly it smelled—but Asher had booked a good table by the window.

The waitress seated us, handed us menus, and poured glasses of water. When she left us alone at our small table, I gazed at Asher, struck by how the romantic candlelight enhanced the angles and shadows of his face, making him even more ridiculously handsome.

The nervousness that had been quietly simmering away during our drive here threatened to boil over. Picking up my menu, I bent my head over it to examine the options, willing myself not to blurt out any more bad puns. While one or two weren't that weird, a whole string of them would be. Neither of us said anything for a long time as we read the menu, and the silence started to get uncomfortable, ratcheting my anxiety up even more.

After a while, our waitress reappeared, her pen poised over her notebook. "What can I get you?"

Her gaze lingered appreciatively on Asher, but he looked at me, clearly waiting for me to order. I gave myself a mini pep talk before I spoke. All I had to do was say the name of the dish and nothing else. Resist the temptation to turn it into a joke. I could do that.

"I'll have the Carbonara please." At least choosing was easy. The cheapest dish on the menu just happened to be my favorite.

"Would you like the large size, or small?" the waitress asked.

"The biggest." I let out an awkward laugh. "You cannoli imagine how hungry I am." The pun escaped before I could clamp my lips over it. "Do you spa-get-it?" I added.

The waitress gave me a sideways look, clearly wondering if I was a recent arrival to the planet who was new to the customs of earthlings.

"You're funny," said Asher. Thankfully, his face betrayed nothing. If he'd given me a frown or a pitying look, I might have jumped up and rushed out.

"Sorry about the cheesy jokes." I gave an inward groan because my apology was another pun. "I'm trying to stop, but I'm afraid I'm pasta point of no return." In despair, I picked up my glass of water and took a big swallow to stop any more puns from spilling out.

"I'll have the lasagna," Asher said to the waitress. He

added garlic bread to the order, and I managed to nod with my lips sealed shut when he asked if I'd like a glass of chardonnay.

When the waitress left, he asked, "Do you always pun when you're nervous?"

I let out a high-pitched chuckle. "What makes you think I'm nervous?"

"You're strangling your napkin."

I looked down to see I'd twisted the white cloth into a tight spiral.

"What's wrong?" Asher asked. "Why are you on edge?" His eyes were unreadable, like polished gray mirrors, and his expression hadn't changed. But he was leaning forward a little, like he was interested in me.

"Um." I was stuck for words. There was no way I could admit it was the dim, romantic lighting and his handsome face that were setting me off. "Guess I'm not used to having dinner with a panty thief," I said instead. And because it came out sounding ruder than it had in my head, which made me nervous all over again, I added, "I'd crack a joke about panties, but I'd like to keep this brief. Besides, I don't have any clean ones."

He raised an eyebrow. "You don't believe my cat's the one with the crime compulsion?"

I shook my head. "It's not pawsible. Your cat couldn't get past Ruff. I don't believe it for a meow-ment."

"You're very punny," he said.

"Bad puns are how eye roll." I emphasized the last two words to make the double meaning clear.

"But a good pun is its own re-word."

He spoke seriously, his face impassive, and it took me a long moment to realize he'd made a joke in return. I was so surprised, I let out a loud and embarrassing snort-laugh, then clapped my hand over my mouth.

His lips twitched. Picking up his water glass, he took a sip. I was almost certain it was to hide the fact he wanted to smile.

"That was clever," I said appreciatively.

"Not as clever as yours. You're very quick."

I let out a relieved breath, grateful he had a sense of humor and hadn't made a dash for the door. It was enough to ease some of my nervousness. And even more eased away when the waitress appeared with our drinks. I took a sip of my wine and sighed with appreciation as the crisp tang hit my taste buds. Maybe it was because my stomach was empty, but the alcohol seemed to have an instant relaxing effect.

"I have my ex-husband to thank for my punning habit," I said. "Not that my ex has a single funny bone. In fact, he was born without a humerus."

"Your ex-husband didn't like jokes?"

I shook my head. "He didn't get them."

"Tell me more." He leaned in further, his attention totally focused on me.

I couldn't help but feel flattered. I was used to Benedict, who'd never been interested in anything I said, or even pretended to listen. He'd been the talkative one, convinced everyone around him would find him endlessly fascinating. Because he was wealthy and privileged, most people played along.

"My jokes confused Benedict," I said. "He didn't like them, but couldn't work out a way to stop me from making puns. It was the one part of my life he couldn't control."

I could even remember the evening that had kicked off my habit. There were fourteen of us at a formal table laid out with so much cutlery, we could have eaten several banquets and still not used all the forks. Two waiters were serving the food while Benedict's family and friends made dull small talk, like an insanely boring episode of Downton Abbey. The only reason I didn't slip into a coma and fall off my chair was because my clothes were so well pressed they'd forgotten how to crease.

Ruff had been a puppy, only a few months old, and impossibly cute. I couldn't bear her heart-rending cries when she was left alone, so I'd smuggled her into the dining room, hidden her on my lap, and fed her table scraps to keep her quiet.

Unfortunately, she'd been quickly discovered and banished to another room.

"A dog is like a classic car," Benedict's mother had scolded me. "It won't be a prize-winner if you give it the wrong fuel."

Then Benedict's father had chimed in. "The girl's probably been used to mixed-breed mongrels that can eat any old food."

"If you keep spoiling the dog, I'll send it to live with the trainer," Benedict threatened in a low voice.

"You wouldn't!"

Benedict's expression darkened. Contradicting him

in public was a serious crime.

"I'm going to Cowdray Park to watch the polo this weekend," he snapped. "Perhaps you should stay here without me."

I'd had to hold in a laugh. An entire weekend without him? Of all the punishments he liked to inflict on me, that was one I'd actually look forward to. Only I clearly didn't hide my glee well enough, because Benedict's eyes hardened. He drew in a sharp breath, but before he could come up with anything worse, one of his upper-crust friends spoke up.

"Oh, you newly-weds," she said with a chuckle. "I remember when Henry would go away and I'd spend all weekend missing him. I'm sure Iola will feel the same."

"You think I'll miss Benedict?" I met her gaze. "Don't worry. My aim's pretty good."

She let out a surprised snort, then coughed to cover it. Benedict and his parents stared blankly as the rest of the guests tittered.

But it wasn't until Benedict changed the subject with an annoyed frown that I realized he was so humorless, he either hadn't understood the joke or thought it was too far beneath him to respond to.

From then on, I'd been hooked.

"Over the course of my marriage, jokes became my *Hunger Games* three-fingered salute," I confessed to Asher. "Only they became too much of a habit, and sometimes I can't stop." I forced an embarrassed laugh to show I knew all too well how ridiculous that was. "Now I've left Benedict, hopefully I'll be able to shake the habit."

"You separated recently?"

I nodded. "I left him a month ago." It was on the tip of my tongue to tell him our separation had been more like a prison break, and that Benedict had threatened to follow me to San Dante, but the waitress was carrying our food over.

"Here you go." As she put my pasta in front of me, I was already grabbing my fork in anticipation. The meal looked delicious, and I could hardly wait to dig in. But the waitress hovered beside us for a moment, looking at Asher. "You're Kade's brother, aren't you?" she asked. "I love his TV show. Never miss it. Could you please tell him he has a big fan here?" Her cheeks were flushing. "You know, in case he wants to come in for a meal or something?"

Asher nodded, his expression neutral. "I will."

"Thanks." She looked embarrassed, and I gave her a reassuring smile to let her know I sympathized. Fangirling over Kade wasn't as embarrassing as blurting a string of bad puns to his brother, so she was doing better than I was.

When she'd left, I tasted my carbonara. The creaminess made it rich and delicious, and the crisp chardonnay was perfect with it. I had to close my eyes for a moment to stifle a groan of pure pleasure. Benedict would never have let me eat something so carb-loaded, and picturing his disapproval only made me relish the dish even more.

I was enjoying the food too much to think of anything to say, but thankfully Asher was focused on his lasagna and didn't seem to be expecting me to make conversation. More tension left me as I realized the silence that fell this time wasn't awkward. It was a relief. Benedict had been petty and vindictive, and whenever I'd been alone with him, I'd spent my time gauging his mood, monitoring the emotions that had constantly played over his face. I couldn't do that with Asher because his face was impassive, not giving anything away. It was surprisingly restful.

Still, while Asher's attention was on his food, I sneaked some glances at him. If I could get used to how handsome he was, I'd be in less danger of reaching bad-joke levels of nervousness around him.

After a while, Asher asked, "How's your meal?"

I swallowed a large mouthful. "Very nice, thank you. Yours?"

"Excellent."

"As good as the food your brother makes?"

He shook his head. "That's a high bar. When it comes to cooking, Kade's food is hard to beat."

"I used to watch Kade's cooking show when I lived in London," I admitted.

"Did you make any of his dishes?"

"I wanted to, but my ex wouldn't let me near the kitchen. I had to leave all that up to his chef. Truth is, I've never really cooked anything."

He blinked slowly, the most emotion I'd seen from him yet. "You've never cooked?"

"Now I have my life back, it's one of the things I want to start doing." I picked up my half-empty wine glass to take another sip. "Honestly, I have a really long list of things I want to try. But learning to cook is right at the top."

"Kade might give you some tips," he suggested.

"Really?" I couldn't help but chuckle at the idea. "Being taught how to cook by Kade would be amazing, but he wouldn't want to bother with a beginner like me."

"He wouldn't mind, only he's going back to LA tomorrow. That's where he usually lives."

"I suppose you can cook?"

He gave a nod, and I took note of his quiet confidence. "It would have been hard not to pick up a few things from Kade." He spoke in an offhand way, and I was instantly sure he was a lot more skilled than he was letting on.

I let out a wistful sigh. "You're lucky to have a chef in your family."

"What about your family?" he asked.

"I'm an only child. No brothers or sisters, unfortunately."

"Where did you grow up?"

"We lived in Mexico when I was young, near Hermosillo. Mom and I moved to San Diego after my parents split up. But when I was twelve, my mom died in a fire." I took a breath. Even after all these years, I still couldn't mention Mom without feeling a moment of loss. "My dad was really busy with work, so I spent the next few years at a boarding school." It was almost the truth. Dad had sent me to boarding school because he'd wanted to keep me away from his business. I hadn't understood at the time, but after he'd confessed his suspicions about

Mom's death, his reasons for shutting me out had become clear.

Asher's gray eyes warmed and though it was a subtle change, I caught a softening of his expression. "I'm sorry." His tone was surprisingly gentle, catching me off guard.

To my shock, I felt my throat tighten and my eyes start to sting.

Was I about to cry? What was wrong with me?

Since arriving in San Dante, I'd been painting night and day, and barely sleeping. I was exhausted, and I'd been tense and on edge all day. It had to be catching up with me.

"Iola." Asher leaned closer, a small line creasing the skin between his eyes. "Are you okay?"

"Yes. Fine." I took a steadying sip of wine, then shook my head to clear the threat of tears. "Sorry. The last few weeks have been a lot, that's all."

I'd been squirreling away money to escape Benedict for a while, but when Dad's lawyer called to say my father wanted me to move into his house, I'd had to make a snap decision. I'd had enough for my plane ticket, a cheap car, and to bring Ruff with me. But to survive longer than a few weeks, I'd known I'd need to start selling paintings quickly. Stealing Ruff and hoping she wasn't too old for such a long plane trip had been stressful enough. With the added pressure to earn money fast, the call from Benedict, Dad's impending trial, and my nervousness about going on a blind date, was it any wonder I felt overwhelmed?

Still, bursting into tears on a blind date would be

more humiliating than letting out any amount of puns. Dragging in a breath, I managed to force a weak laugh instead. "I didn't mean to overreact, but I'm a little emotional."

"Would you like to talk about it?"

I swallowed, because though my first instinct was to say no, Asher's impassiveness, softened with the warmth of sympathy in his eyes, made me want to blurt out all my problems. Though I barely knew him, it was appealing to think he was unlikely to overreact to anything I said. I'd never actually had a session with a therapist, but I imagined confessing to Asher would probably feel like therapy. And if I wasn't still afraid I might cry, I might have taken him up on his offer.

"Thanks," I said. "I'm just glad to be back in California instead of London. Thousands of miles away from my ex-husband." At least I hoped I was that far away from him, and he wasn't on a plane, winging his way here to torment me.

"Your ex is British?" asked Asher. "How did you meet him?"

"My father introduced us. I was in my final year at my boarding school, and Benedict was a business associate of Dad's. He was only in the country for a few weeks, but he asked me to have dinner with him, and that was that. Next thing I knew, I had a one-way ticket to England." I screwed up my nose. "Huge mistake."

Asher's eyebrows crept together. "You were forced into your marriage?"

I had to laugh at the idea. "Nothing like that. The

opposite, actually. Benedict swept me off my feet, and when he proposed, I couldn't wait to say yes." Remembering how enthusiastic I'd been made me feel a little melancholy. Though it had turned into the biggest mistake of my life, I'd been ecstatic at the time.

"You wanted to move to England?"

I toyed with the stem of my glass. "Well, it didn't hurt that Benedict's father is a Viscount. Real English royalty. I'm embarrassed to say I thought marrying him was going to be like that movie where an ordinary girl becomes a princess." I gave a self-deprecating chuckle, and it was only because he didn't laugh at me that I was able to admit the rest. "Benedict was much older than me. He was handsome and kind of a big deal. Powerful and important. When he acted like he was smitten with me, I thought all my dreams had come true. My dad wasn't around much, and I guess I was craving having that kind of figure in my life, and really mattering to someone, you know? So I missed all the red flags that should have warned me how controlling he was."

My cheeks were warming. Asher's way of listening without reacting was nice, but it was also dangerous. It made it too easy to say things I'd never dream of telling a stranger.

A little flustered, I drank the last of my wine. Why had I said so much? He was going to think I was foolish. After so long with Benedict, I'd apparently lost my ability to have a polite conversation without blurting intimate information. And I'd practically admitted to having daddy issues.

"Would you like another glass of wine?" he asked.

"No thanks. I'm talking way too much as it is. I don't know what's gotten into me."

"I like hearing you talk." He put his knife and fork down, his attention focused on me. "And I'm happy you were able to get away from your ex-husband safely."

"Me too!" I said with feeling. "In London, I had no friends or outside support. Benedict even stopped me from having my own bank account. It took me ages to come up with a plan to leave."

"I'm sorry that happened to you." Though Asher's expression didn't change, I could tell he meant what he said. It was surprisingly touching.

"Thank you. But now I've admitted I was an overly trusting fool who let my ex control me, it's your turn to tell me about your past." I glowered at him, pretending to be stern. "Don't think I haven't noticed you're just asking me questions without giving anything away about yourself."

Most people would probably have ignored my self-criticism, but Asher said, "Don't call yourself a fool. It's not foolish to want to believe people are better than they are."

"Have you ever made that mistake?"

He hesitated, taking a slow sip of his wine as though he was thinking hard about the question. I was sure he was about to say no or brush it off. Then he put the glass down and said, "When I was a teenager, my mother struggled with addiction. Every time she was sober, I tried everything I could think of to get her to stay that way. I knew it wouldn't work. I knew she couldn't stop, and that every time I tried and failed, I wouldn't be able to resist blaming myself for not finding the right way to help her. Some of the things I did made her angry. Sometimes they made things worse. I often felt useless and foolish. But I don't regret trying."

"I'm so sorry." Somehow, his matter-of-fact way of speaking made his confession more heart-breaking. Had he always been so reserved? Or had he closed himself off to keep from being hurt by his mother's addiction?

"Nobody outside my family knows Mom was an addict. We've always kept it hidden and with Kade's celebrity status, it's important it doesn't get out. The media would make a huge deal of it and keep hounding Kade for details." His gaze was steady. "Please don't tell anyone."

I blinked, surprised that he'd so easily trust me with something confidential. "I won't. But why did you risk telling me?"

He shrugged, and for the first time his gaze flicked away from me, as though he wasn't sure of himself. "I probably shouldn't have. But I wanted you to know I've also had to deal with someone difficult, and hope I was doing the right thing in a difficult situation. And you're certainly not foolish." His lips quirked a little. "Or if you are, it's something we have in common."

I felt a rush of warmth toward him. He barely knew me, and he'd still shared something private so I'd feel better about my own situation.

"Thank you for telling me," I said with feeling.

## No Fooling Around

He inclined his head. "You're welcome."

We were both silent for a few minutes while we finished our dinner. But I didn't feel any pressure to break the silence. Benedict had been in love with the sound of his own opinions, but Asher only seemed to speak when he had something to say. His words were thoughtful and measured. More valuable for not being handed out so freely.

"Tell me about your father," he said as I was mopping up the dregs of my carbonara sauce with the last piece of garlic bread.

"There's not much to tell," I said evasively. "What about your mom? Is she still an addict?"

He hesitated, and I got the impression he was as reluctant to talk more about his mother as I was to tell him my father was in jail.

"May I get you anything else?" Our waitress appeared back at our table.

"I couldn't eat another bite." I pushed my plate away with a sigh, luxuriating in the knowledge I wouldn't have to hear Benedict criticize my thick waist or flabby thighs ever again. Thinking about it made me giddy with pleasure.

"Dessert?" suggested Asher. "Coffee?"

"I really wish I could squeeze something else in, but I'm about to burst."

"Just the check then, please," he said to the waitress.

"I'm paying half," I said quickly.

"I'd rather pay it all."

"No, thank you." I put a little smile on my lips to

soften my refusal. "I'll joke about everything else, but paying my own way is important to me. Remember, I used to live with a man who wouldn't let me have a bank account. Now it's kind of a big thing for me to use my own money, so please don't argue."

He inclined his head. "Fair enough."

We paid and left, and as he drove me home, we chatted about work. He said he worked in construction, and I told him about a painting I'd just finished. He was so easy to talk to, it seemed like no time at all until we were pulling up at his house.

Asher got out and opened the car door for me, then walked me to my front door. I carried my packet of panties, trying not to think about how weird it was to have collected my underwear from him.

"Thanks for a really lovely dinner," I said, stepping inside. "And I'm sorry about all the jokes. My punning can get out of control when I'm nervous, but like an escaping nun, I'm trying to break my habit." I offered him an apologetic smile.

I'd left the hallway light on, and it lit him from one side, making the features of his face even more dramatic. He really was gorgeous. If only I had a pad and some charcoal handy, I would have loved to capture his image.

"Don't apologize," he said. "I enjoyed your jokes."

"You did?" My smile widened. "That makes a nice change. Most people think I'm weird and annoying."

"I think you're anything but."

Looked at logically, it probably wasn't much of a compliment. But spoken in such a serious tone, from such an impressively thoughtful man? My grin grew so wide I must have looked like the weirdo I was trying not to be.

"Good night, Iola." He started away.

"Wait."

He turned back and I hesitated, not even sure what I wanted to say. Sharing secrets over dinner had felt special, like we'd really connected. But I wasn't sure if he knew how much his disclosure had meant to me, and I didn't know how to tell him. And though I wanted to ask him to have dinner with me again, I was too nervous. When I was younger, I probably wouldn't have hesitated, but I wasn't nearly as confident as I used to be.

"Thanks again for taking me out, Asher," I said after a moment. "Tonight was really nice."

He inclined his head. "It was." But he sounded just a little reluctant, as though he hadn't wanted to admit it. His face was shuttered, with no trace of expression.

"If you'd like to do it again...?" My voice trailed off as he dropped his chin. It said a lot about how economical he was with what he gave away that the small movement was enough to make me sure I'd said the wrong thing.

"Good night," he said with a note of finality, turning away.

Watching him leave, I swallowed a bitter mouthful of disappointment. Whatever door might have cracked open during dinner, Asher had just closed it in my face. And I stared after him with a sense of loss, feeling as though I'd gotten a glimpse of something that could have meant something, before he'd snatched it away.

# Chapter Five

## Asher

The floor of my father's hallway had little gold and silver sparkles scattered all over it. I tried to step gingerly, but it was all but impossible to avoid the glitter. And Dad wasn't bothering to try. He stomped right over it as he led me, Kade, and Natalie into his living room.

Edging around the worst of it, Kade muttered something about unicorn poop. He and Natalie were holding hands, and she tiptoed through it with a grimace.

"Dad, did Trixie Watson send you another glitter bomb?" I asked. My father had been engaged in an ongoing war with his neighbor for many years, and glitter was one of Trixie's favorite weapons.

When Dad turned to answer, he had glitter stuck in his hairy gray eyebrows. They twinkled at me. "That woman is a menace," he growled. "Which reminds me. What time is it?"

"Just after two o'clock. Why?" Kade picked up his foot to inspect the sole of his shoe, frowning as it sparkled at him. I didn't tell him he had more glitter on his jeans, and that Natalie had a patch on the back of her t-shirt where she must have brushed against some of the glitter that was clinging to the wall.

"It's time to make a phone call." Dad headed to the coffee table to pick up his phone. "Be quiet a moment, okay?"

Kade, Natalie, and I exchanged wary glances. Dad ignored us, the phone held up to his ear. I heard the beep of a voicemail kicking in, before Dad spoke in a voice that was lower than his normal one, as though he was trying to disguise it.

"Ah, yes, Ms. Watson, this is your bowel specialist. I'm calling to advise that your farts have recorded toxic levels of stench. Please stay a safe distance from small children and animals." Hanging up, Dad chuckled.

Natalie turned away, suddenly finding something interesting to study at the other end of the room. She was either hiding an eye roll, or trying not to crack up. Knowing her like I did, I suspected the latter.

Kade let out a sigh. "That's childish, Dad."

"Childish?" Dad harrumphed. "You want to hear childish? Listen to this." He hit the speaker button on his phone, then dialed a number that turned out to be his voicemail. The recorded voice announced he had one hundred and fifty-two saved messages.

"One hundred and fifty-two?" I repeated incredulously, over the sound of the voice announcing the first message was about to play. "Why don't you delete—?"

"Shh. I'm saving the evidence in case there's a trial." Dad waved a hand to quiet me as a falsetto voice that was unmistakably Trixie Watson trying to sound like someone else came onto the line.

"This is a message for Edward Lennox," she announced. "Your application to join our nudist club has been unanimously declined." She let out a cackle of laughter and tried to turn it into a cough. "Your photos self-destructed. Almost set my hair alight." She was starting to laugh again as she hung up.

"See what I have to deal with?" Dad demanded.

Grimacing, Kade dragged a hand over his eyes. "I'm almost afraid to ask, but why did you need to make the call at two o'clock?"

"If Trixie sees I'm ringing, she'll blast a foghorn into my ear before I can get a word out. So I leave a message when I know she's busy with her classes."

Natalie was still turned away, and the way her long, dark hair fell over her shoulders meant I couldn't see any part of her face. But her shoulders were shaking. She had to be laughing silently, her hand pressed over her lips. A piece of glitter fell from her back and drifted to the floor.

Kade and I swapped another helpless look. We were in silent agreement that it would be impossible to talk Dad out of making more prank calls. His war with Trixie had been going on for years, and we'd never been able to stop him.

The reason Mom had taken me, Kade, and Mason to Mexico when I was fourteen was because she'd discovered Dad and Trixie were having an affair. Left alone after our sudden departure, and presumably filled with regret, Dad had deflected all blame for their affair onto Trixie. The two of them had been having a very public feud ever since.

Their feud was so showy, it fooled almost everyone. But I'd spent long enough studying body language to be able to pick up on hidden undercurrents, and I suspected Dad and Trixie's feelings for each other were far more complicated—and warmer—than either of them were willing to admit. A few years ago, I'd suggested as much to Dad. But he was so stubborn, he'd rather spend the rest of his life picking glitter out of his eyebrows than confess there was anything more to their battles than long-held resentments.

"Nat and I just came to say goodbye, Dad," said Kade. "We're heading back to LA."

"You're always so busy," Dad grumbled. "Don't they give you any time off?"

"I'm starting to plan the next season of my show and need to spend some time with my team." He glanced at Natalie, who still had flushed cheeks and sparkling eyes from her fit of silent laughter. "And Nat's going to meet with the studio who've optioned her first novel."

Natalie nodded. "Whether they actually make a movie out of it, I don't know. But it's exciting to think they might."

Dad frowned. "What about Mason? Why isn't he here to see you off?"

"He's been busy with Carlotta. They're looking for a house to move into together," I said.

"We saw them both yesterday for a quick goodbye," Natalie added.

"Honestly, there's no way Mason and Carlotta will be up this early." Kade flashed his dimples, his tone suggestive. "We didn't want to ask them to get out of bed for us."

My older brother, Mason, had moved back to San Dante a few weeks ago, and he and his girlfriend were looking for a house. I hadn't seen much of him since he'd been back, but after he'd spent nearly a year away, I could understand him wanting private time with Carlotta. The two of them would probably come up for air sometime soon.

Dad's frown deepened, and when he drew in a sharp breath, Kade and I exchanged a warning look. Carlotta was Trixie's daughter, and reminding him that she and Mason were dating was likely to send him off on a tirade.

"We'd better hit the road," Kade said quickly, cutting Dad off before he could get started. "We'll see you in a few weeks."

Kade and Natalie said their goodbyes, hugged me and Dad, brushed glitter off their clothes and headed for the door.

As soon as they'd gone, I turned to Dad. "I have bad news," I told him. "Your bank wasn't able to reverse the transactions, and they've only recovered a small amount. You'll only get a fraction of your money back."

Dad didn't need to ask what I was talking about. He sat down hard on his couch, as though his bones had gone heavy. "There's nothing else they can do?"

I shook my head. Unfortunately, I'd only discovered Dad had been targeted after he'd transferred his savings to a scammer. It was a sophisticated scam, and I didn't blame Dad for being fooled. I only wished he'd mentioned it earlier so I could have stopped him before his account was empty. And that there was more I could do to help him recover his money.

"The cyber-crimes unit is still looking into it, and I'll keep checking in with them," I said. "Do you have enough money to pay your bills this month?"

"I think so." But Dad sounded hesitant, and his brow was creased.

"I'll put some money into your account," I promised, stifling thoughts of all the other bills I needed to pay. "Then you won't have to worry about it."

"Are you sure you can afford it? Maybe I should ask your brothers for help?"

"No need. I'm about to do a property deal so big, none of us will ever have to worry about money again."

Kade, Mason, and I were a team, but we all had different roles to play. Kade was busy feeding the world with his highly successful TV show. Mason had risked his life as an undercover DEA agent to send a whole lot of drug cartel members to jail. My role was to use my financial talents to keep us safe. Sure I'd had to stretch myself and take a big risk, but it'd eventually pay off. In the meantime, I could juggle things to keep my business operating. And I'd never let my brothers down.

"I don't like keeping secrets," Dad said doubtfully.

"Better than making Kade or Mason worry when I already have everything under control."

"Son, I don't know if it's a good idea to—"

"Trust me, Dad. I can handle this without them." I moved to the door. "I'll see you later. Eat something healthy for lunch, okay? Not too much sugar. Remember what the doctor said."

"You're worse than Mason, hounding me to eat things I don't like. I'm perfectly fine."

Though Dad had already had one heart attack, I knew from experience there was no use arguing with him, so I said goodbye. I had a pile of work waiting for me and couldn't afford to let anything slip. There was a lot at stake. Not just Brenda's livelihood, but two dozen other employees who depended on me to keep them employed.

I was deep in thought as I drove home, figuring out which bills I needed to pay right away, and which could wait a little longer. But when I turned into my driveway, a gorgeous woman was standing at my front door.

I hit the brakes.

Iola turned to look at my car, then started toward me, her graceful walk unhampered by the creature lumbering by her side.

She was wearing a loose white sundress that clung to her luscious figure. Her hair swung around her shoulders, the sun making its silky length glow. With dark sunglasses and red lipstick, she was so stunning I expected nearby birds to burst into song.

In contrast, her dog was like a resurrected creature from *Pet Sematary* that hadn't come back from the grave with the same coat it had when it died. The dog's skin was far too wrinkled and floppy, and the huge jowls hanging from its face swung back and forth as it thundered along beside her.

I watched them approach while I debated what to do. Or rather, how best to create some distance between Iola and me. Her presence in Santino's house was a complication I didn't need, especially when she'd surprised me by being so quick-witted and a master of word play. The fact she'd seemed unaware of how fun she was to talk to had only made her more attractive.

But when I sent in the bulldozers to level Santino's house, I didn't want to be concerned about his daughter.

Iola stopped beside my car window, lifted her sunglasses, and pushed them into her hair. My hand froze and my mouth went dry.

Last night her irises had seemed so dark they were almost black, but the bright sunlight made them warm and smoky. Her skin was a rich bronze, with a faint spray of freckles over her nose like tiny smudges of paint that hadn't quite washed off. The contrast with her elegant dress and long limbs was just right.

When she tilted her head to the side in a questioning gesture, obviously wondering why I was still sitting in my car, I opened the door and got out.

"Hello," she said. "I thought you should know

another pair of panties has disappeared from inside my bedroom. All the windows and doors were shut, and Ruff was lying on my bed." She examined my face as though searching for traces of guilt. "Any idea how to solve this locked room mystery?"

No puns this time. Last night, her nervousness had disarmed me. I'd started the evening with the intention of questioning her, discovering all her secrets, then bidding her a firm and final farewell. But she'd had a vulnerability that had proven impossible to resist. She'd quickly drawn me under her spell, and by the time we were finishing dinner, I'd found myself confessing *my* secrets.

She was waiting for me to reply to her question, but my mind was empty. I was too distracted by conflicting emotions to think of anything to say. So, in the absence of clear and original thought, I used popular culture for inspiration.

"Nemesis has a very particular set of skills," I said. "Skills she's acquired over a long career. Skills that make her a nightmare for people like you."

Iola narrowed her eyes. "Is that Liam Neeson's speech from *Taken*? Are you comparing your cat to an ex-CIA operative?"

"Nemesis is an expert burglar. She's not ex-CIA, though. They wouldn't hire her. She has no respect for authority."

"I don't believe a cat could—"

Her dog barked, a sound so loud it made us both jump. The dog jerked forward, straining at the leash. Iola barely caught it in time, and I had no idea how she managed to hold the dog back.

Nemesis emerged from the side of the house and stalked up my driveway, heading toward us. The dog was barking madly, and I was about to offer my help when Iola spoke.

"Ruff, sit!" Iola's dog stopped barking and obeyed instantly.

"She's well trained," I said, impressed.

"But your cat's still coming toward her. Does she have a death wish?"

"Don't worry. Nemesis can handle herself." When Iola gave me a wide-eyed look of disbelief, I added, "Nemesis is like the feline love child of Lara Croft and Xena. She loves stealing treasure and never backs down from a fight."

As if to prove my point, Nemesis stalked straight at Ruff, her tail held high. Though she was a fraction of the giant dog's size, she didn't stop until she was right in front of Ruff, barely out of reach. Then she turned her back on her and stretched, her movements lazy. She lifted her tail so high it all but tickled Ruff's nose. Her butt was angled up at Ruff.

Ruff looked up at Iola, her eyebrows pulling down at the sides so her eyes looked even more puzzled.

Iola's lips parted, her expression as confused as her dog's. "Is your cat taunting Ruff?"

"I think she's making Ruff's status clear."

Her point made, Nemesis stalked off without a backward glance, heading down the middle of my driveway.

Ruff watched her go without a sound. She didn't seem to know what to make of Nemesis.

"Is that normal?" Iola asked.

"It is for Nemesis."

"I still don't see how any cat could be stealing my panties. She couldn't jump to the top of my clothesline, or break into my house."

"Wait until you get to know her."

Iola pursed her beautiful lips, but I could see amusement in her face. "Are you sure you're not the thief?"

"I'm certain."

She was clearly trying not to smile. "You don't give anything away, do you? I ask if you're a perverted panty thief, and your expression doesn't change."

"You're not the first person to complain. About my facial expressions, that is, not my panty thievery."

"So you're saying you just haven't been *caught* stealing underwear yet?" She quirked a suggestive eyebrow, no longer trying to hide her smile. I had to approve. Her smile was stunning.

"Are you trying to trap me into confessing to a fetish I don't have?" I asked.

"You can have any sexually deviant behaviors you want, as long as they don't involve taking my clothing. But I do have a tip for you. Don't start spanking statues. If you do, you'll know you've hit rock bottom."

I was almost startled into a laugh and had to turn my face away, pretending to look for Nemesis.

"Did you think about laughing just then? I'm pretty sure I saw your lips go up." She sounded shocked.

"Does it matter?" I got myself back under control.

"If you so much as smile, I might get nervous again." She flushed. "Even imagining a smile on your carved-from-granite face makes me want to crack a joke."

"If you make jokes, I'm more likely to smile." Despite my good intentions, I was becoming even more enchanted with her.

"I need you to take smiling completely off the table so I can stop thinking about puns. It's a chicken and egg situation." She twisted the end of her dog's leash between both hands. "And now you have no idea how hard it is for me to hold back a *lot* of terrible chicken-and-egg puns." She closed her eyes and a look of pain settled into her face. Her words came out in a rush. "If you want to know which came first, the chicken went off like a fire-clucker, while the egg was just happy to get laid."

As practiced as I was at keeping a straight face, I'd never found it so difficult.

"I can't believe your ex never laughed at your jokes," I said.

She flicked her eyes back open and grimaced. "I thought I'd left him in England, but I'm actually a little afraid he might turn up here. If you see a strange man hanging around, will you let me know?"

My stomach sunk as I absorbed her words. Complications were exactly what I'd been trying to avoid.

"Your ex is dangerous?"

"Um." She considered it a moment, but I could already see the answer in the way she twisted her dog's leash between her hands, squeezing the end of it as though trying to wring out water. "He's not really violent, mostly just mean and controlling." Her voice had changed, become more hesitant. As though just the mention of her ex made her less sure of herself. "Benedict doesn't like that I left, or that I took Ruff with me. Technically Ruff is his dog, but I'm the only one who ever loved her or told her she's a good girl." She directed the last bit at her dog, and Ruff's tail thumped happily on the ground. "Ruff's too old for breeding, so she's not worth anything to him now. He just wants her back to spite me."

"You really think he may come looking for you?"

"He said he was on his way."

I had to stop myself from groaning out loud. So much for my plan to distance myself from Iola. With her safety at risk, I had no choice but to look out for her. After failing to save my mother, the urge to do whatever I could to keep others from being hurt had been fused into my wiring. If Iola was being threatened by her ex, I could no more keep my distance than I could keep myself from wanting to smile at her jokes.

"We'll swap phone numbers." I took out my phone. "And we should have a signal, in case you're in trouble but don't have time to make a call."

"Like those flags they wave on ships?" Taking my phone, she punched in her number.

"Like a personal alarm. Get one that's small enough to hang on your key chain, and I should be able to hear it from next door."

She laughed. "Right. That makes more sense than

flags." She used my phone to call hers, let it ring once, then hung up. "Thanks for being neighborly, in spite of the way I accused you of suspected panty perversions. Knowing you're willing to help makes me feel safer."

Great. I'd put her father in jail, and now she was thanking me for my good intentions.

Her dog gave a heavy sigh, then collapsed onto her belly as though she'd lost the will to keep standing. Letting out a loud fart, she dropped her massive head onto her front paws.

"Her full name's Lady Ruffington the Third. Can you tell she was a valuable prize winner with a noble lineage?" Looking down at Ruff, Iola shook her head, but her eyes shone with affection. "She used to be worth more than I paid for my car."

"She's louder than your car."

"You almost smiled again." Her voice rose accusingly. "Your lips twitched on one side."

"Don't assume it's normal. Most people never see me smile. I once overheard my team of builders discussing whether I could be an emotionless humanoid android sent from the future."

She gave me a skeptical look. "Is that true?"

"One hundred percent. And just to mess with them, I pretended to drink a glass of motor oil that was really cocoa thickened with molasses."

"What did they say?"

"They didn't say anything. They found another part of the building site that needed urgent attention. Avoided me for days."

Her laugh was as lovely as the rest of her, almost musical, and I was struck once more by the perfection of her lips. They were the lips art students were taught to draw, with a full bow on top and a plump curve below.

Highly kissable lips.

Which was a disturbing thought, seeing as they were precisely the last lips I should ever think about kissing.

# Chapter Six

Iola

Asher was looking at my lips, and I wasn't sure I liked it.

I didn't like the way my heart pounded. I didn't like the heat that pooled in my belly, or the warmth in my cheeks. And I definitely didn't like the sudden urge I had to lick my lips.

Or to lick *him*.

Since escaping from Benedict, I'd resolved to make the most of my freedom. Reclaiming my life meant I was finally having fun, eating all the foods Benedict had frowned at, using the red lipstick he'd called slutty, wearing whatever I wanted. But I needed to rebuild my confidence and take some time to rediscover myself. Was I really ready for a man like Asher?

He was... unexpected.

Stoic and inscrutable, sure. But when he cracked a joke in a flat tone, without so much as a twitch of his deadpan face, it was so appealing I was in danger of falling at his feet.

Ruff had been lying still with her head resting on her paws. But now she jerked up and let out a low, cautious growl as though she wasn't sure if she'd be told off for it.

Asher's cat had reappeared. She jumped onto the fence at the front of his property and sat on top of one of the posts, every bit as cool as Asher.

In fact, as Nemesis leveled an unblinking stare at me, I realized how alike she and Asher were. Both sleek, collected, and giving nothing away. Asher was even wearing black jeans and a dark gray t-shirt, and he had an athletic way of moving that made me think of a cat prowling.

"Maybe people really do start to look like their pets after a while," I said without thinking.

"Your jowls don't hang quite as low as Ruff's." Asher spoke in his usual deadpan way, and I couldn't help but laugh.

"Ruff has me beaten when it comes to jowls. But I think she's beautiful." I glanced down at her big, goofy face. "She looks like a prehistoric teddy bear, don't you think?"

"Mark Twain said the more he learned about people, the more he liked his dog."

"That doesn't answer my question about Ruff's good looks."

"I liked your drawing of her," said Asher.

"Your sketch of Nemesis was good too," I said. "Are you an artist?"

He leaned back against his car, shading his eyes against the sun. "When I was younger, I wanted to be. I studied art at school but decided I wouldn't be able to make enough money that way."

"Smart move. You know what an artist without an alternative source of income is called?"

"What?"

"Homeless." I smiled, though it wasn't entirely a joke. I'd wanted to leave Benedict for a long time, but he'd kept such an iron grip on our finances, I hadn't known how to get away. Creating paintings was the only skill I'd had, the only thing he'd let me do, and the only chance I'd had to support myself. I'd practiced every minute I could, until my art was finally good enough that it was shown in a gallery and I started selling my paintings of landscapes. But it had taken years to get to that stage.

Asher nodded seriously, as though he could tell I wasn't just being flippant. "I needed to be able to support my family."

"Kade seems to be doing okay on his own," I joked. Then I realized that might not be what he meant. "Oh, I never asked if you have kids? I just assumed you didn't." He hadn't mentioned any kids last night, but I shouldn't have jumped to conclusions.

Benedict had expected me to give him children, and to devote my life to raising them. As often as I'd dreamed of having my own family one day, the thought of being forever shackled to him made me shudder. Thank goodness I hadn't gotten pregnant. I might still have time to create the family I dreamed of with someone who'd make a good father.

"I don't have kids," Asher said. "Just Kade, my father, and my older brother, Mason. But if they need anything, I'd like them to know they can count on me."

It was sweet he wanted to provide for them. The realization that his family must be close made me feel a familiar ache. Not jealousy, exactly. More like an old longing I'd tried to outgrow.

"And a cat," I said, glancing around. "Don't forget about her. Where'd she go?"

"On top of the mailbox." He pointed behind me.

"How did she get from the fence to the mailbox without me seeing her?"

"She's made out of shadows." He sounded as serious as ever.

Nemesis swung the back of the mailbox open and fished out a letter with one claw. With the letter in her mouth, she jumped down from the mailbox and slunk toward Asher's house. Ruff followed Nemesis with her eyes.

"What's she doing?"

"She collects other things besides panties."

I watched Nemesis carry the letter around the side of the house and vanish, as Asher had suggested, into a shadow. "So your cat really does steal the panties from my washing line? And she can sneak into my house?" Watching the effortless way Nemesis had opened the mailbox, the last of my skepticism was fading.

"Not just your house. She also turns up with other

people's shoes, socks, and stuffed toys, sometimes from several streets away. She likes presenting them to me. Once she dropped a kid's drawing at my feet."

I blinked at him. The sudden picture I had of Nemesis offering Asher my panties like trophies made my cheeks heat and my brain shift into joker-drive.

"Was it a paw-trait?" I asked. "It sounds sketchy." A thump came from inside Asher's house and Ruff growled again, her head up and her nose pointed toward the sound. "What was that?"

"Nemesis probably took the letter in through the window." Asher looked down at Ruff. "The other day, she brought in a chew toy which might belong to your dog. You should come in and take a look."

"You think your cat would steal one of my dog's toys?" I shook my head. "Ruff weighs a hundred and seventy-five pounds, and Nemesis is what? Eight pounds? Challenging Ruff while she's on the leash is one thing, but stealing her toy?"

"Come in." He turned toward his front door, motioning me to follow.

"What about Ruff?"

"Bring her inside."

Asher's house had been built about the same time as Santino's and it turned out to have the same dated style of tiles on the kitchen floor, along with the original cabinets, counters, and light fittings. But just like Santino's house, the beach view was so stunning it didn't matter that the house still had old fixtures.

Besides, Asher's furniture was modern and tasteful,

and he had some beautiful paintings on the walls. I recognized the work of a couple of up-and-coming painters who were starting to make a real name for themselves.

Looping Ruff's leash around the leg of one of the stools in the open plan kitchen and living area, I told her to sit. Then I walked to the big back doors that lead onto Asher's back deck. My gaze didn't go to the ocean or the people on the beach, but to my own house.

I drew in a sharp breath. "Oh my God. I had no idea you could see my place so well from here. You look over my deck and pool area, and I can barely see your place at all." Pressing my fingers to my mouth, I stared in horror. "Not that I'm in the habit of practicing naked yoga, but I'm glad I found out about your view before I decided to give it a try. Or before I did anything else embarrassing." I hesitated. "Um. You haven't seen me do anything embarrassing, have you?"

I was desperately trying to remember if I'd done anything shameful while on my back deck, like picking my nose or scratching an inappropriate part of my body. Come to think of it, both Asher *and* Kade could have seen me having coffee in my pajamas, or watched me pick my swimsuit out of my butt cheeks before heading to the beach for a swim.

When I glanced over my shoulder, Asher was still in the hallway where he probably hadn't even heard my mini freak-out or the question I'd asked.

He carried a box into the living area and put it down on the kitchen island. "Take a look."

Distracted, I walked over to peer into the full box, my jaw dropping when I saw how many things were in there.

Then I gasped. "This is Ruff's!" I pulled out the squeaky rubber chicken I hadn't even noticed was missing. When I handed it to Ruff, she bit down on it and the toy let out a loud squeak. "Your cat has some nerve."

"She has issues," he agreed in his deadpan way.

"There's Ruff's ball." I grabbed it. "And my missing sock. I thought the dryer had swallowed it." I narrowed my eyes at Asher. "How come you don't return this stuff to its rightful owners?"

He hooked his finger into something pink and fluffy. When he lifted it out of the box, it turned out to be a pair of novelty handcuffs. His eyebrow quirked. "You think I should go door to door with a box that includes sex toys and women's panties, asking my neighbors if they're missing any?"

I snorted a laugh. "What about putting a sign on your front door? *If you've lost your sex toys, please knock.*"

To my surprise, he gave a low chuckle, the sound as sensual and pleasurable as settling into a warm bath. "Or, *No panties, no problem. Step inside and I'll have you covered in no time.*"

I swallowed. Both because it was the first time I'd heard him laugh, and because now the idea of losing my panties with Asher was starting to permeate through my brain. I only wished he'd been facing me when he chuckled, because I'd have given anything to see him smile.

"You'd have them lining up around the block," I said hoarsely, not really joking. I couldn't be the only woman in San Dante to have noticed how dangerously attractive Asher was. A sign like that would probably stop traffic.

When Kade had walked up to me on the beach, I'd thought he was the most handsome man I'd ever met. But Asher had him beat. He may not have Kade's easy charm, but Asher was even more devastating. Maybe because he was more reserved. What woman could resist such a tall glass of dark, mysterious, and sexy?

"You should come to my art exhibition," I said. "Six o'clock tomorrow night at the community center."

He seemed to hesitate, like he was trying to think of a way to turn me down. Did he not want to go? Maybe art exhibitions were unpopular in San Dante. Perhaps I'd wasted money I couldn't afford on wine and cheese, and tomorrow night I'd be left standing alone in an empty room, surrounded by paintings nobody wanted.

My stomach contracted. I'd been trying not to think about tomorrow night because it made me anxious, and now my nerves were returning. "If nobody turns up, I'll try to brush it off," I blurted. "But it'll color things, and my frame of mind could suffer."

"You're nervous about your exhibition?"

I nodded. Nervous was an understatement. Terrified would be more accurate. "I'm afraid nobody will come. So if you could bring several dozen friends along, that'd be a big help." I shot him a smile to let him know I was joking about the last part.

Well, I was kind of joking.

Mostly.

Asher nodded slowly, still not looking as enthusiastic as I'd hoped. "Then I'll be there."

"Thank you." I unhooked Ruff's leash from around the stool. "I'll see you tomorrow."

Walking back down the hallway, Ruff's shoulder grazed against a mostly-closed door, pushing it open. I glanced into what looked like a spare bedroom, the lack of personal belongings telling me it wasn't in use. But when my gaze landed on the window, I stopped dead.

"You can see into my living room." My voice rose with shock.

His window was higher than mine, so he looked down into my house and his window blind gave an illusion of privacy. Because I couldn't see into his house, I'd assumed it worked both ways.

"Yes," he said, his tone suddenly wary.

"Do you watch me?" I demanded.

"I keep the door to this room closed and it's hardly ever used."

"That's not an answer."

He was silent for a moment, his face all but unreadable except for a tiny muscle ticking in his jaw. Then he seemed to come to decision, because he gave an almost imperceptible nod and said, "I watched your father's arrest from here."

My heart stopped beating. I stared out the window, trying to picture it. How many police officers had gone in to arrest Dad? Was anyone else there? What had tipped them off?

Though I had at least a dozen questions, I didn't want

to ask Asher. It wasn't that I was ashamed of my father, exactly. But Dad had been determined I'd never get caught up in his business. He'd wanted me to have a better life than his, without ever having to look over my shoulder. All the years I'd spent at boarding school, I'd wished he wasn't so strict about keeping me away. I'd wanted a real father, and had tried desperately to convince him I didn't care how he made his money. All I'd wanted was to spend time with him.

Then came the bombshell. On my wedding day, Dad had told me he suspected Mom's death might not have been an accident. The fire that had killed her may have been deliberate, set by one of his enemies. That's why he'd wanted to keep me as far from his business as possible.

It had shaken me badly. Afterward, I'd refused to so much as speak to my father. But by the time his lawyer called with news of his arrest, my anger had softened. At least I'd finally understood why Dad had sent me away to boarding school, and why he'd been so eager for me to marry Benedict and move halfway around the world. Dad really had been trying to protect me.

"I wish he hadn't been arrested," I said. "It was a shock when I found out he was in prison."

The lawyer had said he'd fought through the courts to get access to Dad's house, because my father had insisted I should move into it while I still could. Dad and I hadn't spoken for so long, I was surprised and grateful he was so determined to help me get away from Benedict.

"I'm glad they arrested him," Asher stated matter-of-factly.

I gaped at him. "What? Why would you say something like that?"

"Because it's true." Asher's jaw was tight and his gaze was hard. It was almost like he was challenging me to lose my temper.

"That's my father you're talking about."

"He's also a drug dealer. Prison is where he belongs."

I breathed out through my nose, trying to keep my tone even. "Was he a bad neighbor? Did he play loud music all night, or throw trash over the fence?"

"He didn't do any of those things."

"Did he barge over here and refuse to leave? Did you ever go next door to talk to him?" I kept going without waiting for Asher to shake his head. "Or was it the color of his skin you didn't like?"

That got a frown out of Asher. "Of course not. That had nothing to do with it."

"But you didn't actually know Dad, did you?" It was one thing for me to be angry with my father and criticize his choices. It was another thing for a stranger to make a snap judgement and write him off completely. Especially when I'd gotten so sick of Benedict making snide comments about people, mocking everything about them that didn't meet his impossible standards. Nobody had ever been good enough for Benedict. Especially not me.

Asher folded his arms. "I knew the only thing I needed to. He was a drug dealer. End of story."

If he were trying his best to goad me, he couldn't do a better job. So much for keeping my temper.

I stabbed a finger at him. "And you've just decided he's evil and should be locked up forever? I mean, he hasn't even gone to trial yet, but that doesn't matter to you, does it?"

"No, it doesn't. I know he's guilty."

"I'll be the first to admit my dad's not perfect, but he's not completely bad, either. People aren't always black and white. Sometimes they get forced into doing things. Sometimes life isn't fair and people don't get to make easy choices."

"You think your father was forced to deal drugs?" Asher's head shake told me how seriously he took that idea.

"Whether he was or not doesn't matter. My point is, you saw him get arrested and think that's all you need to know about him. And your judgmental attitude is making me angry, so I'm getting out of here." Striding to the door, I tugged Ruff along with me.

"Iola, I'm just trying to be honest with you," he called after me.

"Please feel free not to insult my only remaining family member to my face!" I yanked the front door open.

So much for all that attraction I'd felt. I'd thought Asher was such a great guy, and what had my dad ever done to him? Nothing, I'd bet. Asher had happened to see him get arrested and written him off as a criminal without knowing the first thing about him. And someone who could tell me he was glad my father was in prison obviously didn't much care about my feelings.

Though I paused in the doorway, Asher said nothing. He made no move to stop me leaving, or to apologize. Just like the night before, when he'd suddenly closed himself off from me, slamming the door on anything we might have shared, his expression was totally blank. He just watched me go in silence.

Maybe it was time to do a little door slamming myself —literally instead of metaphorically.

Asher's front door made a satisfying bang as I closed it hard behind me. And as Ruff and I stormed away, I was convinced there was no chance in hell that Asher and I would ever speak to each other again.

# Chapter Seven

## Iola

"See?" said Gloria. "You had nothing to worry about."

"You have no idea how relieved I am." I spoke from the heart, gazing at all the people crammed in around us, filling the community center's gallery space. Showing my portraits to this many people all at once was nerve-racking, but I really needed to sell some pieces, so this was a whole lot better than if nobody had shown up.

"It seems like whole town's here." Gloria sounded gleeful.

"Thanks to you." I wanted to hug her, but settled for putting my hand on her forearm to give it a quick squeeze.

Meeting Gloria had been one of the best things to happen to me since arriving in San Dante. She ran the community center and taught art classes, and I couldn't believe how nice she'd been. Ever since I'd wandered nervously into the community center and introduced myself to the striking woman behind the desk, she'd been enthusiastic about organizing an exhibition of my work. I already counted her as a friend, and hopefully she felt the same way.

Gloria tucked her ultra-long, straight hair behind her ear and grabbed a glass of sparkling wine off a passing waiter's tray. "Everyone loves your paintings," she said. "You've sold a few already."

I smiled gratefully at her. "Honestly, I was afraid people would hate them. This is a new style for me, and it was a risk."

"A risk that's paid off."

Thank goodness it had. In England I'd painted polite landscapes Benedict had approved of, because he didn't like me painting anything more challenging. When I'd disobeyed his rules, he made my life unpleasant. But since arriving in California I'd finally been free to paint whatever I wanted, and I'd found myself creating a series of portraits. My pent-up fear and relief were so strong, the images had seemed to burst out of me onto the canvases. Each portrait was of a person sitting in front of a mirror, their body and surroundings realistic. But they didn't have faces. Instead, each figure had an explosion of color where their face should be.

I felt a tap on my shoulder and turned.

"Excuse me. You're the artist, aren't you?" It was an elderly woman with short silver hair and crinkled cheeks that looked like they'd been folded too many times. Her pink shirt had the word *ViaGranny* embroidered on one pocket, the letters stretched across her very ample bosom. In fact, there were a few older women here who were wearing the same shirt. Maybe they were all members of a bowling team and *ViaGranny* was their team name?

"That's right. I'm Iola Martin. It's a pleasure to meet you, Mrs....?"

"Beatrice Abernathy," she supplied. "I want to buy that painting."

She pointed. But I barely saw which one she was indicating, because my gaze caught on the man standing in front of it. I'd been watching him all evening, my attention constantly drawn to him, my mind distracted by him while I was supposed to be talking to the people who were considering buying my paintings.

Dressed in a smart charcoal shirt and pants, and so handsome it hurt to look at him, he was a steady rock standing firm in the colorful sea of people. While everyone else seemed more intent on chattering to each other and drinking glasses of the cheap sparkling wine I'd scrimped to buy, I'd noticed Asher had found a space in front of each of my paintings to stand and look for a long time, as though to consider each one carefully. He had a distinctive way of standing, evenly balanced with his hands by his sides, like a fighter sizing up an opponent. Though he stood very still, he looked as though he could spring into action at a moment's notice.

Why was he here? Sure, he'd promised to come, but that was before we argued. I'd been sure that watching me storm out of his house would have changed his mind.

And I was equally unsure whether I even wanted him here.

"Good choice," said Gloria to Beatrice. "That painting's one of my favorites."

Beatrice nodded. "I like it too, but I'm not sure I understand it. I want to know what all the colors over the woman's face mean."

"Let's get closer." I was already moving toward Asher, motioning the other two to follow. As I approached him, Asher turned. His gunmetal eyes landed on mine, and I felt my feet stop as though I had no control over them. If only I had a sketchpad to capture the straight line of Asher's lips, his dark, serious eyes, and the sharp angles of his cheeks, nose, and chin.

"So?" asked Beatrice from beside me. "Why doesn't the woman in the painting have a face?"

Though I heard her question, I was so busy staring at Asher while I slashed angry black lines onto an imaginary canvas, I couldn't concentrate on what she was asking. The light in his eyes would be the brightest highlight. The rest would be angles and shadows, a severely handsome face emerging from a black background, his expression inscrutable, trapping the viewer with the force of his sharply intelligent gaze.

I was mentally tracing the only curves in the painting, his charcoal irises, imagining how I'd capture the intensity in them, when Asher looked at Beatrice.

"Because the painting depicts how the woman feels," he said.

With a jolt I realized I must have been staring silently at him for an uncomfortably long time.

Beatrice touched my arm, giving me a puzzled frown. "Are you all right, dear?"

I drew in a breath, trying to push away the vivid portrait of Asher I'd created in my mind. "Um." I blinked at the painting that was actually in front of me and tried to focus on that instead. "Sorry, what?"

"Her appearance is colored by her emotions." Asher tilted his head toward the woman in the painting. "What she's seeing in the mirror isn't real life, but a distortion. See her stiff spine and clenched fists? I think she's trying hard to control it, but her anger's exploding out anyway. The red part represents her fury. She's raging at something outside of herself, but see there, where it's tinged with sadness? She's also mad at herself." His gray eyes moved back to mine as I felt my lips part with surprise. "Have I interpreted your painting correctly, Iola?"

"Yes." The word came out a little hoarse. "That's it exactly." How had he been able to articulate what was in my head as though it were obvious? The clues in the painting were subtle enough that nobody else seemed to have picked up on them.

"It's a self-portrait, isn't it?" Asher asked the question as though he already knew the answer.

I nodded, unable to unglue my eyes from his. "Yes," I said again. As an artist in desperate need of money, I should be talking about the painting, pointing out things that might encourage Beatrice to buy it. But I was lost for words.

Was I completely transparent to Asher? His gray eyes weren't just sharp, they seemed to have power to open me up and peek inside.

"I had no idea it was a self-portrait," exclaimed Gloria. "Why didn't you tell me? But now you've mentioned it, it seems obvious." She waved her half-full champagne flute at Asher. "How do you know so much about art, Asher? You've never come to any exhibitions I've organized before."

"You two know each other?" I asked, looking between Asher and Gloria and feeling a pang of…

Wait. Was that jealousy?

Uh-oh.

Asher might be good-looking enough to make me feel giddy, and maybe his mysterious reserve was appealing, but how could I be attracted to someone who'd told me he was happy Dad was in prison?

"Everyone knows each other around here." Gloria waved a hand to indicate it was no big deal. She looked stunning, as usual, wearing a vibrant blue dress. Her beautiful Asian features and waist-length hair made her even more striking, and standing next to her, I felt plain. Probably should have worn something more colorful instead of a white blouse, black pants, and comfortable, flat sandals.

"San Dante might attract a lot of tourists, but for the people who live here all year round, it feels like a small town," Asher said.

"I want that portrait." Beatrice Abernathy was still

staring at it. "Now I can see the rage in it, I like it even more. You're really angry, aren't you dear?"

My face warmed. I could express my feelings in paint a lot easier than hearing them analyzed. Giving a little laugh, I tried to make light of it. "I have an ex-husband. That explains the anger."

"Just one ex-husband? I have three. When it comes to rage you're still an amateur, dear. One or two more will really develop your temper." Beatrice patted my shoulder. "Now put my name on that painting before Martha snaps it up. She's got her eye on it too, but seeing as she cheats at poker, I'm going to beat her to it."

I gave Beatrice a grateful smile. "Of course. Thank you. I'll show you where to put down your details, and I'll call you tomorrow to arrange payment and collection."

"Let me," said Gloria. "I'll take you to the purchasing sheet, Beatrice." She took the old woman's arm. "Come this way."

"Congratulations," Asher said when they'd disappeared into the crowd. "Another painting sold. Although that's the one I wanted."

"I didn't think you'd come," I said bluntly.

"I told you I would. You didn't believe me?"

"But you said that horrible thing, then I left, and so..." I trailed off, pretty sure I didn't have to spell it out for him.

"We can have a difference of opinion without having to avoid each other afterward." He said it like a fact, as though I couldn't possibly argue.

I shook my head. "Not if you're going to be so blunt about my father. He might be far from perfect, but just because you lived next door to him for a while doesn't mean you know everything about him. And he's the only family I have."

Asher studied me a moment. The only sign of what might be going through his mind was a slight tensing of his jaw. Then he said, "Have you seen any sign of your ex-husband?"

"Benedict? No, not yet." I frowned at the subject change. Was he trying to distract me?

"But you're sure he's coming to San Dante?"

"I'm not *sure*. But he said he was, and it's the kind of vindictive thing he'd do. If he can make my life miserable, he will."

Asher nodded as though I was confirming what he thought. "Then let's not argue."

"You want me to forget what you said about Dad?"

"I respect your loyalty to him. If someone disrespected a member of my family, I'd be angry too. I'm sorry for upsetting you."

I shifted from one foot to the other as my resolve weakened. "You're apologizing for upsetting me, not for what you said?"

"My opinion of your father doesn't matter. What matters is keeping you safe from your ex-husband. I don't want anything bad to happen to you, Iola." When he leaned closer, I felt my breath catch. His voice lowered, becoming more intimate. "Will you forgive what I said so we can be friends again? Please?"

I swallowed. It wasn't exactly the apology I'd wanted,

but the way he said 'please' made me think all kinds of wicked things. It was impossible to stay angry when I was imagining all the stuff I'd be willing to do if he leaned even closer and whispered 'please' softly into my ear.

"Okay," I said a little breathlessly. "Let's be friends."

"Good." He hesitated a moment, looking pleased. "Gracias mi amiga guapa."

I found myself smiling back at him, touched by his use of Spanish. It had been my first language—my language of childhood and happy memories. Not only did it speak to something deep inside me, he'd called me his beautiful friend, which was a nice compliment. His accent wasn't bad, and I loved his deep, rumbly voice.

My gaze went to the hard angle of his jaw, wondering if it would feel as smooth as it looked. He must have shaved before he'd come out. Maybe it was his shaving foam that smelled so nice?

What had I been angry about again? Suddenly it was hard to remember.

"I made a mistake tonight," he said. "The painting Beatrice is buying is my favorite. I should have been quicker about putting my name on it, instead of letting her get in first."

I'd been so focused on Asher, I'd almost forgotten where I was. Forcing my gaze from his face, I glanced around to find the short woman in the pink shirt. "Beatrice is smaller than you are. Just ambush her when she's carrying it out of here and wrestle it away from her," I suggested jokingly.

"The ViaGranny Gang are all tougher than they look.

She'd probably clobber me with her handbag and steal my wallet."

"What's the ViaGranny Gang?" I studied the group of women who were now gathered around the purchasing sheet, gesticulating wildly as they argued over the list of paintings. "They're all wearing the same shirts. Are they a bowling team?"

He nodded. "They also play cards, drink heavily, flirt with men of all ages, and generally cause trouble around town. *'ViaGranny'* is a combination of Viagra and Granny. Because, according to them, it's a good mix."

I snorted a laugh. "They all look around eighty."

"At least."

"I hope they let me join their club when I get to their age."

"You have to have lost at least one husband in highly suspicious circumstances to get in."

I gave a rueful grin. "Don't tempt me."

"Seriously, I shouldn't have let Beatrice get that painting." He glanced after her again, and this time a faint, thin line appeared between his eyebrows. "She won't appreciate it like I would have."

"You could get Nemesis to steal it for you."

"The painting's a lot bigger than your panties. It won't be as easy to take."

I laughed again, mostly at how serious he sounded, as though he'd done the math on the panties versus painting equation. "How do you stay so deadpan, even when you talk about stealing my panties?"

"Oh." A middle-aged woman had approached, probably intending to talk to me. But now she backed away with wide eyes. "I'm sorry, I didn't mean to interrupt your conversation. I'll come back when you're not talking about...um..." The woman turned and fled.

I bit my lip. "Oops. Note to self, don't talk about panty stealing in public."

He leaned in, dropping his voice. "Especially not where the ViaGranny Gang could overhear. Any one of them would happily offer their granny panties to be stolen. If they're actually wearing any."

His low, intimate tone made me hyper-aware of how close together we were, and a shiver ran over my body. His shirt was open at the throat, and the sliver of tanned, muscled chest I could see was ridiculously sexy. I wanted to touch that smooth skin. To undo the rest of his buttons and run my hands over him.

And why shouldn't I? This was my new life, after all. I finally had a chance to experience everything I'd been missing out on. Why not put Asher at the top of my list of new things to try? Especially when the thought of it sent a hot ache of wanting through me.

"Cocktail sausage?" A passing waiter thrust his tray at us.

I jerked back, dragging in a breath.

What was I thinking? We were in a public place, and I needed to focus on trying to sell as many paintings as possible. I had to get a grip on myself.

Asher took a sausage, so I grabbed one too, mainly to have something to distract me from thoughts about his body. As the waiter moved on, I held up the party snack.

"Want to hear a joke about tiny, wrinkled sausages and missing granny panties?"

Asher choked on his sausage.

"Are you okay?"

"Mm-hm." He thumped his fist against his chest. "Just a small sausage malfunction. It went down the wrong way."

"Your sausage slipped into the wrong hole?"

Asher looked surprised for a moment, then his lips twitched up into the biggest almost-smile I'd seen from him yet. And the Fairy of Good Looks and Sex Appeal may as well have taken out her magic wand and clobbered me with it. A deadpan Asher rated full marks on the attractiveness scale, but when his grey eyes crinkled, the scale shattered.

Okay, now the man was officially driving me crazy. Did the community center have a private office out the back? Could I convince Asher to go in there with me, and—

"Is something wrong?" he asked. His brow didn't exactly furrow, but his eyes darkened and pulled down a little, in what had to be an Asher equivalent of a frown.

Noticing it probably meant I was starting to be able to read his expressions. Like learning a secret language. Oh lord, that was even sexier.

"Iola?"

"Yes." I swallowed hard. "Um. You said you're in construction, right? Are you building anything now?"

"My team's finishing work on the town's new library and post office."

"You don't have enough callouses to be a builder. Your hands don't look rough." I couldn't help myself. I touched my fingers to the back of his hand, just because I had to feel his skin. And sure enough, a shiver passed through me.

He didn't move his hand away. Instead he leaned in. His gaze played over my face, moving from my eyes, down to my lips, and back again. His voice was low and intimate. "I don't swing a hammer these days. Mostly I sit at a computer."

I licked my lips. "Let me guess. Are you in management? Or do you own the company?"

"I own it."

"Then you're doing well for yourself." My voice was barely louder than a whisper. Surely I wasn't imagining the heat in his eyes, or the way my lips seemed to be holding his attention?

"I'm not the one creating masterpieces."

Heat travelled up from my neck and I attempted a chuckle. "They're hardly masterpieces."

"You're doing something special. You deserve to be proud." He spoke so deliberately, and his gaze was so intense, so focused, it felt like the best compliment I'd ever received.

My face warmed even more, and I was sure I was turning bright red. "Thank you. I'll be happy if some of them sell. I could use the money."

His eyes darkened. "You're short of money?"

I could have kicked myself. "No, not like that. Don't worry. Well, I need to pay my bills, but it's not..." I shook my head, flustered. "My ex-husband used money to control me, so if I could invent an ideal world, there'd be no money at all."

"Congratulations, Iola!" Gloria's voice was startlingly loud from behind me, and I jumped a little, then turned. To my surprise, the crowd was starting to thin. How long had Asher and I been talking?

"We're starting to wrap things up now. This is for you." Gloria pressed a bottle of champagne into my hands. And it was the real deal, expensive French champagne, not the cheap stuff I'd bought for the event.

"What's this?" I blinked at her. Asher had been taking up so much of my awareness, letting in everything else felt like emerging from a dream. "I should be the one giving you a gift to thank you for hosting my show."

"Sweetie, you need to celebrate selling all your paintings."

My jaw loosened. "Every single one is sold?"

Gloria grinned. "I had a feeling they'd go quickly. As soon as I saw them, I knew your portraits were special."

"That's incredible. Thank you." I hugged the bottle to my chest, wanting to jump up and down. "Shall we drink it tonight? Will you celebrate with me?"

Gloria screwed up her nose. "I wish I could, but the woman I care for hasn't been well. I should get home to check on her."

I turned to Asher. Perhaps I should be wary of how overwhelming my attraction to him was, but I couldn't help myself. "Asher? Will you?"

# Chapter Eight

## Asher

It was a bad idea to accompany Iola all the way into Santino's house.

But still, I went.

Though Kade occasionally complained I was too clever for my own good, if he could see me now, he'd think I was an idiot. My brain had decided to take a break, and it wasn't the organ controlling my feet when I followed Iola into her living room.

She kicked off her sandals and sighed as she flattened her bare feet on the floor. Clad in black pants, her legs were long and shapely, and her white blouse was unbuttoned at the top just low enough to give me tempting glimpses of cleavage. She looked very elegant, and very beautiful.

"Ruff!" she called.

There was an answering bark, and her enormous dog

lumbered up to greet her. Ruff's tail wagged so enthusiastically, it could have powered a small town. The dog thumped her body against Iola's legs then dropped to the floor, rolling over to present her belly. With a laugh, Iola bent to scratch it.

When she straightened, my lungs forgot their purpose.

Iola's hair was glossy and sleek around her face, and her eyes caught the light so they looked a beautiful, warm shade of brown. Her light, smudged freckles were like a treasure map pointing the way to her plump, perfect lips.

"I'm cracking open the champagne," she said. "Make yourself at home."

I winced at her choice of words—she had no way to know I was going to turn her home into my apartment building. I shouldn't have come inside. Seeing how comfortable she looked here would only make me feel worse about what I needed to do.

As she headed toward the kitchen, Ruff lumbering behind her, I considered whether I should make an excuse to leave.

"Will you put some music on?" she called back to me. "Use the record player."

"The record player?" Though I could see into this room from my spare bedroom, the view was limited. I'd never noticed a record player, and it was an unusual thing to have.

"It's in the far corner," she called. "Beside the bookcase."

I crossed over to it, looking around curiously. As

many times as I'd seen into this room from next door, I'd never been inside it before.

Iola had set up an easel against one wall, with a wheeled table next to it that was covered with tubes of paint. The entire room smelled strongly of paint and linseed oil. The rest of the furniture was unchanged from when Santino had lived here, but an enormous dog bed was beside the couch, and dog toys were scattered across the floor.

The bookcase was almost empty. Four lonely books sat at one end of the middle shelf, but I wasn't surprised there weren't more, seeing as Iola had only been in the country for a few weeks. The books were mystery novels, and two had Spanish titles. As I'd guessed from her faint accent and Latina beauty, she had to be bilingual. I'd learned Spanish when Mom had taken us to Mexico and we'd lived in a cheap apartment on the outskirts of Tijuana, but that was a long time ago and I was rusty.

A handful of LPs were stacked on the bottom shelf, and I leafed through them. They were an eclectic mix, everything from indie rock to easy listening.

"I always wanted a record player." Iola emerged from the kitchen carrying two glasses of champagne, Ruff lumbering beside her. "And seeing as this is my first house where I get to call the shots, I figured I should treat myself."

"What do you want to hear?" I asked.

"I don't know. Benedict only liked classical music, so I didn't get to hear much else. I bought a random bunch of second-hand records, hoping I'd find something good." She shot me a smile. "Surprise me."

"How about Florence and the Machine?" I slipped the record from its sleeve, set it on the turntable, then started it turning. The arm moved smoothly over the record, then settled into the groove.

"I like this," she exclaimed when it started. "Good choice."

She thrust one a glass of champagne at me, and I found myself wanting to smile at her for absolutely no reason, which wasn't like me at all.

When I'd navigated the dangerous waters of Mom's addiction, I'd perfected the art of keeping my emotions hidden. But around Iola I forgot my control, as though admiring her physical presence engaged so many of my thought processes there wasn't room for anything but her. And tonight, her incredible talent had left me reeling. Did she have any idea of the impact of her paintings? She seemed humble and unassuming, as though she didn't realize how beautifully unique they were. How was her work not hanging in every art gallery in the country? The instant I'd walked into her exhibition, I'd known her paintings would sell quickly. If I didn't have a short-term cashflow issue, I would have bought them all myself.

As I took the champagne from her, I took a deep breath of the scent she was wearing. She smelled like she'd wandered through an herb garden. Woody and fresh, with a sprinkling of mint.

"With records, you can hear the difference in the

sound," she said. "It's raw, with the tiny bumps and scratches you get on the vinyl. But I like it, don't you?"

"I like it a lot."

She clinked her glass against mine, and I took a sip of champagne, rolling the sweet liquid around my mouth.

"I've never met anyone like you before." She leaned her hip against the table. "Someone so inscrutable. A man of mystery." Her teasing tone suggested she didn't mind a little mystery.

But she didn't know the secret I was hiding.

Being alone with her was too tempting. She was too beautiful, too funny, too talented, too intriguing. As much as I prided myself in controlling my emotions, I couldn't trust myself not to kiss her. When she was this close, it was all I could think about.

I closed my eyes for a moment. When I opened them, I noticed something over her shoulder. A photograph of Santino in a silver frame.

Steeling myself, I turned away from her and walked to the photograph. At some point I'd have to admit to her that I was responsible for her father's incarceration. Only as soon as I did, Iola would shut me out, and I wouldn't be able to protect her from her ex.

There was only one way I'd have a chance of being forgiven. I needed to explain about Mom's addiction first, and she'd need to understand how badly her father and his drug dealing associates had hurt my family. I'd wait until her ex-husband was no longer a threat to admit my role in her father's arrest, but in the meantime, I could start talking to her about my past, making sure she was as sympathetic as possible when I finally confessed what I'd done. Considering her strong feelings for her father, it would be tricky. I'd have to tread carefully. But hopefully I could convince her to see things my way.

"Iola," I started. "I want to tell you about—"

"Wait. Is that your cat?"

I turned. Nemesis was sitting beside Iola's coffee table. Ruff stood stiffly behind her, staring down at her. Then Ruff glanced up at us, her brown eyes confused, as though she had no idea whether to growl, try to bite Nemesis, or pretend she didn't see her.

Nemesis yawned. If she had a magazine, she probably would have flipped through it.

"How did your cat get in here?" Iola asked.

"Maybe she slipped in behind me."

Iola shook her head. "I would have seen her."

"I haven't ruled out the possibility she can walk through walls. Nemesis is an unusual cat."

Iola raised her eyebrows. "Then she must take after you."

Ruff let out a whine. Nemesis lifted a paw and licked it, not bothering to glance at the dog.

Iola put her champagne glass on the counter, then crossed over to me. "I want to dance. Will you?" Taking the glass out of my hand, she set it next to the photograph.

The things I needed to say to her were on the tip of my tongue, but her hands slid around my neck and her body moved into mine.

Then the warmth and softness of her curves were pressed against me, and my brain short-circuited. All thoughts became cave-man-like grunts, and the only words in my head had one syllable. *Mine. Want. Take.*

I slid my hands around her waist, holding her to me as we swayed to the music. Bending my head, I dropped my nose to her hair to breathe her in. Then I brushed her hair back from her ear. "Mi hermosa," I whispered against her ear, because she was so beautiful, I couldn't help but tell her. She shivered with pleasure, and the intensity of my desire to kiss her was overwhelming. But I'd only known her, what? A few days? And she'd barely escaped a seven-year marriage.

Then I felt the warmth of Iola's breath on my neck, and her lips pressed against my skin. Another hot wave of lust surged through me. Her hands were on my back, pulling me tighter against her. I found myself starting to slide my hand under her blouse to touch her bare skin and forced myself to stop.

"You've only just separated from your husband," I murmured, my voice tight with the effort of keeping control. "I don't want to rush you into anything."

"My marriage was a sham. This doesn't feel like a rush." She nuzzled my neck again, her breath on my skin making my heart pump faster. "You smell really good."

She ran one hand up my torso and her finger brushed my nipple. At the same time, her lips pressed into the base of my neck, and I felt her tongue flick against my skin.

I closed my eyes.

I shouldn't let this go too far too soon—not until I was ready to tell her what I'd done to her father. But my hands weren't obeying my commands to withdraw. One was stroking her back, the other was pulling her hips closer. I was hard, and the most primitive part of my brain was focused on wanting to feel her softness rub against me.

"Iola..." It came out as a groan as I struggled to shove my inner Neanderthal back into his cave.

Ruff barked and a moment later, I heard footsteps.

Iola and I jerked around as a man appeared in the doorway.

"Hello, darling," he said.

It was the man I'd seen in the newspaper picture, though he was seven years older and his eyes looked meaner. As his gaze moved from Iola to me, then to Ruff, his thin lips tightened with anger.

Searching online, I'd learned the Honorable Benedict Appleby Junior was forty-five, which made him seventeen years older than Iola. He wore a dress shirt and slacks, and a heavy gold watch. Unlike Iola, he was wearing a wedding ring.

I had to admit his features were even, so some people might consider him handsome. He had a long, straight nose, white teeth, and a golden tan. His hair's blond highlights were salon perfect, his nails were professionally manicured, his eyebrows shaped, and I was fairly certain his tan was fake. He'd chosen a shirt that had the *Versace* logo across its front pocket and his watch was one of the biggest Rolexes on the market. He clearly spent a lot of time and money on his appearance.

But even if I hadn't known who he was, I would have

distrusted him on sight. His upper lip had an obnoxious curl, there were no laughter lines around his eyes, and his expression seemed to fall naturally into a contemptuous sneer.

Iola's face went white. "Benedict? How did you get in here?" Her voice was breathless and she sounded panicked.

I stepped in front of her. An automatic reaction, one I couldn't have stopped if I'd tried.

The man's eyes narrowed. "Fast work, Iola. You've already found yourself a boyfriend to pay your bills?"

"Who are you?" I asked, because it would serve no purpose to let on that I knew.

The man drew himself up. "I'm Iola's husband."

"My ex-husband," she snapped. Her shock was turning to anger, the red of her cheeks getting darker.

"If Iola doesn't want you here, you need to go." I sounded bored. When faced with a threat, my mind always went clear and my thoughts sharpened. The logical side of my brain took over the driver's seat, while my under-developed emotional side took a nap in the back.

Benedict's top lip curled even more. "It's none of your business. This is between me and my wife." As he spoke, he looked me up and down, obviously evaluating what might happen if our confrontation got physical. Benedict Appleby and I were a similar height, but I could read his posture well enough to be confident he'd be a coward in a fight.

I didn't have bulky muscle like my brother Mason,

but I regularly bench pressed two ninety. And I'd been in enough fights that I felt little fear at the prospect of another, even though I'd been badly beaten a few times. When I was fifteen, I'd received some valuable lessons that way on the kind of targets not to pick for the hustle Kade and I were running to earn money.

Iola's fists were clenched, and I could feel waves of anger radiating from her. "I'm not going back to England," she snapped. "You can't make me."

His gaze raked her up and down. "You're already getting fatter." He tsked. "See darling? You need me. Without me, you fall apart."

"You have no power over me here."

"If you won't do the right thing and come back where you belong, I'll take Lady Ruffington."

At the mention of her name, the dog lumbered to Iola and sat down next to her. Nemesis was nowhere to be seen.

"Over my dead body." Iola dropped a protective hand onto Ruff's head. "She hates you, and I won't let you take her."

"The dog belongs to me."

"Careful, or I'll order her to bite you."

Benedict let out a hard humorless laugh that sounded more like a slap. "The dog's too well trained for that, darling. And I thought you knew better than this. You owe me an apology for making me come all this way. Not to mention a debt of gratitude. What would have happened if I'd let you run out of money over here on your own?"

She spoke through gritted teeth. "I'm doing just fine without you."

He scoffed. "You were nothing when I met you. Nobody wanted you, did they darling? I took pity on you, gave you luxury and status beyond your wildest dreams, and this is the thanks I get?" His voice hardened. "If you turn me down now, I'll make you regret it for the rest of your life."

It was taking every bit of my self-control to let them talk without interruption, but when Iola hissed, "Get out, Benedict," I took it as permission to enforce her request.

"You heard what she said. Leave now, and don't come back." Though I still sounded bored, I moved toward Benedict with purpose, and he took several fast steps back toward the door.

"I'll leave." He narrowed his eyes at me. "But remember what I said, Iola, and don't test my patience."

He turned and strode out, the front door slamming shut behind him.

Iola dragged in a loud breath, her eyes still bright with fear. "How did he get in here?"

I went to the front door, opened it and looked out. Benedict was getting into a car across the street. "The door was unlocked," I called to her.

"I must have forgotten to lock it. How could I have done that?" The music switched off abruptly. She'd clearly had enough of it.

Once Benedict's car had disappeared around the corner, I turned the latch and tested the front door to make sure it was secure. But even with the house locked, I wasn't about to leave Iola unguarded.

When I went back to the living room, Iola was on her knees beside Ruff with her arms around the dog. "I won't let him take you," she was saying. "We're family. I'll protect you, no matter what."

I waited by the door for her to give Ruff a last squeeze, then cleared my throat. "I'm going next door to get my toothbrush and a change of clothes. I won't be longer than five minutes. Lock the door behind me, and don't open it again without being certain it's me."

"What?" She got to her feet keeping one hand on Ruff's head. "Why are you—?"

"I won't leave you here alone. I'll sleep on your couch."

Her lips parted and her eyes widened. "You'd do that?"

"Of course."

Telling her what her father had done to my family would have to wait. I couldn't risk upsetting her more. And confessing that I was responsible for her father's arrest was out of the question. I couldn't protect her from her ex-husband if she was so angry with me, she refused to see me. The worst possible situation would be to live next door to her if she needed my help but wouldn't allow me to give it. That would be unacceptable.

"But I don't like asking for favors," she said. "I'd have to pay you back somehow."

"Then agree to sell me a self-portrait, once you've painted another one."

Her smile was small and shaky, but I was relieved to see it. She was so pale, even the tiniest smile was a win.

"That doesn't feel like me paying you back," she said.

"Believe me, it is."

"You don't need to take the couch. There's a spare bedroom through there." She pointed.

I shook my head. "The living room's central to the house, so if anyone tries to break in, I'm more likely to hear him from the couch."

She swallowed. "You really think Benedict would come back in the middle of the night?" Before I could answer, she choked out a mirthless laugh. "What am I asking? Of course he would. He followed me all the way from London."

She looked so scared and angry, I wanted to smooth away her frown and promise everything would be okay. But she bent to give Ruff another hug. "Don't feel bad if you can't bite him, baby. I promise I'll keep you safe."

I stuck my hands in my pockets, feeling rueful. The last bit was almost exactly what I'd wanted to say to her.

"Benedict doesn't strike me as much of a dog person," I said.

"Ruff has won a room full of rosettes and trophies, including Best in Show at Crufts."

Ruff had won trophies? The ugliest dog I'd ever seen had been Best in Show?

Maybe when she'd said Crufts, she hadn't meant the famous British dog show. Perhaps I'd misheard, and there was a parody dog show called Mutts.

"But now Ruff's too old for all that, Benedict just

wants her because he knows how I feel about her." Iola went to the counter to pick up her glass of champagne. She took a big gulp of its contents, then turned to me.

"The thing about London is all the rich people go to the same schools, which means a lot of them know each other. Benedict lunches with the manager of the bank where we have our accounts, he plays polo with the lawyer who's representing him, and he golfs with the judge who's going to hear our divorce case. With all the power and privilege on his side, he's always been able to do whatever he wants."

"That's corruption."

"They call it the old-boy network."

I picked up my own half-full glass of champagne that was growing warm and losing its fizz. The thought of a system so rigged against Iola made everything inside me want to rebel.

"I'll help you fight him."

"He's too powerful to fight." She went to the fridge and took out the open bottle of champagne. "But I've finally been able to open a bank account that Benedict can't touch, and all the money I earn here will go into it. I have my own life now, and the only thing I want from my old life is Ruff." She topped up my glass, slopping the champagne because her hand wasn't steady.

"We won't let him have Ruff," I told her.

Shooting me a quick, grateful smile, she grabbed her glass and filled it to the brim. "I'm glad you're in my corner, Asher. I have a feeling nothing gets past you."

Although I didn't particularly want any more to

drink, I clinked my glass against hers, sealing my pact to protect her. Taking a symbolic sip, I saw Nemesis on the windowsill with Ruff's squeaky chicken toy dangling from her mouth. My cat must have stolen the toy back from Ruff and sauntered straight past us, jumping soundlessly up to the window ledge without so much as a squeak from the toy.

Nemesis flicked the latch with her nose and nudged the window open. The security catch stopped it from opening more than a thin crack. Nemesis carefully maneuvered the toy out of the tiny opening, worked her head through, then somehow squeezed her body out. She hung for a moment by her hips, and I was certain she was stuck. But with one final wriggle she dropped out of sight with her prize.

"That's right," I promised. "Nothing gets past me."

# Chapter Nine

## Iola

"Omph!"

There was a heavy weight on my chest.

Shocked out of sleep, I opened my eyes and stared into a bristle of whiskers, a triangular black nose, and piercing yellow eyes.

"Nemesis," I gasped.

The black cat stared back at me, her front paws pressing painfully into my breasts. How could a small, slinky cat weigh so much? She was a feline version of the Tardis, only instead of being larger than she looked from the outside, she was heavier, like she'd eaten lead weights for breakfast.

She wasn't blinking. Her piercing gaze seemed to be trying to tell me something, but my brain was too fuzzy to understand. It was probably something about how she could have killed me with one paw while I slumbered, and I should ply her with endless gratitude and mountains of panties for allowing me to live.

"How did you get in here?" My voice was croaky with sleep. Daylight was leaking under the curtain, so it was probably time I woke up. But I would have preferred my regular alarm clock to being woken by a feline ninja.

Nemesis stepped off me slowly, taking her sweet time about it, then jumped lightly onto the floor. Snoring was coming from the dog bed in the corner. Ruff was fast asleep.

"Ruff?" I croaked.

Giving a little sigh, my dog's front paws twitched as though she was dreaming about all the cats she wanted to chase. Then she snored harder.

Nemesis sauntered past Ruff's head, choosing a route that took her a bare inch from the dog's nose. Her small whiskers probably brushed against Ruff's giant ones. Still, Ruff didn't move.

The black cat leaped onto the wooden dresser that held my clothes. Its top drawer was broken and I couldn't get it to close all the way. The gap was just big enough for a cat's paw to slide into. After fishing around in the drawer for a moment, she hooked a pair of panties with one claw and pulled them out.

"Ruff?" I demanded, my voice an incredulous squeak. "You're really not going to wake up and do something?"

This time, Ruff's snoring didn't even falter.

Though I could have sworn my bedroom door was closed when I went to sleep last night, it was now halfway open. Nemesis jumped down from the dresser and sauntered out with my panties hanging from her mouth.

"Ruff!" I threw the pillow at her.

She jerked her head up and gave me a reproachful stare.

"Seriously, you call yourself a dog?" I pulled myself out of bed. "Come on, there's still time to redeem yourself. Follow that cat and get my panties back!"

Ruff struggled to her feet, her tail wagging. She clearly had no idea she'd been disrespected by an animal smaller than one of her jowls.

I'd started toward the hallway before the events of last night came flooding back. Benedict had turned up. And Asher had slept on my couch. Was he still here? I might have woken him up by talking to Ruff, and I was only wearing a t-shirt and sleep shorts.

Peeking into the living room, I saw Asher was sitting up on the couch.

"Hey, you're still here," I said.

"It's early." He stood, stretching his back as though the couch had made him stiff. He wore gray pajama pants and a black t-shirt, sticking to his habit of wearing dark clothing even in bed. Freshly awake, he was as good-looking as ever. His hair wasn't messy, no drool, and I hadn't heard him snore. Not that I was likely to have heard him over the noise Ruff made, which came close to the volume of a plane repeatedly taking off and landing.

I ran a hand over my messy hair and smoothed my t-shirt, conscious of how disheveled I must look. Benedict would have made a snide remark about it. At least with the lingering aroma of my oil paints in the air, I didn't have to worry about Asher getting a whiff of my morning breath.

"Did you see Nemesis?" I asked.

He shook his head, not looking surprised by the question. "Did she steal anything?"

"Forget it. Doesn't matter." I couldn't admit to losing another pair of panties before I'd had a cup of coffee.

"I checked all your windows were secure before I went to sleep."

"I think you were right. At least one of her parents had to be a shadow."

He ran his hand over his hair, roughing it up. But when he dropped his hand, his hair settled perfectly back into place.

Like magic.

"Maybe you're a warlock, and Nemesis is your familiar," I mused aloud.

Small creases appeared in the corners of his eyes, telling me he was amused. "You guessed my secret. Has my spell been working on you?"

I opened my mouth to say a heartfelt 'Yes', then shut it again, because he was clearly joking and I definitely needed coffee before I blurted any embarrassing truths.

"I'll get cleaned up, then make coffee." I started out of the room. "I'd make you breakfast to go with it, but the best I can do is toast and even then, I might burn it."

"I'll cook breakfast," he offered.

I stopped to give him a bright, beseeching smile. "Are you offering to whip us up a gourmet meal?"

"My brother's the chef in the family, but I'll do my best."

"Funny that you and Kade are twins when you're so different. You don't even look alike."

"Most people think we do."

"Kade's lighter than you are."

"Lighter?" His lips twitched. "You think I'm heavy?"

He was obviously teasing, but I tried to explain. "If Kade was a painting, he'd be pop art. Like an Andy Warhol screen print."

"Don't let Kade hear you compare him to a Campbell's soup can. He makes his soup from scratch."

"Okay, maybe he's one of Banksy's quirky artworks. *Gorilla in a Pink Mask*."

Asher's eyes lightened, and the creases in their corners deepened. "Do me a favor and tell him that when I'm around. I'd like to see his face."

I was warming to my theme and wouldn't let him throw me off. "And if you were a painting, you'd be a…" I considered it a moment.

"Don't say a Van Gogh." He lifted his hand to the side of his head. "I like my ear where it is."

"Oh, you're definitely a Van Gogh. He's my favorite artist. His paintings are deceptively simple, with layers of amazing brush work."

His eyebrows hooked up. "That sounds like a compliment."

He was clearly pleased. I was getting the hang of reading his small facial cues, like a diner discovering the delights of subtle flavors.

"A big compliment. Huge. So now you'll make me pancakes for breakfast?" I arched my brows.

He let out a chuckle that was so warm, I wanted to melt into a puddle at his feet. The thing about him being frugal with showing emotion was the wallop it packed when he did.

"You're devious." He gave an approving nod. "I like that about you."

Ruff plodded to the back door, and I opened it so she could go out to the back deck and poop on the fenced strip of grass that ran down the side of the house.

"I'll go next door for a shower, then come back and make breakfast," Asher said. "I won't be long. Lock the door after me."

He was still wearing pajamas and bare feet when he went out, clearly not caring if anyone saw him, though to be fair, his house was right next door.

I showered quickly, changed into shorts and a t-shirt—similar to my sleepwear only clean, and with the important addition of underwear—and let Ruff back inside. When Asher knocked, I was sipping strong coffee from my biggest mug. He was freshly shaven and carrying a bag of groceries. He smelled so good, I wanted to use syrup on him instead of the pancakes.

I trailed him into the kitchen where he put the groceries on the counter, then handed him a cup of coffee.

"Thanks." He took a sip. "That's good."

When he put his coffee back down, I moved close.

"Thank *you*," I said sincerely. "I slept better knowing you were on the couch."

Actually, it had taken me forever to get to sleep because I was so tempted to tiptoe out to the living room and cuddle on the couch with him. But he didn't need to know that.

"You're welcome." He angled his face to me, looking so handsome, my heart did a backflip. How did he manage to walk around looking the way he did and not get jumped by every woman he met?

I barely realized I was moving closer until we were a hand's width apart, as though my body had been caught in a powerful attraction tractor beam and I couldn't resist his pull.

My hands went to his waist, and I rose onto tiptoe so I could press my lips against his. For one long, glorious moment, he kissed me back, his mouth hot and tasting of coffee. Then he broke the kiss.

As he pulled back, my heart was beating so hard it felt like it was auditioning to play the opening notes of Beethoven's Fifth Symphony, and my body was trembling like a violin string. I was practically a one-woman orchestra.

"Iola, we should take things cautiously." His voice was a low murmur that sounded a little hoarse.

My heart sank. Had I got this all wrong? If Asher didn't want to kiss me, I must have been mistaken about the chemistry between us. What if he'd been repulsed by my kiss? Did I have bad breath? Did he think I was a terrible kisser?

Or maybe I'd wanted to kiss Asher so badly, I'd just imagined seeing the same longing in him, and he was currently trying to figure out which lawyer he needed to call to get a restraining order.

"Okay." I took a step back. "Never mind. I'm sorry."

I saw the change in him at once. His eyes softened and he stepped in and took hold of my arms.

"Don't do that," he said softly.

"Do what?" I lifted my chin, challenging him with a direct gaze.

"Don't get the wrong idea." His eyes dropped to my lips and his steel-gray irises seemed to darken. This time I was sure I couldn't be imagining the heat I saw.

Bending his head, he brushed his lips against mine. There was a tension in him that was obvious in the way his fingers tightened on my upper arms and the stiffness in his spine. It was as if he was fighting some internal battle.

Why was Asher holding back? The question ran through my mind like lightning, then vanished in an exhilarating rush of sensation.

Asher was a great kisser. But his lips felt too soft against mine. They were like velvet over steel, and behind the softness was a tantalizing hint of hardness. An inner strength I craved.

The gentle graze of Asher's mouth did nothing but leave me hungry for more. No, not hungry. Ravenous.

The ache inside me was like nothing I'd ever felt. I tried to press myself against him, but his hands were tight around my arms, frustrating my efforts.

I stopped pushing forward and pulled back instead. "What's wrong? I don't understand what I'm doing—"

My phone rang.

Asher let me go. He stalked to the windows at the other end of the room, running his hand roughly through his hair as though he was angry or frustrated.

I grabbed my phone off the counter. "Hello?" I barked, not bothering to check the screen to see who was calling.

"Iola? It's Gloria. I have bad news." She sounded so upset, my stomach clenched. "Someone broke into the gallery last night."

"What?" The shock in my voice was so sharp that Asher spun to face me. "Did they take anything?" I asked.

"They weren't here to steal anything. There was a little money in the cash drawer and they didn't touch it. All they did was..." She broke off with a huff of breath. "I'm so sorry. I hate to tell you like this, over the phone."

My face felt bloodless. "What did they do?"

"They destroyed your beautiful paintings. Why would anyone do that?" Her voice became a wail. "It makes no sense."

I put out a hand to steady myself on the counter.

It made perfect sense. Benedict had always used money to control me, and the paintings were my ticket to independence. He was going after me the way he knew best.

"I'm on my way."

I told Asher what had happened, trying to sound

calm and not like I wanted to scream. Then I clipped on Ruff's leash before heading to the car.

"You're too upset to drive." Asher followed me to the garage. "Let me."

"You don't need to come."

"I won't leave you to deal with this alone."

Even in my upset state, I was grateful. I'd become so used to being treated like I didn't matter, I'd come to expect it. But Asher was nothing like Benedict.

"Thank you," I told him. "You're right. I'm so angry, if anyone cut me off, I'd probably drive into them." Realizing my hand was fisted so tightly around the car keys they were cutting into my skin, I forced myself to suck in a deep breath before handing the keys to him.

All my paintings had sold last night, at least on paper. But the new owners hadn't actually paid for them yet. If the paintings had been destroyed, did that mean I was broke again?

We loaded Ruff into the back seat, and Asher drove like I'd expect, quickly and efficiently. When we pulled up outside the community center, two workmen were nailing wood over its broken window.

"You go in," he said. "I'll park the car and follow."

I braced myself before walking inside, but the devastation still hit me hard. Benedict had sliced up my canvases so thoroughly, they hung from their frames in tatters. He hadn't done it coldly. There was passion in the destruction. I must have made him furious.

"You're here." Gloria emerged from the back of the gallery and threw her arms around me, hugging me to her. I was engulfed by her hair, a straight black waterfall that flowed to her waist and smelled like a flower garden in full bloom. "Oh, Iola, I'm so sorry."

"I'm the one who's sorry, Gloria." I hugged her just as tightly. "I think my ex-husband did this, which means he's the one who broke the window as well."

She let me go, drawing back with wide eyes. "Your ex-husband? Why would he do this?"

I shook my head helplessly. "I'm sorry you were dragged into it."

"Don't blame yourself. Some men are just plain bad." The way she said it suggested she could be speaking from experience.

"Have you called the police?" asked Asher, coming into the gallery. His tone was even, and his expression hadn't changed, but I could see his anger. It was in the way his gaze raked over the ruined paintings, the tension of his skin around his eyes, the hard line of his bottom lip, and the stiffness of his spine. He looked almost as furious as I was.

"They're on their way," said Gloria.

"I didn't take payment for any of the paintings yet," I said. "Does the building have insurance?"

"The building does. The broken window will be covered, but your paintings won't. We only have a standard policy."

I turned away, rubbing my eyes and trying not to cry. The financial loss was a heavy blow. I'd spent weeks finishing those paintings, working every waking minute while the little money I'd been able to escape with slowly ran out.

Now I had to start again with no safety net. I'd have to look for a job so I could feed myself and Ruff, and paint when I wasn't working. Which meant it'd take at least two or three times as long until I had enough work for another small showing. Probably longer.

And that was assuming I could *get* a job.

I had my back to Asher and Gloria when I felt hands close around my upper arms. "You okay?" asked Asher softly. He didn't pull me back against him, but I could feel his warmth.

I nodded, crossing my arms to put my hands over his. And knowing I wasn't alone made me feel better.

"Thanks for being here," I said.

"Ruff's still in the car, and it's not safe to leave her there." He gave my arms a squeeze then let me go, turning to Gloria. "Do you mind if I bring Iola's dog inside, Gloria?"

"Go right ahead." She stared after Asher, watching him leave. After the door shut behind him, she raised her eyebrows at me. "I didn't realize it was serious between the two of you, but I approve. Asher's a sweetheart."

"I don't know what I would have done without him last night." When her eyes widened, I realized how it had sounded and shook my head. "Oh, I didn't mean... I mean, we didn't sleep together. My horrible ex turned up and Asher slept on my couch so I'd feel safe."

"That sounds like something he'd do." Her lips

curved up slowly, as though she was remembering something he'd done for her.

"How well do you know Asher?" I asked.

"Honestly?" She hesitated. "I used to have the biggest crush on him, but that was a while ago. We've always just been friends." She put a hand on my arm. "I don't think of him that way now, so please don't think I was trying to hide something from you."

"Of course not." Resting my hand over hers, I squeezed it before letting go.

Gloria lifted a piece of canvas that was hanging by one corner. "Maybe your work can be repaired?"

"I wish it could." Lifting another piece, I fit it against the one she was holding before dropping it. Benedict had gone wild with a boxcutter, and there was no fixing any of it. My eyes stung again, and I scrubbed my hands over my face.

"Oh, sweetie. Will you be okay?" Gloria put her arm around my shoulders.

"I just can't face all this right now. Tell me more about Asher. Take my mind off the carnage."

"Well." She lowered her voice to a murmur. "As long as I've known Asher, I still can't tell what he's thinking. Can you?"

"I'm getting better at it."

"The Lennox boys are lucky they didn't get their mother's temperament. All three of them are real gentlemen, which is a miracle considering how they grew up."

"What was their mother like?"

"I was terrified of her as a child. She was unpredictable. One day she'd be running the bake sale, the next day you'd want to check her yard for buried corpses."

"That must have been hard on her kids."

"Very hard. But the worst part was—" The door opened and Gloria shut her lips over whatever she'd been going to say.

Ruff's paws clacked on the hard floors. Her tail wagged when he saw me, and her jowls swung as she lumbered over.

"Hey, girl." I rubbed her ears the way she liked. "You're okay. I'm right here."

Asher had clearly been thinking about something while he was gone, because he started talking while he was still approaching. "Iola, I haven't paid you for the portrait I asked you to paint. Most commission pieces are paid for up front, so it's only fair I do the same. I'll arrange it immediately."

It was a tempting offer, but I didn't want charity. It felt too much like Benedict's financial prison.

"Thanks, but I don't want an upfront payment,' I said. "If you want to buy a painting, you should get to see it first."

"But—"

I held up a hand. "Thank you. I appreciate your kindness, but I'll be okay. I only want you to pay for a painting if you've seen it and you like it."

"Iola, I'd expect to pay upfront if I was commissioning any kind of—"

"No, please. I realize I'm being weird about this, but that's because of Benedict." I gave him a weak, apologetic smile. "Even though you're nothing like my ex, he's given me a kind of phobia. I can't accept any money until I can give you the painting."

I'd survive without a handout, because I couldn't bear to do anything else. And if only Ruff and I didn't need to eat, maybe we really would be okay.

# Chapter Ten

## Iola

My lack of qualifications meant getting a job that paid enough for me and Ruff to live on wouldn't be easy. Art was the only real skill I had, but my paintings took time to create, and I was running low on dog food.

After getting up early on Monday morning to check the job ads, I managed to convince Asher I'd be okay on my own for a few hours if I promised to keep the door locked and my phone right beside me with his number on speed-dial. He'd slept on my couch again last night, but hadn't so much as kissed me, and now I was more confused than ever. I wanted to ask where things stood but didn't want it to be embarrassing or awkward. Especially seeing as I was a lot less worried about Benedict with Asher sleeping over, and I didn't want to accidentally drive him away.

I spent the day working a new painting while trying

not to worry about the financial pressure I was under. After finishing in the afternoon, I was looking for Ruff's leash when Asher came back.

"Just checking in," he said when I answered the door. "Everything okay?"

"No sign of Benedict." I opened the door wider. "I'm about to take Ruff to the dog park. She needs some exercise." Beside me, Ruff wagged her tail harder, recognizing the words.

When Asher stepped inside, I moved away to give him room, trying to pretend I was cool with the way he was holding back from me. When we'd kissed and he'd pulled away, he'd said I shouldn't take it the wrong way. But what was I supposed to think? Had I been too pushy? If only I wasn't so inexperienced, I'd know how to handle this and what I should have done differently.

Taking another step back, I hoped by putting extra distance between us I'd be less affected by Asher's sexy cologne, devastating good looks, and magnetic presence.

Only, nope.

"I'll come to the dog park with you," he said.

"Um." With difficulty, I swallowed what was about to be a totally inappropriate joke about staying in and doing it doggy style instead.

"You shouldn't go alone," he said. "Your ex might be trying to catch you out of the house to approach you again."

I was only half listening, busy frowning down at the area past the hem of his t-shirt, trying to work out what was bulging out of the front pocket of his jeans. "Um," I said again. "Is that Ruff's rubber chicken, or are you really pleased to see me?"

His eyes creased with amusement as he tugged it free of his pocket. "I found it in my living room."

"Again?" I handed it to Ruff who bit down on it, making it squeak loudly.

"I found these too." He pulled some silky fabric from his other front pocket. "They were in my bedroom."

Grimacing, I took my panties from him. "Three pairs? I swear, every window is latched. Every door is locked. What more can I do to keep Nemesis out?"

"And this." Reaching into his back pocket, he pulled out Ruff's leash.

I gaped at it for a moment, then clenched my jaw. I'd just wasted twenty minutes searching for it. "I'm sorry Asher, but if I catch your cat in here again, I'll have to..." I trailed off because I couldn't think of anything I could do to Nemesis other than scold her, and that hadn't exactly been working for me so far.

Asher cleared his throat. "You do know she's over there, right?"

"What?" I swung around. Sure enough, Nemesis was curled up in the middle of Ruff's oversized dog bed beside the living room couch. The sleek, black feline looked like she was asleep, until one eye cracked open and she stared at me for a second. Then she closed it dismissively.

Turning to Ruff, I huffed out an outraged breath. "A cat's asleep in your *bed*. Are you going to put up with that?"

Ruff's eyebrows drooped mournfully as she gazed back up at me. The rubber chicken squeaked in her mouth.

Asher pressed his lips together like he was trying not to laugh. "Want me to see if I can get her out of here? Not that she listens to me, but I can try." He clearly hadn't received any memo about keeping his distance, because he moved disconcertingly close to me. One whiff of his cologne and I had to hold myself back from burying my face in his neck.

I swallowed hard. "No, leave her. At least while she's sleeping, she's not stealing anything. Let's go to the dog park."

"I should drop into my father's place to check on him," Asher said. "Would you mind if we stopped on the way?"

"I don't mind." In fact, I was intensely curious about other people's families, and I wanted to know everything about Asher's. If Asher and Kade were any indication, their father would be a handsome silver fox. He'd be dignified, funny, highly intelligent, and charismatic. I couldn't wait to meet him.

We crammed Ruff into the back seat of Asher's car, and had barely turned onto Calle Colina when I spotted a huge flock of birds hovering low in the sky, acting strangely. They were diving down and wheeling back up, the flock only a few blocks away from us. And as we drove closer, I could hear them screeching.

"That's odd." I craned my neck to watch them.

"Mmm." Asher sounded thoughtful.

We turned the corner onto a quiet residential street, and the full flock came into view.

They were seagulls. Hundreds of gulls. They'd completely covered a house, flapping around it while they squawked and quarreled, squabbling with each other the way they did when they were fighting over food.

"That's Dad's house." Asher sounded perfectly calm, like he wasn't shocked at all. He pulled the car over a short distance away, out of range of the birds.

My jaw was slack. "It's like a Hitchcock movie."

"More like a cartoon." He pointed out a small woman wearing a bright yellow raincoat with a matching yellow safety helmet jammed over her long gray hair, and high rubber boots. She was holding a pump-action water gun that was bigger than she was. With her feet planted wide, she was leaning back to fire it, her body braced as though it was a rocket launcher.

The woman looked like she was laughing maniacally as she shot liquid over Asher's father's house, but with the windows up and the gulls screeching, I couldn't hear her. I could hear her dog, though. A Bassett Hound was bounding around her with his tail wagging, happily barking at all the birds.

Ruff barked in response, her mouth so close to my ear she all but deafened me. "Shh," I told her. "Be quiet. There's a good girl."

"That's Trixie Watson," said Asher. "She's Dad's neighbor. And her dog's name is Xul the Destroyer."

"What's she doing?"

"Shooting something onto Dad's roof that the birds

like to eat. Can't be birdseed, it'd cause blockages in the water gun's firing mechanism." He tapped his chin thoughtfully. "Could be fish paste dissolved in water. The smell would attract gulls."

He was as matter-of-fact as ever, and it made the whole thing more surreal. Was it actually happening, or some kind of weird hallucination?

"Why?" My head was spinning.

"Seagulls like fish."

"No, why would she do that?"

The small woman strode over to a large bucket of slushy liquid to reload her weapon, though there was a disturbing amount of bird poo splattered around the house already. No wonder she was wearing a raincoat and helmet.

"My father's been feuding with Trixie for years," said Asher. "Believe me, this is nothing. You should have seen the yard wars a few years ago."

"Yard wars?"

"Remind me to tell you about it later." His brow creased. "The only strange thing is that Dad's not—"

A pot-bellied, gray-haired man with enormous hairy eyebrows came bursting from inside the house onto the front porch. He was wearing a long trench coat and carrying the most enormous water gun I'd ever seen. Even bigger than Trixie's.

"Ah," said Asher. "There he is. That's my father. And he's carrying the Soakinator Gargantuan 2000." A hint of admiration leaked into his voice. "I always wanted one when I was younger. They were easily the best on the market, but too expensive for me and my brothers."

His dad let out a war cry so loud I could hear it over the barking of Trixie's dog and the squawking of gulls. He leaned back and fired his water cannon from the waist, like Rambo spraying an entire army with a machine gun. A long, hard jet of purple liquid sprayed out. It shot into Trixie's face, drenching her. She shrieked, lifting her own gun to shoot him back. But before the stream reached him, he ducked behind the porch rails, bending and running like a much younger man.

Trixie ran sideways, still firing. She was aiming at Asher's father now instead of at his house. Asher's father dodged, jumping out from behind his porch rails to fire back.

I craned forward, wanting to see what would happen when Asher's father got wet. Would his hairy eyebrows flatten over his eyes like a curtain?

Incredibly, Asher was relaxed behind the wheel. He didn't even look as interested as Ruff, who was panting excitedly. She was too well trained to bark again, but her eyes flicked between the dog and the two senior citizens as if she was dying to jump out of the car and join in. Couldn't say I blamed her. I'd never had a water fight, and I'd clearly been missing out.

"Shouldn't we do something?" I asked.

Asher shook his head. "The exercise is good for Dad. The doctor told him to get out more, and this is the most active I've seen him in a while."

I gasped as Trixie scored a direct hit, and Asher's dad

spluttered out fishy liquid. Incredibly, his eyebrows barely sagged. I wanted to get out of the car and cheer.

"You didn't have your heart set on meeting my father today, did you?" asked Asher. "Better to come back another time."

"You're really not going to stop them?"

"Why disturb them when they're having fun?"

I opened my car window, gazing with open-mouthed wonder at the scene in front of me. As soon as the window came down, everything was louder. The birds screeched, the dog barked, and I could hear the colorful insults Trixie was yelling.

"Take that, you cretinous old coot!" she shouted. "You rotten pit of maggot larvae!"

The small woman's raincoat and helmet were dripping purple liquid. The grass and sidewalk were also splashed with purple, and a purple river was running into the gutter.

"Is your father shooting paint?" I asked.

"Food coloring. Dad wouldn't shoot paint onto his own grass."

With the window down, a strong fish smell was drifting in. Asher's father was drenched with the liquid and the gulls were starting to dive-bomb him. Trixie landed another direct hit to his face and even though his hair was slicked against his head, somehow his eyebrows still refused to droop.

"Seen enough?" Asher started the car. He pulled away from the curb and I craned around to watch his father and Trixie disappear as we rounded the corner.

"That was the weirdest thing I've seen in a while." I settled back in my seat.

"Dad likes things that way. He's easily bored."

A familiar ache had started in my chest. But now I'd seen Asher's eccentric father and chatted to his charming twin brother, how could I not be jealous?

"Your family's amazing." I didn't bother to keep the envy out of my voice.

He shot me a sideways look. "That's not most people's reaction to my father."

"I wish I had a close family who did kooky things."

"Kooky is the word you've chosen to describe Dad?" His tone was dry. "Your restraint is admirable."

"You were going to tell me about his yard wars?"

"Oh yes." He stopped at a traffic light and turned to face me. "Trixie planted a large topiary in her front yard and cut it into a rude shape aimed in Dad's direction. A giant hand with its middle finger extended. An impressive feat. She must have taken a topiary shaping class."

I snorted a laugh. "What did your dad do? Dig it out?"

"He planted one in his own yard to return the favor, though his shaping wasn't as good. Rudimentary, but still recognizable. Then Trixie got more plants, and so did Dad. For a while they had dozens of matching topiaries in their yards, all flipping each other off."

I sighed wistfully. His family was the best.

"What happened to the plants?" I asked.

"Someone made a complaint, and they were forced to pull them out."

"I wish I could have seen it."

"I have a photo. Remind me to show you."

The light turned green, and he went through the intersection, heading toward the park.

"How come your father and his neighbor hate each other so much?" I asked.

"Hate each other?" He shook his head. "I'm not sure they do. It's probably closer to love, but they don't want to admit it."

"Love?" I gaped at him. "You really think they love each other?"

"It's only people in love who make each other that crazy."

"You're serious? You really think that's what love looks like for them?"

"That's what love does to most people. I've seen it over and over. First with my father and mother, then Dad and Trixie. Even Kade and Natalie when they split up and made each other miserable. Then there's my other brother, Mason. His girlfriend Carlotta was in trouble, so Mason did something dangerous. He risked his life for her."

I fell silent, trying to think of couples I knew who were in love to check whether his theory might apply. But I couldn't think of any couples who were actually happy. Benedict's friends had mostly married for money or status. Or in Benedict's case, because he'd wanted to mold a vulnerable girl into an obedient wife.

"My parents separated when I was little, so I've never really been around people in love," I said.

"You were never in love with Benedict?"

My laugh was bitter. "When I first met him, maybe. Until he started treating our marriage like a certificate of ownership."

Asher nodded. "Love makes people do things they wouldn't if they were thinking more clearly."

"Like marrying a guy whose birth certificate should be an apology letter from the condom factory?"

His eyes crinkled. "Exactly."

"Have you ever been in love?"

"No, and I never want to be."

"Never?" I frowned, taken aback. "Not ever?"

"Why would I want to put myself through that?" He gave me a sideways look. "You of all people should feel the same."

"Hmm," I said distractedly. With Benedict, I'd gone through a lot. But was that a reason to give up on love?

He pulled over and I realized we were at the park. But I was so busy thinking about what he'd said, I got Ruff out of the car in a daze. Was that why Asher didn't seem to want to kiss me? I hadn't thought to ask Gloria if Asher had dated much, because how could a man with his looks not be in hot demand? But if he was that serious about never falling in love, maybe he didn't date at all. Either way, I needed to be careful. In the short time I'd known him, I already liked him better than any guy I'd ever met. If I didn't watch out, I could be setting myself up for heartbreak.

When she realized we were at her favorite place, Ruff surged forward, distracting me from my thoughts. She was too well trained to yank hard on her leash, which was a good thing seeing as a dog of her size could pull me right over. But her tail wagged furiously as she led Asher and me through the big park, past the gazebo, to the fenced, off-leash area for dogs at the far end.

I'd brought a ball along for her and when I threw it in the off-leash area, Ruff bounded after it with her jowls swinging. One problem with her obedience training, it had been designed to make her a winner at dog shows and hadn't included any kind of play. Ruff had no idea she was supposed to bring the ball back to me and I didn't want to make it less fun for her by ordering her to come. So I spent a lot of time chasing her to pull the ball from her jaws, and she seemed to think running away was the best part of the game.

"Help!" I laughed, calling to Asher as Ruff kept evading me. "We need to corner her."

"Stay there. I'll shepherd her toward you."

Sure enough, when he ran at Ruff, the dog came thundering straight at me. I launched myself at her and Ruff dodged to the side. Drops of dog saliva spattered from her jaws, hitting my arms as I dove into a tackle.

Unfortunately, when the dust cleared, I was on the ground and Ruff still had the ball. Asher stood over me, stretching down a hand to pull me up. And as I reached up to grab it, Asher's lips stretched into a wide, real smile.

My body went weak.

The small hints of smiles he'd given me before didn't begin to compare. This smile didn't just break the attractiveness scale, it laughed in its face. And like how soft drugs are supposed to be a gateway to harder ones, I knew right away I was a goner. Getting Asher to dazzle me with more real smiles would be my new compulsion. From now on, I'd have to trail him like a junkie, desperately cracking jokes until he gave me what I needed.

And how dumb was that?

I'd just escaped my terrible marriage, and now I was swooning over a guy who kept pushing me away. How self-sabotaging must I be?

Asher hauled me to my feet, and I wobbled a moment before forcing my limbs to stop being ridiculous.

"You okay?" He dusted me off. "That was an impressive dive. Would have gotten any high school quarterback laid."

Ruff trotted back over to me and dropped the saliva-covered ball at my feet. Tail wagging, she gazed up at me with her enormous pink tongue dangling, almost hidden by her huge hanging jowls.

"Oh no," I told her. "I'm not falling for your tricks again. I'm going to sit down and let you run around without me."

There was a bench in a shady corner of the park, and Asher and I sat down together while Ruff ambled around, exploring the park on her own. She had to sniff every fence post and watching her made me smile. Maybe there were some men I couldn't trust, but I could count on Ruff. During my marriage she'd been one of the only good things in my life.

"When I was with Benedict, Ruff saved my sanity," I

said. "I don't know what I would have done if I hadn't had her to take care of."

"I'm glad you had her."

Letting out a sigh, I leaned back on the hard wooden bench. "What I'm trying to say is that Ruff means everything to me. No matter what Benedict does, I won't give her back. She's my family."

"I understand."

"You don't think I'm being foolish?"

He blinked as though surprised by the question. "Of course I don't."

"Good." I gave him an apologetic smile. "Sometimes I wonder about my own judgement and whether I can trust myself, seeing as I was dumb enough to marry Benedict before I even knew him. The last few years have shaken my confidence."

His expression stilled, his irises darkening. I noticed him take in a breath as though weighing something up.

"Iola, I'd like to tell you about my family," he said after a moment.

"Okay." I had the feeling whatever he was going to say was important to him. There was a stillness to him, though the air around him seemed to be vibrating with tension. So I folded my hands in my lap and waited for him to speak.

"When I was fourteen, our mother took Kade, Mason, and me to Mexico." He stretched his legs out in front of him, gazing at his sneakers as though he suddenly found them interesting. "I mentioned she was an addict, didn't

I? It was alcohol first, then drugs, which were worse. When she used drugs, her personality would change. Her moods would be extreme. But there were some short periods of sobriety when she tried to quit. Whenever she was herself again, I tried everything I could think of to keep her clean. I was obsessed with trying, as though there might be some switch I could flip, some way I could cure her, if I could only find it. And I clearly wasn't trying hard enough, because I hadn't made enough money to send her to rehab. I hadn't found the right person to help her, or figured out the right words to say to her. I made her continued addiction into a failing of my own."

His eyes lifted and I was caught in his gaze. He had the most curious, intelligent eyes I'd ever seen. If I hadn't just rediscovered my freedom, I'd be in serious danger of losing my heart to the power of those eyes.

"What I'm trying to say is that making mistakes is easy," he said. "Not beating ourselves up for them is the bit that's almost impossible. It's clear that your ex hid his true nature until he had you trapped. The only part that reflects on you is your strength in surviving and your courage in getting away."

My face heated at his compliments. While Benedict had torn me down, Asher seemed determined to build me back up. It was nice. And it made me wish more than ever that he wanted to kiss me.

"Where's your mom now?" I asked.

"She died of a drug overdose, and I'll never forgive the drug dealers who got her hooked. Never." His hands were resting on his thighs, and he squeezed them into fists as though channeling his anger into them.

No wonder he'd judged my father so harshly. "I'm sorry that happened to you," I said softly. Before I could think better of it, I covered one fist with my hand.

His fist uncurled and he flipped his hand over, linking our fingers together. "I wouldn't have got through it without my brothers. We looked out for each other."

"Now I get why your family is so close."

"But you had nobody."

"I had my dad. What he did for a living was wrong, and inexcusable, but he still looked out for me."

He gave a slow blink. "Did he, though? You said he sent you away to a boarding school." His tone was dismissive, and it made me instantly defensive.

"Dad had a good reason for that. He wanted to keep me far away from his business."

His jaw hardened. "Your father didn't have to deal drugs. He could have made his money legally."

"Dad grew up an orphan. He ran away from an abusive foster home and had to live on the streets from a young age. I know it's not an excuse, but he wanted my life to be better than his. His illegal activities were a bad way to go about it, but it was the only way he knew." Though my voice was defiant—almost angry—my answer sounded hollow, even to me. I could have done without the expensive boarding-school, but instead I'd had to manage without my father.

Maybe Asher saw the conflicting emotions in my face, because his eyes softened and he squeezed my hand. "You're a good person, Iola. You think the best of people."

I lifted my chin, still defensive. "Dad's made a lot of mistakes. I hated that he sent me away to boarding school and I never got to see him. I can't stand that he was tempted by promises of big money, and that he transported some illegal shipments and wouldn't just stick to his legitimate business deals. In fact, I've been angry with him most of my life, but he's all the family I have, and now I have him to thank for being in San Dante instead of London. I'd like to believe we still have a chance to reconcile."

"I'm happy you're here." Asher's smile was a peace offering. It was rare and precious, and it melted my insides, making all traces of anger and defensiveness disappear.

"Thank you," I said, taking a breath. "I'm glad to be here. I'm still not sure where I would have gone if Dad's lawyer hadn't called to say my father wanted me to stay in his house."

Asher stroked the back of my hand with his thumb. It felt good, and was highly distracting. I couldn't stop wondering whether it meant that kissing might make it back onto the table.

"You must have planned on going somewhere when you left your ex-husband?" he asked.

"I just dreamed of getting away, it didn't matter where." I gave a self-deprecating laugh, because it sounded like I'd been incapable of putting together a firmer plan when the truth was that I'd been afraid to get my hopes up too high. "Maybe I would have joined the circus," I joked. "Only I've never actually been to one, so that might not have worked out."

He did one of his slow blinks. "They don't have a circus in England?"

"Lots. But according to Benedict, those sorts of things were for commoners. He'd never let me lower myself. I have a whole list of things I've never done."

"Like what?"

"Um." There were so many things, it was almost too hard to pick examples. "I've never been to a drive-through movie theater. I've never shot a water gun like the ones your father and his neighbor were using. I've never—"

"You've never fired a water gun?" he interrupted. "Not even as a kid?"

"Nope. And I've never thrown a snowball, or even danced in the rain." I winced as I heard the words leave my mouth. "Uh-oh."

"What's wrong?"

"I sound like an eighties song. What was it again, the one about liking Piña Colada?" I laughed, feeling silly. "I'm twenty-eight years old, and I've never made love at midnight, driven through Paris in a sports car, had the time of my life, or been the wind under anyone's wings."

His hand tightened around mine for a moment before he let go. "Then you need to do all those things."

"Actually, I've been making a list."

"A bucket list?"

"I'm calling it my New Life List. I'm going to do

everything I've never done, and this time I'm not letting anyone stop me."

His eyes were warm. "Good for you. In fact, maybe you should tick something off your list right now."

"What do you mean?"

He got up from the bench. "Put Ruff on her leash. I need to make a phone call."

I did what he asked, though I was mystified as to what he was doing, especially when he walked away to make his call so I couldn't even eavesdrop.

"Okay, we're all set," he said when he got back. "Come on. We only have five minutes."

"Five minutes for what?"

"You'll see." He grabbed my hand, leading me out of the off-leash area with Ruff padding happily beside us. "This way." We were angling toward the deserted ball park instead of toward the car.

"Where are we going?"

"You said you've never danced in the rain. It's something you can do now."

I looked up at the blue sky with a puzzled frown. "What rain?"

There was a sputtering sound, then the park's sprinkler system came on, jets of water spraying upward in high arcs and showering down on the grass.

"See." Asher sounded smug. "Rain."

"But how—?"

"San Dante's a small town. I called a friend and asked for a favor."

"You're crazy!"

"Incorrect. Ask anyone and they'll tell you I'm reserved and serious, and the last person who'd ever do anything crazy." He motioned to the sprinklers. "There. Rain. Dance." Taking Ruff's leash out of my hand, he added, "Ruff and I can turn our backs if you'd like some privacy."

I widened my eyes at him. "Oh no, there's no way I'm doing this alone. You have to dance with me."

"That wasn't the deal."

"Come to think of it, I don't actually need you to agree." Stepping backwards into the spray of the closest jet, I shrieked then laughed as the cold water rained down on me.

Asher smiled at me, a dizzying real smile that made the shrieks die in my suddenly thick throat. If I did something reckless after a smile like that, he only had himself to blame.

Standing still, I let the water soak me while I met his gaze. "Last chance." My voice was a little hoarse. "Either you dance with me of your own free will, or..."

"Or what?"

I looked down at Ruff, sitting quietly at Asher's feet. "Here girl."

Ruff surged forward at once. Asher laughed as my giant dog dragged him into the cascade of water so fast, she tore her leash right out of Asher's hand. I'd been a little afraid Asher might get angry at me for forcing him under the sprinklers, especially as Benedict would have been beyond furious, but Asher's eyes were sparkling with amusement.

"Clever." He lifted his hands, letting the water soak him. "And tricky."

"Do you know how to waltz?" I flicked my wet hair out of my eyes. "We waltzed at school, and I also learned to rhumba, tango, and foxtrot."

"Foxtrot? Where did you go to boarding school, the nineteen twenties?" He slid his hands around my waist. "I'm pretty sure I can waltz, though it's been a long time."

He led, and I matched his steps while the rain fell and Ruff lumbered around us. Our dance sped up as Asher spun me, then dipped me. When he lifted me, I grabbed hold of his shoulders. Water trickled over the angles of his face, slicking down his hair. Somehow he managed to look even more gorgeous wet, especially because his t-shirt was plastered to his chest. His good looks made me dizzy, even before he twirled me again. And it was a good thing the water was cold, otherwise my skin might have caught fire in all the places he was touching me.

Pulling me closer, he dropped his face next to mine. The rough skin on his jaw tickled my cheek in the nicest way, and I leaned into him. His hands were firm around my waist, his chest wide, his scent all male. He danced with serious intensity, guiding me effortlessly, as though he'd practiced this dance every day of his life.

He was so sure, so confident, that in his arms I felt completely safe.

When he dipped me again, supporting me with his powerful arms while he gazed into my eyes, his lips pulled up into that incredible smile. I couldn't help laughing with joy, which made him smile even wider.

We only had five precious minutes in the water, but I wanted it to last forever.

And when the sprinklers finally sputtered to a stop, my mind had gone clear and I knew two things beyond a doubt.

The first thing was that there'd never been any other woman in the world as lucky as I was, getting to dance with Asher in the rain.

The second was that I wanted to do a lot more with him than dance.

# Chapter Eleven

## Asher

After getting soaked under the sprinklers, I went to my own place to shower, change, and feed Nemesis.

I was still sleeping on Iola's uncomfortable couch in case her ex came back, but I was wary about things moving too fast between us before I'd told her I was responsible for her father's arrest, so I ate dinner alone, packed an overnight bag, and waited until it was dark to go next door.

When she opened the door, Iola was wearing a simple black dress that was loose and straight. Instead of drying her hair, she'd pulled it back into a short ponytail. Her face was scrubbed clean of makeup, and her legs and feet were bare. Theoretically, she should look plain. Only she didn't. I'd come to appreciate how open and guileless she was, and her unadorned look seemed to match her genuine nature.

"You're beautiful," I blurted, because apparently her appearance had dissolved the normally efficient series of filters between my brain and mouth.

When she smiled, the lift of her lips had a corresponding effect on my heart. No other woman had ever made my breath vanish from my lungs, but Iola seemed to do it effortlessly.

"Thank you." She gave a laugh that sounded both pleased and a little embarrassed, lifting one hand to tuck back a shorter strand of hair that was slipping free from her ponytail. "Come in. I was just about to let Ruff out of the other door for a last pee before going to bed."

I followed her inside as she went to the side door to open it for Ruff. I watched her hips sway, mesmerized by her movements. A picture of her laughing as she danced under the sprinklers flashed through my mind. I'd never seen anyone so breathtaking.

It was becoming apparent I couldn't trust myself around her.

The right thing to do would be to go slow and give her the time she needed to adjust to being newly single, while I finished telling her about my past and how her father was one of the drug dealers responsible for my mother's death. Theoretically, both goals were complimentary. Moving slowly would help ensure I wasn't exploiting her newly single status *and* enable me to convince her to see things my way, so she didn't slam the door in my face when I confessed my role in her father's downfall.

Only I didn't want to wait.

Even knowing I should stay on her couch and keep my attention focused on protecting her, I couldn't stop thinking about sharing her bed.

Putting my overnight bag on the couch, I prowled around the house, looking in every room to check all the windows were locked. When I went back into the living room, Iola had moved my bag onto the floor and was sitting on the couch with a bottle of red wine and two glasses.

"Drink?" she asked, already pouring. "Don't say no or I'll have to drink them both." Her chuckle was an octave too high. "Actually, that's a balanced diet, keeping a glass of wine in each hand."

I sat next to her and took the glass she offered, though being so close to her wasn't good for my willpower. Especially not when her dress had ridden up her thighs, revealing three new freckles I hadn't previously noticed.

"Thank you for today." She clinked her glass against mine. "You're wine in a million." Taking a sip, she added, "I always say, why have mer-little when you can have a merlot?" Her cheeks flushed. "I hope you don't think wine puns are in pour taste. Shall I put a cork in it and keep them bottled up? Or do grape minds think alike?"

I put my glass on the coffee table. "What's wrong?"

She swallowed. "I don't know. I'm suddenly feeling nervous around you, because of what you did for me at the park and how it made me feel." When she leaned closer, our knees pressed together. The tie holding back her ponytail was too loose, and more strands were coming free. "I like you, Asher. I mean, in a strongly physical way." She flushed. "But I know you don't want to go too fast, and that's okay. I don't want to make you do things you're not comfortable with, like some kind of sexual predator." Her cheeks went even redder and she took a big gulp of wine.

I sucked in a breath, not sure whether I should laugh or be mortified I'd given her the wrong impression. "You're not a predator. And it's not that I'm not comfortable with being physical, it's that I don't want to hurt you."

"How would you hurt me?" Her brow furrowed as she put her glass next to mine on the coffee table.

"You haven't been single for long, and you're being threatened. My priority is to make sure you're protected."

"You can't protect me and kiss me at the same time? Or is that your polite way of saying 'thanks but no thanks'? If so, that's okay. You can tell me, and I promise not to get upset."

She bit her lip, looking into my face with her clear, bright eyes, and all I could think about was how her courage put me to shame. She'd had such a bad marriage, most people would probably want to shut the whole world out. And I'd given her so little encouragement, I couldn't blame her if she'd decided to write me off. But no. She still wanted to kiss me, and even more bravely, she wasn't afraid to tell me.

I couldn't keep holding back. I had to show her how amazing I thought she was.

Reaching up, I brushed the loose strands of hair back from her face. Instead of dropping my hand, I caressed her cheek. Her soft freckles were barely there, all but fading into her skin. They were impossible to count, which seemed just right. Everything about her was an enticing mystery, drawing me in.

"I like you too, Iola," I whispered. "In a strongly physical way."

Then I took her lips with mine, and I was lost.

Iola kissed the way she did everything, with energy and enthusiasm. Like she'd been in training for this moment and was determined to ace the test.

I smiled against her mouth, but when she made an eager breathy sound, my body responded instantly. I pulled her closer, needing more contact. Needing more of her.

Her scent was intoxicating. I ran my hand up the back of her neck and into her hair, tugging more of it loose from her ponytail. When I twisted my fingers into it, she responded instantly, pulling herself into my lap.

Her hands tugged at my jeans trying to fight them off. She was impatient for the end game.

Warning bells rang in my head. Would it be fair to her to let it happen so quickly?

"Wait." With self-restraint a monk would be jealous of, I gripped her waist and lifted her from my lap, setting her on the couch beside me.

"What?" Her eyes were wide and worried. "Am I doing something wrong?"

I took her hand in mine, trying not to think about how much my mouth was missing the feel of hers. Especially when she pulled her lower lip between her teeth.

"No, you're perfect," I told her. "But we don't need to move that fast."

Her expression fell. "It's too fast for you? I'm sorry, Asher, I didn't—"

"Stop." Linking her hand in mine, I lifted it to my mouth to brush my lips against her skin. "I'm not worried about myself."

"Well, I don't need you to worry on my behalf. I'm finally free after being stuck in marriage prison, and I want to do all the things I've never done. This is top of my New Life List." She dropped her gaze as though suddenly embarrassed. "I've never slept with anyone but Benedict, and after the first couple of years, I got pretty successful at keeping him from touching me."

I leaned in to kiss her softly, needing to hide a surge of raw anger. I wanted to pull off every one of the fingers Benedict had used to touch her. I didn't like violence, but in his case I'd make an exception.

"When you kiss me it feels so good," she murmured against my mouth.

I dropped my mouth to her jaw, running my lips to her ear. She shivered as I kissed the sensitive spot under her lobe.

"I really like that." Her breathy voice made me throb with want. She had no idea what she was doing to me. I might seem calm, but inside I was the battle scene from Braveheart, with my lust and protective instincts charging into war against each other, swinging broadswords and yelling "Freedom" at the top of their lungs.

"I feel like I've never done anything," she added.

"Now I want to do everything, and I want to do it with you."

I groaned silently, closing my eyes for a moment to see if I still had any dregs of self-control left. But the one thing I'd always prided myself on seemed to have taken a vacation.

This woman was too much. Too gorgeous, too sexy, too tempting to resist. Every part of my body needed to touch her. Needed to *own* her.

Iola took advantage of my hesitation to climb back onto my lap, straddling my legs. Her dress rode up so high I caught a glimpse of black lace panties, and I could feel her heat on my crotch, making me strain against my jeans.

She slid her hands under my t-shirt, running her fingers across my abs. Then her palm brushed my erection and it throbbed harder, my need for her so strong I couldn't fight it.

I couldn't hold back.

Taking hold of her dress, I pulled it up. She lifted both arms, helping me tug it over her head. Underneath, her breasts were encased in a soft white bra, like beautifully wrapped gifts. Her black lace panties didn't match, but somehow the combination was even sexier than if her lingerie had been a set.

I didn't have much time to appreciate the gift wrapping though, because she reached back to unhook her bra and it dropped away.

My hands moved to her breasts without my brain activating them, drawn to their irresistible weight. Her stomach was slightly rounded, soft and feminine.

I'd pictured her naked many times, but my breath caught at just how stunning she was. Her nipples were already hard, and when I bent my head to worship them with my mouth, they pebbled even more, making her gasp.

"Everything you do to me feels so good."

"You have no idea all the things I want to do to you." I didn't realize I'd said it aloud until she moaned.

"Yes, please. I want everything. All of you."

Every word out of her mouth only made me throb harder. I was losing my mind, and I couldn't bring myself to care. Running my fingers down to her panties, I stroked her over the fabric.

She gasped again, letting her head fall back. Her panties were soaked and she ground her hips forward, pressing herself into my hand. Her quick, needy movements told me how much she needed this. She'd been waiting for *years*. I needed her to have everything she'd missed out on, to make up for everything she'd suffered.

Touching her wasn't enough.

"I want to taste you." My voice was like gravel. Some part of my brain was processing the fact I wasn't following my decision to move slowly with her, but that part was being overruled by the more important fact Iola was mostly naked and rubbing herself against my lap.

"Taste me?" she sounded uncertain. "As in...?"

I slid my hand between her legs, slipping my fingers under the elastic of her panties to dip into her wetness.

"Asher," she groaned, squeezing her eyes shut.

Kissing her neck, I stroked her clit. "I want you in my mouth."

Her hands were digging into my back, her voice breathless. "I've never done that."

"Then it's time to tick it off your list."

Lifting her off me and onto the couch, I dropped to my knees on the floor and pulled her panties off. She helped me get them off, but when I spread her legs and moved between them, she went stiff.

I hesitated, frowning up at her. She was too rigid. Her eyes were closed, and she gripped the couch tightly, squeezing the cushions in her fists. Her body quivered with nerves, as though she were in a doctor's surgery, waiting for an examination. Her buttocks were clenched tightly together, and her thighs pressed against my upper arms as though she wanted to close them.

I wrapped one hand over her fist and squeezed. "Hey. It's okay if you don't want me to do this. Or if you want to try it and don't like it, I'll stop."

She cracked one eye open enough to peek at me. "The thing is, I don't know if *you'll* like it."

"Oh, I'll like it.'

"Are you sure?"

"Cross my heart." I let myself smile a little, so she'd know I was already enjoying myself. Just getting to feast my eyes on her was extremely enjoyable. Her body was every bit as gorgeous without clothes as I'd spent the last few days imagining it would be. She was soft and rounded in all the right places, and there were so many previously-undiscovered soft freckles covering her stomach and breasts, I felt like the first astronomer to ever glimpse a new galaxy. They were fascinating new worlds I couldn't wait to explore.

She closed her eyes again, scrunching her face to emphasize the action. "Okay. Go."

I licked between her legs softly with the flat of my tongue, my pressure feather light. Her body jerked a little in response, and her face scrunched even more.

"Okay?" I asked.

"I think so." She sounded hesitant.

I moved my face closer, so when I spoke my breath would drift over her most sensitive parts. "I'll stop any time you like." This time I didn't wait for a response before gently licking her again.

"Ohh," she breathed.

"Still okay?"

"Mmm." Some of the tension eased from her body. When I licked her again, her legs relaxed and opened a little wider. "That feels good. I mean, really good."

I smiled, letting my tongue drift over her and enjoying her soft groan of pleasure. "Are you sure you don't want me to stop?" I teased.

"Do you want to stop?" A note of worry leaked into her voice again. "It's okay if you do."

"Why would I want to stop?" I ran a finger over her, following it with my tongue, then eased my finger inside her. She gasped, her legs parting even more as I showed her with my mouth and hands just how turned on I was.

Forgetting her nervousness, she bucked under my mouth, making wild, uncontrolled sounds. Each sound, each movement, turned me on even more. As my mouth feasted on her, my eyes did too. With her hair wild, her lips parted, her nipples pebbled, and her magnificent breasts swaying up and down with each panting breath, I'd never seen anyone more breathtaking. How could any man have denied her anything?

She grabbed the hair on the top of my head, twisting her fingers into it. Then, with a scream, she lifted her entire body, bending her spine backward as she shuddered and clenched under my tongue.

Her orgasm was long and strong. As it slowly ebbed, she relaxed back onto the couch, and untangled her fingers from my hair. Some may have been torn out at the roots, but when she gave me a dazed, incredulous smile, I didn't care.

"Oh." Her voice was little more than a gust of air. "I can't believe I did that. I've never done anything like that."

I was hard and throbbing, my own need for release urgent. But I ignored the feeling. Moving up onto the couch, I pulled her onto my chest to cradle her. "You've never what?" I asked, making sure to sound offhand. "Orgasmed?"

"I have, but not with Benedict. Only on my own." She gave me a lazy smile. "That was much better."

Gently and tenderly I kissed her forehead as I pictured myself ripping off all of Benedict's limbs, one by one, while he screamed and begged for mercy.

"Are you angry?" She blinked at me, her eyes still dazed. "Being able to see what you're thinking is like learning a secret code. Your jaw tightens when you're angry." She ran her finger along my jaw and it rasped across my emerging stubble. "Did I upset you?" she asked.

Though images of revenge were still running through my mind, I kept my voice as calm as ever. "Benedict used you for his own pleasure, without considering yours. That makes me furious."

"It might make me angry too, if I wasn't feeling so nice right now." Her languid smile made my chest ache. Why was it always the best, kindest, nicest people who suffered most?

"But let's forget about you-know-who," she added. "I'm too relaxed to let him into my head. I don't want him to have so much as a single brain cell."

"It's a deal." I pushed my anger away to focus on how good she felt in my arms. She was right. Why let anyone spoil this perfect moment?

"I'm as limp as a soggy rag," she said. "But you're not." She shifted against me, rubbing her lower body against me. It felt so intensely pleasurable, I stifled a groan of need. "You're as hard as a rock, and we should do something about that." She moved her hand down to stroke me where I was trying to punch a hole through my jeans.

I covered her hand, stilling the action. "Don't worry about me yet." In spite of my resolve, my voice was tight with the effort of keeping control.

"What?" She raised questioning eyes to mine. "Why not? Don't you want to go further?"

"In a minute. We've just ticked a very important thing off your New Life List, and I need you to take a breath first, so you can enjoy this feeling of limpness before I add another orgasm or two to your evening." I released her hand so I could lift a knuckle to her chin and run it across her jawline. She was so damn beautiful, I felt almost unbearably tender toward her. So tender I ached with it. "We have all night," I promised. "Take a breath, then we'll move into the bedroom. The next thing on the list can't be done on a couch. At least, not the way I want to do it."

Her eyes widened before a wicked smile lifted her lips. "I'll be able to walk in just a minute," she promised. "Or maybe you'll have to carry me in there and throw me roughly on the bed before having your way with me." She lowered her voice to a whisper as though revealing a dirty secret. "I've just added that to my list."

I laughed softly, and she blinked at me.

"Wait," she said, pretending to be shocked. "Did you just laugh?"

"You've heard me laugh before."

"Hardly ever. I'd like to hear you laugh a lot more often. Your laugh is so lovely, deep and rich, like black coffee."

"I'll put a reminder in my phone," I said, teasing. But she was right. Laughing felt great, so why didn't I do it more? I couldn't blame my messed-up childhood, not when Iola had survived far worse. At least when my mother had died, I'd had my brothers to lean on. Iola had been alone. Her longing for family was so obvious, it was heartbreaking. And all the men in her life had treated her like garbage.

But here she still was, not just a survivor, but thriving. She was brilliant and wildly talented. Most perplexing of all, she could still see something worthwhile in someone like me. Someone with secrets, who hadn't done anything to earn her trust.

Iola made a startled sound and jerked her head up. "Drop that!" she ordered. "Nemesis, stop!"

I turned my face to where she was looking, but I needed have bothered. Nemesis jumped onto the arm of the couch right next to our heads. When I'd freed Iola from the burden of wearing panties, I'd dropped them on the floor. Now they were dangling from my cat's mouth.

"Put them down!" Iola pushed off me, trying to snatch them back. "I was just wearing those. They aren't clean!"

Nemesis didn't even look like she was trying to evade Iola's grasping hand. One moment she was on the couch next to us, the next she was a sleek black missile flying through the air. She landed soundlessly near the side door that led out to the strip of the grass next to the house. After leveling a contemptuous stare at us, she sat down in front of the closed back door, the panties still hanging from her mouth and her tail flicking angrily from side to side.

"She's getting worse," Iola exclaimed. "Now she's not even trying to hide her thievery. Unless that's her psychopathic way of getting our attention so we open the door for her?"

I frowned, studying my cat. "That's strange. Nemesis never bothers with doors. She thinks they're too mundane."

Iola blinked at me, her eyebrows high. "Your kleptomaniac cat is carrying my dirty laundry away like some kind of offering to the god of perverts, and you think the bit that's strange is that she wants us to open the door?"

A cold feeling was creeping up from the pit of my stomach. "Where's Ruff?"

Iola's eyes widened with sudden shock. "Oh no. I couldn't have left her outside all this time? She always scratches to come in."

Scrambling up, she ran to the door stark naked and threw it open. "Ruff? Come here, girl. Where are you?"

I got up and moved next to her, unease churning in my gut. Nemesis slipped outside carrying her trophy, but Iola either didn't notice her disappear into the darkness, or didn't care.

"Ruff!" she bellowed.

I cursed my own stupidity. Watching Ruff while she was outside should have been my priority. I'd calculated high odds of Benedict breaking in to take the dog, yet I'd been so preoccupied, I'd left Ruff unattended.

Iola turned to me, her face pale. "She's gone."

# Chapter Twelve

## Iola

"Drink this." Asher handed me a steaming mug of hot chocolate.

I sat on a stool at the kitchen island and sipped the drink without really tasting it. I'd put my clothes back on before we went around the block calling for Ruff, though we both knew searching for her was pointless. The side gate had been padlocked when I'd let Ruff out, but I'd found the remains of the padlock on the ground. Benedict must have invested in bolt cutters.

Tugging my cellphone out of my pocket, I put it on the countertop and stared at it while I drank, willing it to ring.

Asher sat on the stool next to me. He wasn't saying much, and I was grateful. I was too upset to hold a conversation, but just having him with me was a comfort.

If he was worried, he didn't let it show, and his silent, capable presence was more reassuring than I could say.

My phone's shrill ring made me jump and almost spill my drink, even though I'd expected the call. The screen said *Private Number*.

I dragged in a breath, meeting Asher's gaze and drawing strength from his calm gray eyes before I answered the call.

"Benedict," I said instead of hello, trying to project Asher's level of cool and not quite managing to.

He chuckled, the bastard. "You must know by now I have my dog back."

"Hurt Ruff and I'll kill you."

"Calm down, Iola. It's only an animal."

"You're the animal. You've never loved anything in your life." With the hand that wasn't gripping the phone, I reached for Asher. He caught my hand and held it, lending me more of his strength and control. Without him, I'd probably be trying to sob and scream at Benedict at the same time.

"Be sensible, darling. You have no way to support yourself in California. Come home with me, and we'll say no more about your vacation. I'm still prepared to forgive you."

"Forgive me?" My voice rose. "You destroyed my paintings!"

"And you embarrassed me." His voice was hard. "The night you left, we were supposed to be at Lord Pardington's wedding. By disappearing, you put me in an extremely uncomfortable position."

"Why do you even want me back? Didn't you always tell me I'm more trouble than I'm worth?"

"You're my *wife*, Iola. That's a commitment you don't get to shirk. And when you behave properly, you can be a decent wife. Even my mother admitted as much, and she never thought I'd find anyone good enough for me."

Ugh. His mother was the worst. In the first years of my marriage, I'd tried to make the best of things, hoping Benedict would let me have more freedom as we got to know each other. Eventually I'd asked his mother for help. But she was no ally. She said men of Benedict's class and lineage were used to being obeyed, and told me off for disrespecting him.

"You're delusional, Benedict. Really. You need professional help."

He let out a loud sigh, as though he couldn't understand why I was being difficult and was almost done humoring me. "Remember your manners or I might change my mind about taking you back."

"The day I go back to you will be the day the devil goes ice-skating through hell. In a tutu!"

"Very well, Iola. It'll take a day to have the dog's paperwork arranged, so you have twenty-four hours to change your mind. Then I'll revoke the offer to return to England with me, and that door will permanently close."

"I've already told you—"

"And if you're not in London to look after the dog, I'll have no reason to keep it alive."

My skin went cold and I squeezed Asher's hand even tighter. "What? No. You wouldn't kill Ruff."

"I won't bother taking the dog to the vet to have it done. I'll just use my hunting rifle. Though last time I went pheasant shooting, I only wounded one of the birds and it took a long time for it to die."

"I won't let Ruff leave the country. I'll go to the police."

"The dog is legally mine." His tone was harsh. "If you try anything foolish, you'll be the one who's arrested."

"Then you'll never get me back."

"Be grateful I'm offering you a chance to return to England with me at all. I'll call you tomorrow evening to hear your decision. You should think long and hard about how you're going to make up for your behavior and show your appreciation for my lenience."

I started to tell him how much he disgusted me, but found myself talking to a dead line. Benedict had hung up on me.

Fuming, I turned to Asher and found I was still clutching his hand, probably squeezing all the blood from his fingers. And even after I realized, it took a moment before I could force myself to let go.

"Are you okay?" Asher flexed his hand, but to his credit, he didn't wince.

"Benedict's going to call tomorrow night, so I have to steal Ruff back from him before then. Only I don't know how to find him."

Asher tapped his chin, his expression thoughtful. "Maybe there's another way."

"You know a professional assassin-for-hire who'd be

willing to kill Benedict and offers a 90-day payment plan?"

"That could be a problem. All the assassins I know only take cash."

"Then what's your idea?"

"Would Benedict accept money in exchange for Ruff?"

I shook my head. "I don't have any to offer him."

"I could—"

"If you're about to say you could offer him money on my behalf, thanks, but I couldn't accept it, and he wouldn't take it anyway. Benedict's already rich. He inherited millions, and he cares more about his reputation than making more money."

Asher nodded slowly. "Then what if you called his friends and explained the situation? They might shame him into giving Ruff back."

"That would be a good idea, only you haven't met Benedict's so-called friends. They're all as bad as he is."

"His parents?"

I let out a huff of air. "If I called them, they'd remind me he was my husband and therefore the boss, tell me not to be selfish, and order me back to England where I belong."

His mouth twisted. "They sound like delightful people."

"I'll introduce you. If you like stuck-up, bigoted misogynists with no empathy or compassion, you'll love them."

"I'll add them to my Christmas card list."

"Any other ideas?" I picked up my mug of hot chocolate with shaky hands and tried to take a sip. My stomach was churning so much, it only made me feel sicker.

"Only one."

"You're thinking what I'm thinking?" I put the mug down. "That we should kill Benedict ourselves, take Ruff, and flee to Canada?"

He shook his head. "My plan's a little different."

"You think we should flee to South America?" I bit my lip, hating my need to make light of things when I was so worried about Ruff. It might have helped me get through the awful Benedict years, but I didn't need to do it anymore. If only it were easy to stop.

"I'm pretty sure you won't like what I'm going to suggest," he said.

"Try me."

"We could set up Benedict and blackmail him."

I searched his face. His expression was serious and his gaze was level. No sign of any tell-tale shiver in the muscles under his eyes.

"Are you for real?" I asked, just to check.

"I didn't think you'd like it. Don't worry, I'll come up with something less drastic."

My heart sped up, a sliver of hope making me feel less grim. "I like it a lot."

Asher put his elbows on the counter, leaning closer. He examined my face as closely as I'd searched his. "You're willing to resort to blackmail?"

"Would I be willing to blackmail the man who controlled me for years, stopped me getting access to my own money, destroyed my paintings, and is threatening to kill Ruff just to get back at me? Honestly, I'd still rather have Benedict assassinated, but blackmail comes a close second."

Asher's gaze grew warm. "I'm surprised."

I flushed, thinking about how Benedict had disapproved of just about everything I'd said and done. "In a bad way?"

"The opposite. I'm impressed you'll consider something so… unconventional."

"I can't let Benedict kill Ruff." I toyed with the handle of my mug, just to have something to do with my hands. "If I can't get her back, I'll have to go back to England."

Asher gave a slow blink, his version of shock. "You'd go back to Benedict to save Ruff?"

"Ruff's my family, remember?"

The problem was, Dad was my only other family member and if I left the country, I wouldn't get to see him. My visitation permit would be approved any day, and I wanted to be here to support him through his trial.

Pushing my mug away, I rubbed my hands over my eyes.

"We'll get Ruff back," Asher promised.

"How? What can we blackmail Benedict with?"

"I have an idea, but I want to sleep on it and work through the details before we discuss it. And in the light of day, you might decide blackmail isn't your preferred option."

Ruff's chewed-up giraffe was on the floor beside me,

and I got off my stool to pick it up and squeeze it. My chest hollowed out when I thought about how confused Ruff must be. She'd miss her toys, and her bed.

"By morning, I might have figured out a way to murder Benedict and get away with it."

Asher's gaze dropped to the chew toy. "Stay at my place tonight. Sleep in my spare room. You won't be surrounded by Ruff's things, and you won't need to be afraid Benedict might come back."

I stared at his face, searching for a hint of what he was thinking, but it was like trying to read a blank page. "Thanks," I said after a moment, trying to sound normal. Asher was offering me his spare bed instead of his own? Was he retreating inward again, putting the barriers back up between us? Or maybe he was just being considerate, thinking I'd be too upset about Ruff to feel sexy.

"I'll get my pajamas." I stood up with a sigh. My body had gone weak and I felt drained. I was already exhausted, so I didn't have the energy to try to figure out whether Asher was regretting what we'd done or not, and I still had a long night of worrying about Ruff ahead of me.

# Chapter Thirteen

## Asher

I told Iola my plan the next morning while we ate scrambled eggs on toast in my kitchen. She was still subdued, obviously missing Ruff, and the dark shadows under her eyes said she hadn't slept well.

"How will we get Benedict to tell us where he's keeping Ruff?" she asked when I'd laid out the details of what I thought we should do.

"Leave that to me."

"Can we torture the information out of him?" She stabbed her eggs with her fork, her brows pulling together. "Quiero matarlo," she muttered darkly.

Though my Spanish was a little rusty, I had no trouble understanding. "We should abide by the Geneva Convention," I said with more than a touch of regret.

"Do we have to?" She ate another mouthful of the eggs she'd so violently murdered. "Delicious breakfast, by the way. Perfectly fluffy. Are you sure we can't torture Benedict?"

"We're going to blackmail him, remember."

"He threatened Ruff. He should count himself lucky if he can walk out of here after I'm done with him." She sliced her remaining piece of toast in a hard, swift downward stroke, as though she were picturing his throat as she cut into it.

Maybe I was crazy to find her anger sexy, but it was all I could do to keep my hands wrapped around my knife and fork and my brain focused on scheming instead of how badly I wanted to kiss her.

"If everything goes well, you'll be able to stop worrying about him," I said.

"I like your plan, in spite of not getting to exact painful revenge on Benedict. But all that really matters is getting Ruff back."

"And making sure Benedict never bothers you again." Finishing the last of my breakfast, I placed my knife and fork on my plate.

She flashed me a grateful smile. "Thank you for helping me. You have a wonderfully devious mind."

"I've had practice."

"Really? Tell me about it. Distract me from worrying about Ruff." She picked up the last piece of her toast to finish, pushing her empty plate away.

"When we lived in Mexico, Kade and I sometimes used to hustle money from tourists. We'd ask people to guess which cup a ball was in, and they'd always lose."

"Will you show me?"

After putting our plates in the sink, I got five cups out of the cupboard and set them upside down on the kitchen island. Then I took two walnuts from the pantry. Hiding one in my palm, I put the other on the table.

"Pretend that's a ball." I put a stool on the other side of the island so I could sit opposite her.

"Okay." She nodded. "It's a ball."

"The cups are all empty." I lifted them two-at-a-time to show her the interiors of all the cups. As I put the last cup down, I slipped the hidden walnut inside it.

Then I picked up the other walnut and made a show of putting it under another of the cups. But I palmed it at the last moment, slipping it into my pocket.

Though it had been almost fourteen years since I'd last executed the trick, my movements were quick. My muscles still remembered exactly what to do. And performing the actions triggered all my old memories, so I could almost feel the heat radiating off the sidewalk, hear the laughs and chatter of the tourists staggering past, and smell the stale beer wafting from the nearby bars.

"Kade would talk through the trick," I said. "He had this patter he'd do, complimenting the target while he advised them to keep their gaze fixed to the cup with the ball in it. Or in this case, the walnut."

While I spoke, I moved the cups quickly around, switching their places.

"You still know where the walnut is?" I asked Iola.

"That's easy." She tapped one of the cups.

I lifted the cup to show it was empty and her eyes

widened. When I lifted another cup, she gaped at the decoy walnut.

"That's amazing! How'd you learn to do that?"

Her expression was so full of wonder, I couldn't help but smile. The delight she took from such a simple trick was touching. It made my own cynicism melt.

"Not long after we moved to Mexico, Mom started dating one of the chefs at the restaurant she worked in. He liked doing magic and taught me the basics. Then I got hold of some books to expand my skills."

"So you started doing the trick for money?"

I nodded. "Kade and I would sit at a makeshift table we'd tucked out of the way so most tourists would walk right on past, and I'd nudge Kade when the right target came by."

"How could you tell they were the right target?" Her face was alight with interest as she leaned forward. I was so captivated by her expression, I found myself talking without reservation, telling her more than I was usually comfortable with.

"I studied body language. Bachelorette parties were the best. The women were usually half drunk, determined to have fun, and happy to stop for a few minutes of entertainment on the way to the next bar. I'd tell Kade which one was the bride, and he'd go right over to draw her into our trick."

"How would you know which was the bride?"

"I could always tell."

"And Kade would convince her to come over to your table?"

I shrugged. "He was a smooth talker."

She smiled, her eyebrows lifting as she shot me a knowing look. "I bet he came out of the womb that way."

"He'd tell the bride how pretty she was and act heartbroken because she was taken."

"I can imagine. I'm sure he was almost as charming then as he is now."

I pictured my brother the way he was back then, lanky and non-threatening. His hair had kept flopping into his eyes so he had to keep tossing it back, and though he had faint traces of acne on his cheeks, the women still blushed when he pretended to have fallen for them.

"He'd tell them they just had to put up five dollars," I said. "And they could walk away with ten. He'd say they had to take advantage of it now, because after they were married their husbands wouldn't let them have any fun."

"You'd give them ten dollars if they guessed where the ball was, but they only lost five dollars if they were wrong?"

"Exactly."

"Did you ever lose?"

I shook my head. "But a few times when we first started, I picked the wrong targets. If we chose people who resented losing, it got nasty. And occasionally we had boyfriends suddenly turn up and decide they didn't like the way Kade was flirting with their women."

She leaned in, her expression shocked. "It got violent?"

"I got better at picking targets." I sidestepped her

question. "Ones who didn't mind paying a few dollars for Kade to make them laugh."

"Did you have a patter as well?"

"Kade did all the talking. I just did the magic."

"You were silent and mysterious?"

"That was the act."

Only it'd been more than just an act. Maybe my brothers hadn't grasped how serious our situation was, but I'd been all too aware of the dangers. By picking the wrong target, I could have gotten us badly hurt. And if I didn't find any target at all and brought home no money, Mason would suffer the consequences.

I couldn't afford to let our targets see how much we had riding on the game, and I used the same skills at home to minimize the chance of accidentally triggering one of Mom's mood swings. Sometimes all it had taken to set her off was a frown.

Hiding my emotions hadn't just been part of our trick, but the way I'd survived.

"You're really clever." She tilted her head. "You know that?"

"Not clever enough." The words slipped out before I could think better of them.

"What do you mean?"

I hesitated, because I'd wanted to take her mind off her current predicament, not drag the conversation into gloomier waters.

"We'd often go home with enough money for a meal," I said reluctantly. "But there were also quiet days, when it rained, or we couldn't convince any tourists to bet on the game."

Those were the nights when Mason would have to slip out late at night to steal food or money, not that I could tell her that part of it. Mason had hated stealing, and wouldn't thank me for telling anyone.

"It wasn't your fault it rained."

"But if I'd been smarter, I would have been able to come up with other ways to make money."

Anything would have been better than having to worry that Mason might get caught. And then there were the rehab facility brochures I'd collected. I'd been convinced they could cure Mom and solve all our problems, if only their high fees hadn't been so frustratingly out of reach.

Iola started to say something else, but I wanted to change the subject. Some of my memories of that time were almost more than I could bear.

"Have you had enough to eat?" I got up to clear away the cups and walnuts I'd used to demonstrate the trick. "Another coffee?"

She stood up too, catching me around the waist. "Hey." She stepped into me, so I had to put my arms around her. Her face angled up to mine. "You don't want to talk about it, and that's okay. But I still think you're the cleverest person I know. So there."

Her eyes flashed, her expression defying me to contradict her.

But as it turned out, I didn't need to.

My own actions proved the lie in her words. If I were clever, I would have been enough of a gentleman not to make love to her before putting my plan into action. First I needed to make her understand why my role in her father's arrest was forgivable, and that putting him behind bars had been the right thing to do. And if I were clever, I wouldn't start kissing her again now. But Iola's lips parted under mine, and she made a soft sound, wrapping her arms around me. When her body pushed into mine, I felt like I'd downed five tequila shots in quick succession. My limbs loosened, and a wild, fierce passion burned through my body. All I could think about was my *need* to give her more orgasms, to make up for all the years she'd had none.

But my conscience had a loud and annoying voice.

The voice in my head kept reminding me how duplicitous I was being. The longer I spent kissing Iola, the worse it became for me to keep my secret hidden from her. And seeing as I'd made no progress on convincing her to see things my way, she was likely to be furious with me if she found out before I was ready.

I wanted to strangle that voice.

Reluctantly, I pulled back from the kiss. Gazing into Iola's deliciously hazy eyes, I had no idea what excuse I could give for stopping, when any sane man would only draw back for the purpose of clothing removal.

Then Iola's gaze sharpened, and she examined my face as though she found it suddenly fascinating. "Is everything okay?" she asked.

"Why do you ask?"

"The muscles around your eyes have gone tight."

"Have they?" I made an effort to relax my face.

"What's wrong?" She stepped backward, pulling away from me. Behind her, sunlight was streaming through the glass doors, casting light around her head as though she had a halo.

That Iola was able to read my face should have been disturbing. Only Kade and Mason could read me like that, and I had too many things to hide from Iola to be comfortable with her insight.

But weirdly enough, her perception didn't just make me feel more vulnerable. It also loosened something inside me, as though it were almost a *relief* for her to be able to see the emotions I wanted to hide.

Which was contradictory, ridiculous, and made no sense at all.

"I need to ask you something about your father's property." I braced myself for whatever her reaction might be. "Did you know there'll be a criminal forfeiture hearing for his assets?"

"Oh." She frowned. "Are you talking about his house being seized? Dad's lawyer filled me in. But they'll only be able to take it if Dad's found guilty at his trial."

"He's guilty. You can count on him being convicted."

Her frown deepened. "What do you know about it? You're not trying to upset me again, are you?" She sounded confused rather than angry, but I was aware of the need to tread cautiously.

"I just want to make sure you have somewhere to go when his house is seized, and you won't be forced onto the street."

She blew out a breath, her expression troubled. "Dad's lawyer went to a lot of trouble to get me access to his house before his trial. I figure Dad thought it'd give me enough breathing room to be able to find a job and another place to live. And he probably wants me to move his personal belongings somewhere safe, in case he's convicted. Hopefully when I get to see him, he'll let me know."

"They're letting you visit your father?" The question came out a little too sharp.

"Not yet, but hopefully soon." Her brown eyes were darkening with suspicion. "Why are you asking? What's going on?"

"After the trial, you and Ruff can stay with me. No strings attached. I have plenty of room for you to stay as long as you like." My conscience pricked me again. Offering her my house to stay in was false comfort when I planned to tear it down soon afterward.

Her expression softened. "Thank you. *If* Dad's house is seized and I haven't figured anything else out by then, it's nice to know I won't have to live in my car."

I steeled myself for the conversation to get even more difficult. "Good. Now we've agreed on that, I'd like to tell you about my family." I pulled out a stool for her at the kitchen island, deciding this was a talk we should have while seated. The balancing act I had to walk was a tricky one. I couldn't reveal my role in Santino's arrest until after we had Ruff back and Iola's ex-husband had been neutralized. But I needed to start winning Iola over before she got visitation access to her father. I wasn't sure how much Santino knew about the circumstances around his arrest, but if I hadn't told her the truth by then, he might.

Worst of all would be if I was called as a witness to testify against Santino, and Iola was watching from the gallery. Would I even be able to go through with it? It wasn't a choice I wanted to have to make.

Iola eased onto the stool, her gaze staying on my face. "You want to tell me about your brothers?"

"And about my mother." I sat next to her. "You should know more about what happened to her, and the impact it had on—"

Her phone rang, cutting me off. She snatched it off the counter, the sudden rigidness of her body showing how afraid she was that her ex-husband might be calling her again. But when she checked the screen, the tension eased out of her. "It's Gloria. Do you mind if I answer it?"

"Go ahead."

"Hi Gloria." She paused, listening. "Okay. Great, thank you. I'm on my way." She hung up and shot me an apologetic look. "The police are finished at the community center, and Gloria wants me to collect what's left of my paintings. She needs the space cleaned up before another exhibition she has scheduled." She scrunched up her nose. "I'm sorry. I know you wanted to talk, but is it okay if we do it later?"

I nodded, not liking the sense of relief I felt. It wasn't usually in my nature to avoid difficult conversations. Was I subconsciously sabotaging my plan, and was that why I hadn't gotten as far with it as I should have?

"Wait," I said as she got up, remembering something. "I have your money. It's the deposit for the painting I'd like you to do for me." Taking my wallet out of my pocket, I pulled out the wad of cash I'd put aside for her. Though technically I couldn't afford to give away money right now, Iola needed it more than I did.

She shook her head, not reaching for the money. "I can't take any payment until the painting's finished and I know you like it."

"I'll like it."

"I appreciate you wanting to help, but I need to stand on my own two feet." Iola gave me a quick kiss, then headed for the door. "I'll see you later, okay?"

"Call me if you need anything." As soon as the door closed behind her, I took out my cellphone and dialed Gloria's number.

"Hello, Gloria? It's Asher. I need a favor."

"Hey, Asher. What do you need?" Gloria sounded a little preoccupied, like she was busy with something at the community center.

"Iola was counting on the money from selling her paintings. Now she needs financial help."

"Oh. The poor thing." I could tell I now had Gloria's full attention. "What can I do?"

"Convince her it's standard practice for people to pay for commissioned paintings up front, or at least give her a deposit for them. I tried to pay in advance but she wouldn't take the money. Maybe if you suggest it, she'll understand it's not charity but good business."

"Sure, I'll bring it up with her today."

I thanked her and said goodbye, but after hanging up, I still felt hollow inside. It wasn't enough, not by a long shot. I'd been willing to put my company on the line to deliver justice to Santino while making my family financially secure. Now I was afraid my plan would hurt Iola, the person who least deserved it.

And even if I wanted to change how my scheme was playing out, I couldn't. The contract I'd negotiated with the bank to buy Santino's house and build the apartment building had fixed conditions. If I defaulted, or didn't follow through on my plan, the penalties could drag my business under, putting two dozen loyal, hard-working employees out of work. I couldn't risk that. Not when Brenda had two kids and a mortgage.

I'd thought my plan was fiendishly clever, but it was a runaway train hurtling full steam ahead with no way to stop it, no matter who was tied to the tracks.

# Chapter Fourteen

## Iola

Every time I saw Gloria, she was wearing a bright dress. Today's yellow one was the brightest yet. With her long black hair loose, she looked like she could walk down a runway at a moment's notice. But now I was getting to know how nice she was, I was becoming less intimidated by how she looked.

Gloria had taken down my ruined canvases and stacked them against one wall, but seeing them again was almost as bad as the first time. Even after bracing myself, I was shocked all over again. I felt the blood draining from my face, and wasn't surprised when Gloria made a tsk-tsk sound before hugging me.

"Are you okay?" she asked.

"Yes," I lied. Then I sighed. "It's just that I worked so hard on those paintings. I got up early each morning and painted until I couldn't keep my eyes open every night. And they were all destroyed so quickly."

Gloria gave my arm a squeeze. "Let's leave them here for a few minutes and head down to Mack's Place. You look like you could use a coffee."

"Is that the café on Calle Colina? I've driven past it, but never been in."

"You haven't?" Gloria looked surprised. "Mack's Place is a landmark around here. Coffee will be my treat."

The café was just down the road. We took a table by the window, and the waitress brought over a couple of coffees.

"Can I ask you something?" Gloria regarded me over her coffee cup. "What happened was devastating, but do you think you'll be able to do some more portraits to replace the ones that were lost?"

I nodded. "Those portraits were about letting out my anger, and I still have plenty of that." Though I didn't see how I could concentrate on painting with Ruff still missing and the threat of a forced return to England hanging over my head.

"I'm glad you're doing more portraits, because your work is special. And I need to give you this." She pulled a folded piece of paper out of her jeans pocket and handed it to me.

Unfolding it, I saw it was the list from the exhibition of everyone who'd put their names down to buy the portraits Benedict had destroyed. My stomach curled in on itself. Gloria had given me a reminder of what I'd lost?

"What should I do with this?" I asked.

"They're the people who want to buy your pieces. Let them know you're working on new paintings, so they can place their orders. And make sure you ask for a deposit right away." She gave me a stern look over the top of her cup. "Don't feel bad for asking for some money upfront, okay? It's standard business practice. They'll be glad to do it."

My heart lifted. "You really think they'd be interested?"

"Of course. When I called to tell them the paintings had been damaged, I heard how disappointed they all were."

"You already called them for me? Oh no, I should have done that."

She waved a dismissive hand. "It was nothing. It had to be the last thing you felt like doing."

It was such a thoughtful thing for her to have done, I felt a little like crying. "Thank you."

She tapped the piece of paper. "You need help calling them back?"

"You've done so much already, I don't know how I'll ever repay you."

Gloria barely knew me, but she'd done more for me than anyone had in years. And she seemed to think it was no big deal.

"No payment necessary," she said. "Though if you ever want to come and talk to one of my art classes about your work, I'm sure they'd be excited. They'd love to get some tips from an artist of your caliber."

"Of course I will. Anytime you like."

She put her cup down, her expression concerned. "Seriously, are you okay? If you need help, I'll do anything I can."

I blinked hard, still a little afraid tears might leak out and embarrass us both. "Is everyone in San Dante this nice?"

"I can't speak for the tourists, but we locals like to look out for each other." Her voice held a hint of pride. "A lot of us went to the same school. It's that kind of place."

"Thanks for your offer of help, but please don't worry. I'll get by. Ruff and I won't go hungry."

"Sweetie, any time you get hungry, come over to my place. I'll make you an unforgettable Korean feast. Come to think of it, the only thing that can make you forget my spicy rice cakes is the soju cocktails I'll make to go with them." Her grin was full of mischief.

"I'd love to come." I wouldn't cry. Nope. No way. No matter how grateful I was to have made a friend like her.

"Great. Then how's next Friday?"

"I'll bring desert." I crossed my fingers under the table, desperately hoping I'd be able to go. Everything hinged on whether I could get Ruff back.

But it was unthinkable that I wouldn't. I'd do whatever it took. And with Asher's help, I had to succeed.

"Hey, I might need to move out of Dad's place soon," I said. "You haven't heard about any cheap apartments to rent, have you?"

"Actually, I've had my eye out for one too. They're hard to find around here."

"You're looking for a new place to live?"

Tucking her long hair behind her ear, she leaned in and lowered her voice. "The woman who owns the house I live in hasn't been well. I hate to think about her passing on, but eventually I'll need to find a place where I can keep four ancient cats, a parrot, and an overgrown rabbit. Only it'd be hard enough finding an affordable house if I were on my own."

I grimaced. Being a beach town so close to LA, I should have guessed San Dante housing would be in high demand. That made things more difficult. "I wish I could just stay in Dad's place," I said with a sigh. "I wonder how much it would sell for?"

I realized I was talking as though Dad had already been convicted and his house seized, and felt a moment of guilt. But wasn't it better to prepare for the worst while you hoped for the best?

"I don't know, but I have a friend who would," Gloria offered. "Violet Eaves. She's the best realtor in town."

"If Benedict signs the divorce papers, I'm supposed to get a settlement. Honestly, I don't care about the money as long as I'm free of him. But it'd be nice to have somewhere to live that was my own."

"I'll give you Violet's number so you can ask her how much you'd need." Gloria picked up her phone. "Vi won't mind. She takes a life drawing class with me. Basically it's a group of women who meet up occasionally, whenever I can organize it." Gloria's face lit up. "Why don't you join us next time? I can't believe I didn't think of it before. We take turns bringing along the mixers to make different cocktails, and we drink and chat while we draw. To be honest, we're not terribly serious, and you'll be by far the best artist. But did I mention we have cocktails?"

I smiled back at her. She was so sweet, I wanted to bottle her. "You do life drawing? With a nude model?"

"One of the ViaGranny Gang poses for us. Beatrice loves getting naked. We pay her in cocktails."

"Not Beatrice Abernathy? Isn't she eighty?" I blinked rapidly as I tried to imagine the very well-endowed woman posing naked for an art class.

"Eighty-two." Gloria frowned at her phone, looking for Violet's phone number. "You seriously think you could buy your dad's place? Isn't it right on the beach?"

"It's a long shot, but maybe. *If* I can get my ex to sign the divorce papers."

Gloria told me Violet's number and I punched it in. I introduced myself to the cheerful-sounding woman who answered and explained there was a forfeiture notice against my father's house, so it might be seized and sold. Then I gave her the address.

"I know the house well," said Violet. "I sold it to your father."

"Do you know what it might sell for now?"

"Hmm." She was silent for a moment. "Only two bedrooms and in need of renovation, but a wonderful location. Best street in San Dante." Another pause while she thought about it. "I'll give you a ballpark figure, but don't quote me, okay? Rough estimate, somewhere around two million dollars."

I swallowed. That was a lot of money. "Would you mind telling me about the process if it gets seized?"

"There's not much to tell. By the time I get the listing, the house is likely to go on the market like any other property. It'll probably be sold by auction, so you can bid on it if you'd like."

"How long would it all take?"

"If I'm the one who gets the listing, which is likely, I'll do a three-week marketing campaign before holding the auction."

"So, if I wanted to buy it, I'd have three weeks to get the money?"

"That's right. Want me to save your number and call you if I get the listing?"

I thanked Violet and gave her my contact information before hanging up. "Dad's trial is only a week away," I told Gloria. "They'll seize the house if he's found guilty. Then I'll have three weeks before the auction. My ex would need to sign the divorce papers soon for me to have any chance of being ready in time. *And* the settlement would have to be big enough to buy something that expensive." I sighed wistfully. "It was a lovely dream, but I should set my sights a lot lower."

"No, you shouldn't. Dreaming big is never a bad thing. That's how you make things happen."

I blinked at her, surprised by the earnestness in her voice. "Maybe you're right. I'm making a New Life List, which has all the things I want to do on it." Mentioning the list made me think of Asher. Certain acts with him were currently holding all the top positions on my list. I wanted to have all the orgasms I'd missed out on the other evening, after the shock of realizing Ruff had disappeared.

When I'd been married to Benedict, sex with him had started off as disappointing, progressed to terrible, eventually become a battle of wills involving strenuous objections if he so much as touched me, and finally turned into a punishment he'd threatened me with, but thankfully never followed through on. How was it fair that Benedict was *still* managing to mess up my sex life?

"Put buying your father's house on your list, then try to figure out a way to make it happen," Gloria suggested.

"Okay." I reached for my coffee cup. I'd been so intent on our conversation, I'd forgotten to drink my coffee. But when I took a sip, Gloria screwed up her face.

"Hasn't it gone cold?" Her own coffee was long finished.

"It's still good," I said.

"Like revenge. Best served cold," she joked.

"Like revenge," I agreed, thinking about Benedict's upcoming phone call, and how different it had been fooling around with Asher than anything I'd done in the past.

The thought made something connect in my head.

"You know what?" I said slowly, turning the idea over in my mind. "I might have just come up with a way to get my ex to sign the divorce papers."

"Really? What are you going to do?"

"Hit Benedict where it'll hurt him most. His pride,

and his precious reputation. He'd do anything to save that."

She leaned in. "Go on."

"First I have to call my lawyer in London. Then I need to make sure Benedict believes how badly I could embarrass him."

When I told her exactly what I planned, Gloria gave a delighted laugh, her eyes lighting up with glee. "You wouldn't?"

"Actually, I think I would."

"Hilarious." Gloria held up one hand for a high-five. "I'm so glad we're friends."

# Chapter Fifteen

## Iola

I got home around eleven to my carefully secured and locked house, mentally preparing myself to spend a long, anxious afternoon alone while I waited for Benedict's phone call.

When I walked into the living room, Nemesis was sitting on my couch.

"How do you keep getting in here?" I rolled my eyes. "Never mind. Just don't steal anything on your way out and we'll call it even." Sidling toward her, I attempted to grab her.

Nemesis dodged me effortlessly. She jumped onto the coffee table and sat down, as though daring me to chase her.

"Nope. No way. I'm not going to race around the house after you, making a fool of myself for your amusement."

Stomping into my bedroom, I shoved the broken dresser drawer as hard as I could, trying to force it shut. With an inch to go, it stopped and refused to go in any further. Tugging it back out, I frowned at the open drawer.

Where had all my panties gone?

"Nemesis!" I marched back out to my now-empty living room. "Nemesis? Where are you?"

I checked around the furniture, peered behind doors, and looked under beds. Some of the cupboards in the kitchen didn't close properly, and I yanked them open, half expecting a pair of yellow eyes to be staring back at me. I tore from room to room searching for her, until I realized I was racing around the house, making a fool of myself. I could practically hear her laughing.

There was a knock on the door. I froze, my heart speeding up. Could Benedict be here? Had he decided to turn up unexpectedly instead of calling me like he'd promised?

Then I heard Asher's voice.

"It's me, Iola. Are you there?"

Letting out a relieved breath, I went to open it.

Asher was on my front step looking as gorgeous as ever. He had a paper bag in one hand and several pairs of panties in the other. "Are all of these yours?" he asked.

"How did Nemesis...?" I shook my head, throwing my hands up. "Wait, I've finally figured this out. You're a magician, and Nemesis is your assistant. You must be practicing for your Vegas show."

"If that were the case, I'm fairly sure Nemesis would be in charge, and I'd be the assistant who gets sawn in half."

He held out the panties, and when I took them, they rustled. I frowned down, then pulled out a note that had been slipped inside them.

On the note was a simple but beautiful cartoon drawing of Nemesis. It was a police mugshot, with her holding up a mugshot letterboard in her front paws.

Below the drawing, in three neat lines he'd written:
*Wanted for having a bad cat-itude.*
*Probable claws for arrest.*
*No chance for a paw-don.*

I snorted a laugh. "You did this just now? I thought you were at work."

"My forewoman has everything under control at the building site, and I couldn't concentrate or leave you here fretting by yourself." He lifted the paper bag. "So I picked us up some lunch."

*Swoon.* Not only was he clever and funny, but incredibly sweet. Had I discovered the perfect man?

"This is a beautiful drawing," I said. "You're talented, you know that?"

"Coming from you, that's quite a compliment."

His navy t-shirt and dark jeans fit him to perfection, and he looked so handsome I wanted to throw myself into his arms. When he stepped in to kiss me, I almost crushed our lunch with my enthusiasm. Though I could have kissed him all afternoon, he pulled back way too soon.

"We need to eat quickly," he said, leading me into the kitchen.

"Eat quickly? Why?"

He set the paper bag on the counter and pulled out two sandwiches. "Because after lunch, I'm taking you out."

"What?" I blinked, sure I must have misheard him. "Where do you want to go?"

"It's a surprise." He got plates out of the cupboard and unwrapped the sandwiches. "Sit down. Eat."

Asher set our food on my dad's little dining table, and I found myself sitting down with a sandwich in front of me, though my mind was still full of questions.

"It looks nice, but I'm sorry, I'm not really hungry," I said. "And we can't go anywhere. Benedict's going to ring this afternoon, remember?"

"Are you worried about his phone call?" Asher took the chair next to mine.

I nodded, though I wasn't just worried about the call, I was terrified.

"What if I mess it up and Benedict doesn't take the bait?" I asked.

"You're too clever to mess it up. I have complete confidence in you."

Because he was so thoughtful and everything he said sounded so considered, whenever Asher paid me a compliment, I felt a surge of pride, like I'd won an award. My nervousness also faded a little, which seemed like a minor miracle. Though I was still too nervous to do more than pick at my sandwich while I watched Asher eat his.

"You're not going to eat?" he asked when he finished. "You should keep your strength up."

I shook my head, aware that I'd tensed again. I was so used to Benedict telling me what to do and coming up with petty punishments anytime I disobeyed, I was waiting for Asher to get irritated with me for not eating the sandwich he'd so thoughtfully brought me. But Asher's face stayed as impassive as ever. Come to think of it, I wasn't sure I'd ever seen him get irritated.

A flood of gratitude surged through me. Over the last few weeks, my relief at finally being away from Benedict had kept hitting me at odd moments. This time it was strong enough to make me feel overwhelmed.

Asher covered my hand with his and gave it a squeeze.

"Hey." His voice was gentle. "It's okay. We have several hours before the phone call and I want to take you out to keep your mind off it, so you don't spend the time fretting."

"You won't tell me where you're taking me?"

"You'll see when we get there." He stood up and carried the plates into the kitchen.

I shook my head. "Thanks," I called after him. "I appreciate your thoughtful offer, but I'm too worried about Ruff."

"That's exactly why we need to go," he called back.

"Asher, I—"

"Please." Walking back to the dining table, he offered his hand with a smile that made me let go of my objections and stand up. His smile was like the Pied Piper's flute. One glimpse and I'd follow him anywhere.

"Okay," I said. "But you won't even give me a hint about where we're going? Not even so I know what to wear?"

Running his gaze over my sundress and sandals, heat flickered into his eyes as though he liked what he saw. "You look perfect. Don't change a thing."

My legs weakened.

I loved that look in his eyes. It gave me serious tingles. If Asher really wanted to take my mind off my nervousness, staying in and exploring where that look might take us would be a lot more effective.

"Come on," he said with a little laugh as though he could hear my thoughts. "If you don't hurry, we'll be late."

"Late for what?"

Still refusing to say where he was taking me, he hustled me into the car. But we'd only been driving for half an hour or so when I realized we were heading for a group of large, colorful tents.

"You're taking me to the circus?" I asked incredulously.

"You said you'd never been. Don't you want to tick it off your New Life List?"

I was speechless. All I could do was gaze at his profile as he drove. I already knew he was sweet, but this was next level. A friend had once told me she thought the hotter a guy was, the more likely he was to be an arrogant narcissist. When it came to Asher, her theory couldn't have been more wrong.

Swallowing hard, I managed to force out some words. "Thank you. I mean, you remembered. That's... wow. But do we have time?"

"The afternoon show's about to start. It'll be finished by three thirty. Benedict won't call before then."

"How do you know about the afternoon show?"

Instead of answering, he just shot me a sideways glance, one side of his mouth slightly lifted. My heart burst out singing, and it was some kind of operatic number. Very romantic. He must have checked out the timetable in advance.

Just like when I'd found out what Gloria had done for me, tears came dangerously close. Was being so nice a San Dante thing, or had I somehow gotten lucky and stumbled on the most thoughtful people in the entire state?

I barely managed to get my emotions under control by the time Asher parked outside the big top. He insisted on buying the tickets, and we found our seats just before the show started.

From the moment the ringmaster stepped into the central ring, the show didn't stop. A miniature car careened into the ring after him, racing around in fast circles. I couldn't stop laughing as clowns somehow poured out of it, more squeezed into the tiny vehicle than I could believe possible.

I leaned over to murmur in Asher's ear. "Crazy as it sounds, I've never seen clowns in real life before."

"Then they have big shoes to fill." The smile lines around his eyes crinkled at his own joke, and I laughed before turning back to the ring where the clowns were jumping onto unicycles.

"I didn't think they did stunts, but—" I gasped as one after another, they flew over a ramp, doing somersaults while still on their unicycles. "Can you believe this?"

He took hold of my hand. "Save some amazement for the other acts. It's only just begun."

I wrapped the fingers of my other hand around our joined ones, and lost my worries in the spectacle unfolding in front of me. Next came the acrobats, then the tightrope walkers, and two contortionists who had no bones in their bodies at all.

Then the trapeze artists appeared, and all the air left my lungs as I watched them fly at the top of the tall tent, totally weightless.

The clowns came back to close the show, and when the bright overhead lights came back on, my hands were sore from clapping.

"What did you think?" asked Asher.

"It worked. I forgot about how nervous I am." I looked longingly up at the top of the tent. "One day I want to take trapeze lessons."

"You want to climb up there?" He sounded surprised.

"What, you don't?"

"Not even a little."

"Scared of heights?"

He nodded. "Of heights, but mostly of falling."

The words reminded me of how matter-of-factly he'd

told me he was never going to fall in love. That he'd never be able to trust anyone enough.

Something twisted in my chest.

I didn't want to fall either. But I did want to soar through the air, high above the ground.

If only Asher wanted to fly with me.

# Chapter Sixteen

## Asher

There was probably a mathematical equation to calculate how long a circus-induced feeling of happiness should usually last. But whatever the typical duration, for Iola and I it ended when we stepped out of the big top.

I took Iola back to her place, where she sat stiffly on the couch, holding her phone in both hands. She stared at it, willing it to ring, her face pale and serious.

As for me, I was trying not to let on how much I wanted to be the one who'd talk to Benedict. I didn't like not being in control, and the whole situation was pushing me out of my comfort zone.

"If you can, put a little fear into your voice when you talk to him." I leaned against the table to keep from pacing. "At least at first. Try to sound like you're gaining confidence as the conversation progresses."

She nodded. "I can be afraid. I'll just think of what could happen if we don't get Ruff back." She put her phone down on the coffee table and twisted her fingers together. "What about if I add a whole lot of anger to my act. Would that work?"

"If I said no to anger, would you be able to hold it back?"

"Not a chance." She picked her phone back up, her hands clearly restless. "Around three o'clock this morning, I came up with a list of offensive websites and I'm going to register his email address on all of them."

I nodded approvingly. "Revenge is better than anger."

She gave me a weak but grateful smile. "That's exactly what I was thinking."

"I'll get us a drink." I headed toward the kitchen.

"Just water for me. I need to keep a clear head."

Opening the cupboard door to get the glasses, I noticed it didn't shut properly and made a mental note to come back with my toolbox.

But that was a foolish thought. There was no point in fixing it when I'd be pulling down the entire house soon.

Stifling a sigh, I filled two glasses with cold water before carrying them into her living room. It smelled of paint. She'd started a new painting, and already I could see its potential. I had a feeling it'd be her best yet.

She took one of the glasses from me and her dark eyes met mine. I saw sadness in them again, as well as worry, and my desire to take that sadness away and make her smile was intense.

"Thank you." Her voice was soft. "I'm glad you're here."

My heart thumped against my ribs, like it only seemed to do around her. "I wouldn't miss it," I said in a level tone, careful to keep my face impassive.

Her phone rang and she jabbed the speaker button to connect the call.

"Benedict?" she demanded.

"Hello, darling." With the speaker on, Benedict's voice rang out clearly, his aristocratic accent making him sound deceptively polite. I sat on the couch next to Iola, keeping my movements slow so her ex-husband wouldn't hear me.

"Is Ruff okay?" Iola asked.

"The dog's healthy enough, for now. A veterinarian just issued the papers for her flight home."

She glanced at me, her lips tightening and her eyes flashing murder. "Benedict, why do you want me back?" she asked with just the right amount of fear and anger in her voice. "Our marriage was never happy. We fit together like pubic hair and a yanked-up zipper."

"No Appleby has ever been divorced."

My jaw clenched at the stupidity of his answer. What kind of reason was that?

Iola drew in a breath and let it out again, as though drawing on hidden reserves of strength. "I'm not going to England. I need you to give Ruff back and sign the divorce papers. You can't keep our bank accounts frozen when some of that money belongs to me."

Benedict chuckled. "I had dinner with Frank before I left. You remember the president of our bank, don't you darling? He's been a great friend through all of this unpleasantness."

Iola rubbed her palm up and down her thigh. She was doing a brilliant job holding back her rage. Maybe even better than I could have done, though it pained me to admit it.

"You broke into the community center. You smashed a window and vandalized private property. Now you're in serious trouble."

"I don't know what you're talking about, but if they suffered a recent break-in, I'm not surprised. The crime rate in this country is a disgrace. The town must be full of vandals and thieves."

Iola met my gaze again, and a calmness seemed to settle over her. She was playing this conversation perfectly, and was about to lead Benedict from confidence to uncertainty like a matador coaxing a bull toward the sword.

"Next to the community center is a realtor's office. You may have noticed it? The woman who runs it displays her listings in the window."

"Iola, it's time to accept—"

"Apparently over the years, teenagers have found it funny to make changes to those listings by scribbling on the glass. That's why the realtor has a security camera focused on the sidewalk outside her shop. When I checked, I found the camera covered a large area."

She paused, but Benedict was silent. He had to see

where she was going with this. With any luck he was having a panic attack.

"It captured the man who smashed the community center's window. The shot was clear. And when I asked the realtor for the footage so I could pass it on to the police, she was happy to let me have it. One thing about San Dante, it's a very friendly town. The locals are almost too nice."

"You're bluffing." Benedict's voice was an unpleasant snarl.

"I haven't taken the recording to the police yet, but I imagine you'll be charged with destruction of property. You don't know any judges here in California, do you, Benedict?"

He let out a derisive snort. "I know you're bluffing."

"And what if someone sent the recording to British newspapers? The gossip rags love running stories about upper-class twats embarrassing themselves." Her voice sharpened. "Can you imagine your parents reading about it? What if Frank-who-owns-the-bank discovered you'd been committing crimes? Do you think he'd still come to dinner?"

Benedict was silent again, and Iola looked like she was holding her breath. Her wide brown eyes met mine and her expression was half fearful, half hopeful.

"I don't believe any such recording exists," Benedict said finally. "But if you have something with a man who looks like me, I want to see it. I'm sure the resemblance will be shaky, to say the least."

"Be at my house at nine o'clock tomorrow morning,

and bring Ruff with you. I'll have her ownership papers waiting. Once you see the recording, you'll give Ruff back to me and sign her over to me."

"Nine o'clock it is." His voice hardened. "If I don't see a credible recording, I'll expect you to be packed and ready to get on a plane to England."

"Agreed."

Iola hung up and dropped the phone on the table as though it were hot. Blowing out a loud breath, she leaned back "I really hope this works."

"You were incredible." I spoke from the heart.

A slow, relieved smile spread over her face. "You think so?"

"I was awestruck. You were perfect."

Her smile grew and her cheeks flushed. She looked both pleased and breathtakingly beautiful. I wanted to kiss her more than I wanted to breathe.

"I hope he takes the bait," she said.

"He will. Now I have to prepare. You're sleeping at my house tonight, so grab whatever you need."

She shook her head. "I'm staying right here."

"Absolutely not."

"I'm staying here." Her voice was firm and she lifted her chin to shoot me a defiant stare. "This is still my house, even if it won't be for long."

I swallowed a hard lump of guilt at the reminder. I should be getting used to the taste of it by now.

"I need you out of harm's way," I told her. "If anything happened to you, it'd be on me."

"I can't stay next door. Don't ask me to do that, because I won't. Whatever happens, I need to be here."

Her jaw was set so firmly, what else could I do but give in? I just hoped I wouldn't come to regret it.

# Chapter Seventeen

## Asher

After Benedict's phone call, we spent some time setting up the house with the equipment I'd picked up. Then we ordered pizza. By the time we were done eating, the sun had dropped below the horizon and the house was getting dark.

Leaving the lights off, we retreated into Iola's bedroom and closed the door behind us.

Iola sat on the bed. I turned on a dim, low-wattage lamp next to the bed and handed her the pair of handcuffs Nemesis had turned up with a few months ago. In spite of the fluffy pink fur, they seemed as strong as regular cuffs.

"Time to play?" Iola dangled them from one finger and quirked a suggestive eyebrow. "I could joke about handcuffs, but I'll restrain myself. Even if I wanted to unlock some off-the-cuff puns, my hands are tied."

"Don't be nervous. It'll be okay."

"I'm not nervous, I'm terrified. By the way, what do you call a potato that likes being handcuffed? A mashochist." Her cheeks flushed and she gritted her teeth. "Must. Stop. Talking." She threw herself down flat, bunching the pillow under her neck.

"You don't have to do this. Go next door where you'll be safe." It came out sounding too much like a command, so I softened my voice. "Please."

Though the dim light meant her face was in shadow, I still saw her eyes flash. "I'll tell you a million bad jokes, but I'm not leaving."

I settled on the bed next to her. "Then I'll stick close. I won't let anything happen to you."

She rolled onto her side facing me, and I did the same. Lying close without touching, I waited for my eyes to adjust to the darkness. Though I couldn't make out her freckles, I mapped and memorized the fine bones that shaped Iola's face. Her breathing slowed a little and some of the tension eased from her body. My proximity seemed to calm her, even as hers had the opposite effect on me.

She was close enough to kiss. Close enough that if I put my hand on her hip, I could pull her against me.

My muscles tensed with the effort of remaining still, of not touching her. Of not kissing her.

"I have a surprise for you," I whispered.

"A good surprise?" Her breath was warm and a little minty.

"I think you'll like it."

"Is it in your pants?"

I huffed a quiet laugh. "It's not that kind of surprise."

"Then what is it?"

"You'll find out later." I leaned in until my nose lightly brushed against hers. "Tell me a joke," I whispered.

"Did you hear about the vampire who jumped a snowman? He got frostbite."

I chuckled.

"And cow farts come from the dairy air," she added. "In case you were considering a moo-ve to the cow-ntry."

"You're hilarious. Keep going."

"A perfectionist walked into a bar. Apparently it wasn't set high enough."

I kissed her nose. "Another."

"Once I was kidnapped by mimes. They did unspeakable things to me."

There was a thump from outside the window, then a muffled curse. A man had stumbled over something.

Iola's eyes widened, glinting in the dim light. We were both frozen, holding our breath. Then she grabbed her cellphone.

Something rattled, and it sounded like the house's side door. That was the logical entry point for an intruder seeing as it wasn't visible from the road or the beach. That door hadn't been well maintained, and the lock was rusty. It had become even more defective after I'd removed several screws.

Sure enough, a hard thump and the crack of screws breaking free of the wood told me the intruder had broken the lock with a swift shoulder blow.

The hinges creaked as the door opened. I heard soft footfalls that meant the intruder was making his way into the living room.

Soundlessly, I eased off the bed and padded over to the bedroom door, positioning myself on the side where I'd be hidden behind it when the door opened.

A faint beam of light slipped under the door, then vanished. Benedict was shining a flashlight around, searching for the recording Iola had baited him with.

She shifted on the bed, and I put my finger to my lips, silently willing her not to move. Benedict wouldn't have come here without a weapon. There was a chance he may have a gun, though it was more likely he'd be carrying a baseball bat or knife. And sneaking around a strange house in the dark, he'd be on edge.

In my original plan, I was going to be here alone. Now Iola was in danger, I kicked myself for not arranging backup. She had her cellphone in hand, ready to call 911 if things went wrong, but I should have asked Kade or Mason to be here in case we needed help.

Benedict's footsteps approached the bedroom and stopped outside the door. The door handle turned, then the door swung open, blocking my view of the person coming in.

"Benedict!" Iola sat up on the bed, her face pale. His flashlight found her face and she flinched back against the headboard, lifting one hand to shield her eyes. "What are you doing here?" She sounded panicked and afraid, but she'd remembered to keep her other hand under the covers so Benedict wouldn't see her phone.

"Hello, darling." Benedict's voice was unpleasant, but at least he lowered his flashlight so it wasn't shining in her eyes. "You shouldn't have threatened me. That wasn't nice."

"Don't make me go to England with you," Iola whimpered. "I'll give you the recording." She darted her gaze to the nightstand where I'd left the biggest memory card I could find. It was illuminated in the dim glow from the lamp, and in case Benedict was slow on the uptake, I'd written 'CCTV Footage' in black marker on the label.

Benedict's flashlight jerked over to it, and he chuckled. "I'll take that—"

His demand cut off with a yelp as he stepped into the tripwire I'd strung just below knee height.

His momentum carried him forward and Benedict went sprawling. His flashlight flew out of his hand and crashed into the wall. Another object skittered after it. I was on Benedict in a second, pushing my knee into his back to keep him on the ground, while I twisted his arm up.

Benedict grunted, trying to throw me off, but I had my full weight on him and I was stronger than he was.

"Here!" Iola threw me the pink fluffy handcuffs, and I fastened them around his wrists.

"You got him," she crowed as I stood up.

Hooking a hand under Benedict's arm, I pulled him to his feet. With his hands cuffed behind his back, all the fight had gone out of him. He looked petulant.

"Let me go," he spat. "This is illegal. It's kidnapping.

If you don't release me right now, you'll have to deal with my lawyer."

I turned on the bright overhead lights and looked at the object he'd dropped with his flashlight. Instead of a baseball bat or knife, it turned out to be a canister of pepper spray. Huh. Just went to prove that predicting everything was impossible.

"Who the hell do you think you are?" Benedict twisted to glare at me. He was trying to yank his hands out of the cuffs, but I'd fastened them so tightly, he didn't have a chance of getting free.

"I'm the guy who's kidnapping you," I said.

"Where's Ruff?" demanded Iola.

"I'll never tell you," he snarled.

She stepped closer to him and jabbed her finger into his chest. "You'd better tell me where Ruff is before I decide to hurt you."

"What exactly do you think you're going to do, Iola? If you so much as scratch me, I'll make sure you serve jail time."

I cut the tripwire, then put my hand on Benedict's shoulder and propelled him out of the bedroom. "Come on." In a softer voice I said to Iola, "Remember I said I have a surprise for you? It's through here." Pushing Benedict through the living room, I flicked on the lights as we went.

"Where are you taking me?" Benedict growled. "You have no idea how much trouble you're in. When my lawyers get through with you—"

I shoved him into the laundry room and he almost

stumbled into the wall before turning to face me. The room was small, with a small drain set into the tiled floor so excess water could drain away. Beside the washing machine, leaning on the wall, I'd hidden my surprise gift for Iola. It was big enough that I used two hands to pick it up and offer it to her.

She gaped for a second, then a wide grin spread over her face. She took it out of my hands, her face displaying enough reverence to make my inner child smile.

"Is this what I think it is?" she asked.

"The Soakinator Gargantuan 2000," I confirmed. "Still the best water gun on the market, and it's fully loaded and ready to shoot. You said you'd never been in a water fight, and I'm afraid this one will be one-sided, but hopefully you'll enjoy it anyway." I took a moment to savor the glee in her eyes.

"Don't be ridiculous." Benedict growled. "You'd better not even think about using that thing on me."

Iola responded by hoisting the big gun and aiming it at him. "Where's Ruff, Benedict?"

"This is an expensive jacket. And my passport is in my pocket, an official document. If you damage it, that's a serious crime."

"You're right." Reaching into his jacket pocket, I pulled out his passport and car keys. "I'll hold onto these for you."

"You wouldn't dare shoot me, Iola." Benedict cringed backward until his back hit the wall. "Don't be foolish. This benefits nobody."

"One more chance," she aimed it at his chest. "Where's Ruff?"

"Iola, for heaven's sake—"

She pulled the trigger and a torrent of water erupted from the Soakinator.

He shouted as the water hit, twisting to try to get out of the way. Iola laughed with delight, drenching him from head to toe. When the stream stopped, her eyes were dancing. "This is fun!"

I smiled back. "At some point in the future, we should both get guns."

"Yes! Get your own gun and we can have a war, like your dad and his neighbor."

Benedict was gasping. "Iola, you bitch! I'll kill both you and the dog. I'll make that mongrel suffer—"

Iola let out a war cry as she fired, and his threats turned into splutters.

Leaving her to her fun, I went outside. A number of cars were parked on the street, but when I pressed the button on Benedict's key, the lights of one flashed. And as I walked to the car, a familiar face peered out from the back window.

"Hi Ruff," I said.

The dog barked. She seemed pleased to see me. I let her out of the car and she butted my leg with her head, her tail wagging furiously.

"Iola's inside," I told her.

Ruff barked again, lumbering to the door ahead of me. I let her inside, and her claws clacked on the floor as she raced straight for Iola.

"Ruff!" Iola dropped to her knees to throw her arms around Ruff's neck.

"That dog isn't yours." Benedict drew himself up, shaking with outrage. His face was bright red, and his clothes were soaked and clinging to his frame, but he seemed to have recovered some of his bluster.

I put a hand on Iola's shoulder. "Are you finished with the Soakinator?" I asked.

She hesitated. "Well, I guess so."

"We should move to the next phase." I eyed Benedict. He was even wetter than I'd expected, and he'd drip water all through the house, but there was no way to avoid that.

I stepped forward and took his soggy arm. "Come with me."

"Where are you taking me?" He tried to plant his feet, but with his hands cuffed behind him, it was easy enough to pull him forward.

"To the dining table. Sit down and I'll take the handcuffs off."

That got him moving under his own steam, and he sat in the chair I pulled out for him.

"We have papers signing over ownership of Ruff to Iola," I said. "When I take the handcuffs off, I expect you to sign them."

He leaned forward, lifting his hands behind him. "Take them off."

"First, I want to play you a recording."

Iola carried in a couple of towels. She dropped one on the floor under Benedict's chair and laid the other on his legs. She put a pen and the change of ownership papers for Ruff on the table in front of him, then sat on the chair next to him.

"You have footage of the community center?" asked Benedict.

Iola shook her head. "No. I was bluffing."

I opened my laptop, found what I was looking for, and pressed Play before swiveling it to face Benedict.

"What's this?" He frowned at the black screen. "There's nothing there."

"You'll notice the camera in the corner of the living room." I pointed away from the laptop, at the camera I'd installed only a short time ago. "It uses the latest infra-red technology. In a moment you'll see yourself breaking into Iola's house. Breaking and entering happens to be a felony. You broke the law, whereas handcuffing an intruder isn't defined as kidnapping. We broke no laws, but simply detained a burglar before calling the police."

Sure enough, a light appeared in the corner of the black recording, and a figure became visible. It was clearly Benedict creeping through the door.

"That's a good shot of the pepper spray he's holding." Iola leaned forward to peer at the screen. "Isn't that classed as a weapon, Asher? Wouldn't the police take that seriously?"

"Very seriously. Breaking and entering with a weapon isn't an easy charge to defend."

"I'll call the police." She lifted her cellphone.

Benedict's jaw was tight, his teeth grinding together. His face was even redder than it had been before. "I'll sign your damn papers," he spat. "Keep the mongrel. I hope it gives you rabies."

"Lean forward." I pulled out the key for the handcuffs. "And just so you know, the recording has been automatically saved to the cloud, and the camera's still recording us, so doing anything foolish like trying to destroy my laptop would only get you in more trouble."

His teeth ground together even harder, but when I released the handcuffs, he snatched up the pen and scribbled his signature on the papers.

"Now destroy the recording," he demanded.

I shook my head. "Not until you're back in England."

Benedict jumped to his feet. His fists were clenched, and he was shaking with anger, little droplets of water flying off him. "I'll make you regret this."

Iola leaned back in her chair and looked up at him. "There's one more thing." Her voice was so cool and biting, it made pride swell in my chest. "I sent my lawyer a statement about our marriage. It's a sealed document detailing exactly how controlling you were, and how you threatened me and made me suffer. And in case you find a way to justify how awful you were, I also included information about our marital relations. Because it's an unfair world, the fact you never even tried to give me an orgasm won't make any legal difference, but if you contest the divorce, the document will be unsealed and read out in court." She tapped her finger against her lips as if she'd just thought of something. "Wait a minute. Don't you play golf with the judge? Aren't you members of the same club?" She tsked. "Having such intimate details read out could be embarrassing for you. I hope he doesn't gossip, or every single person you know could hear about it."

It was almost impossible to keep from smiling. She hadn't told me she'd embellished the plan, but it was brilliant. *She* was brilliant.

Benedict's face had gone from bright red to a deep shade of purple. "You wouldn't embarrass yourself by telling lies about our private life, Iola."

"They aren't lies. And seeing as I never plan to go to England again, I don't care if everyone in the country finds out every detail of how awful you were to me." She stood up to face him, her chin lifted and her eyes as hard as flint. "Signing the divorce papers is the only way the envelope stays sealed."

He gave his head a disgusted shake. "You were a nobody, and I gave you my name. Becoming an Appleby was a privilege you didn't deserve, and now you've thrown it away. You should be ashamed."

"Get out." She folded her arms. "I have nothing more to say to you."

"Come on," I told Benedict. "I'm going to drive you to the airport. Once I've seen you get on a flight, I'll delete the recording."

Benedict drew himself up and squelched out, his wet shoes leaving a soggy trail across the floor.

Iola put her hand on my arm before I could follow. "Thank you, Asher, but I can't ask you to take him all that way."

Lifting her hand, I kissed her knuckles. "I'll message

you when his plane takes off so you know he's gone for good."

"Come back here afterward."

I shook my head, heading for the door. "It'll be late. You and Ruff should get some sleep. I'll call you in the morning."

Once Benedict was gone, Iola would be safe, and I'd have to tell her my role in putting her father in jail. The knowledge filled me with dread, but what choice did I have? My conscience wouldn't let me keep delaying it.

Tomorrow, I'd have to confess the truth.

Tomorrow, I could lose her.

# Chapter Eighteen

## Iola

"Why are we back here?" I asked Asher as we parked in front of the circus tents the next morning. What made it stranger was that it was quiet, with not many cars around, so it didn't even seem as though a show was about to start.

"Not that I'm complaining," I added before Asher could get the wrong idea. "I enjoyed it so much the first time, I'm happy to see the show again. But I wouldn't have thought you'd want to come back so soon."

Last night's plan had gone so perfectly, I'd still been riding a high this morning. Asher had said he was taking me out to celebrate, but wouldn't say where. And he'd been weirdly insistent, even asking Gloria to take care of Ruff so I wouldn't worry about her while we were gone.

All that trouble to go to the circus again? It didn't make sense.

"Come on," he said, sliding out of the car. "I'll explain on the way inside."

I got out too, and we started toward the big top. When he'd told me to wear workout clothes, I figured we'd be doing something active. "Okay, what's this all about?" I demanded.

"I wanted you to have a special day." His face was unreadable. "Today we celebrate. Tonight we'll talk."

"Talk about what?"

He shook his head, and I frowned at the tightness around his eyes. "That's for later. Today, we're going to swing."

"Swing?"

"I've arranged for a trapeze lesson."

"Really?" I let out an excited whoop, bouncing on my toes. "I guess you're not going to do it with me?"

"I am."

"But you're afraid of heights."

"It's not the heights that worry me, it's the possibility of falling. I had a bad fall when I was younger."

"What happened?"

He took my hand as we walked into the big top. "I'm going to tell you everything, I promise. But first, I'll let them know we're here."

I couldn't see any performers, but there were some workmen in the ring, laying fresh sawdust. Asher spoke to one of them, and the man strolled away through the back of the tent, presumably going to fetch someone.

"We're a little early." Asher motioned me toward one

of the seats at the side of the ring. "Let's talk while we wait."

"Are you going to tell me about your fall?"

"It happened when we were in Mexico," he said as we sat down.

"Are you sure you want to talk about your fall right before a trapeze lesson?" I was half joking, but as I settled into my seat and turned to face him, I saw the tension around his eyes and realized how serious he was being.

"I need you to know everything about my past," he said. "But it's difficult to talk about. When my brothers and I came back to San Dante, we made a pact we'd never tell anyone what had happened in Mexico, and I've never wanted to break that promise."

"So you've never spoken about this to anyone?" It was obviously important to him, and my heart expanded at the thought he was willing to share it with me.

He nodded, taking a breath as though he was bracing himself to say something difficult. "When we first arrived in Mexico, Mom got a waitressing job. Money was short and things were hard. She was drinking a lot after years of being sober, but she wasn't doing drugs. Not at first. Most of the time, she was still in control."

"That's when you learned your cup and ball trick?"

"Mom wasn't earning much, so we all did what we could to help pay rent and buy food. When Mom drank a lot, it wasn't pleasant. But we were scraping by."

His tone was so matter-of-fact, I could tell how hard it was for Asher to talk about that time of his life. And he was sitting stiffly, staring into the gloom of the tent's furthest corner.

"It must have been difficult." I took his hand.

"Mom started dating one of the chefs from the restaurant she worked in, and despite her mood swings, her boyfriend stuck with her for a long time. Without him, things would have been a lot worse."

"He was a nice guy?"

Asher nodded. "He was a stable influence. After he and Mom split up, that's when she met Four-Finger-Frankie."

"Another boyfriend?"

"Scum." The word was toneless. "A drug dealer with delusions of grandeur. He gave her drugs and used her." His eyes were unfocused, his face as blank as though he was wondering what type of sawdust the workmen were laying. "He broke her. She was sick and vulnerable, and he finished her off. Thanks to him she developed psychosis. She'd have big highs and deep lows, and they'd happen so fast, none of us knew how to cope. She needed serious help, but he had her convinced she only needed him."

I wrapped my other hand around the one I was holding. My stomach was churning. I felt a deep pity for a woman I didn't know, and her three boys. How terrible it must have been for Asher and his brothers.

When my mother had died suddenly, the pain of losing her had been worse than anything I could have imagined. I couldn't imagine how helpless Asher must have felt watching his mother suffer through such a serious drug addiction when he couldn't do anything to stop it.

"The drugs made Mom so paranoid that she started locking us in the apartment all night while she went out with Frankie. One day, she didn't come back."

I frowned. "What do you mean, she didn't come back? You were still locked inside? How long did she leave you?"

"After three days, we knew we'd have to get out on our own."

*Three days?* My mouth dropped open and I made a muffled sound in the back of my throat, but Asher kept talking.

"The apartment was on the third floor. The door was too solid to break, and the deadlock was about the only thing in that rathole that worked like it was supposed to. The only way out was through a window, but there was no fire escape, and the windows all had safety latches to stop them opening far enough."

I squeezed his hand, wishing there was something else I could do. My face felt bloodless, but I was trying not to let him see how horrified I was.

"One of the windows opened a little more than the others," he said. "I was the only one who could fit through it, so I went out that way to get help."

"You climbed out a third-floor window? What was below it?"

For a moment, I wasn't sure he'd heard me. His eyes were haunted. It was like he was back in that long-ago apartment, staring out the window, judging the distance to the ground.

"It opened onto a side alley. A narrow passage, concrete below. The walls were sheer. There wasn't anything to climb onto. I just had to drop."

My mouth opened and shut. I cleared my throat. "When you went out the window, you knew you'd fall?"

He nodded. "But it wasn't nearly as bad as it could have been. I only broke my arm."

I swallowed hard, picturing Asher going out a high window to get help for his brothers. How scared he must have been. That moment when he'd let go of the sill and dropped… I shook my head, both awed by what he'd done and horrified he'd had to do it.

Could I have done the same thing in his place? Would I have been brave enough?

"What happened to your mom?" I asked. "Did she ever come back?"

A muscle pulsed in his jaw. "By the time we got out, someone had already discovered her body. Her pockets had been emptied, and the police hadn't known who she was or where she lived. They couldn't give us a time of death, but I'm sure it happened at least a day or two earlier."

"I'm sorry." The words sounded insubstantial, made from nothing but vapor.

"That's why Mom hadn't come back to the apartment. She wouldn't have left us without food for so long otherwise. I have to believe that."

His eyes finally came up to meet mine, and I saw

their seemingly hard gray surface was just a shield to hide his pain.

"I'm sorry," I said again, hating how inadequate the words were. There should be something else I could offer him, another way of telling him how much I wished he hadn't suffered like that.

After my mother's death, my life had turned upside down. My home was gone, burned to the ground. The boarding school Dad sent me to was in Washington State, and I'd had to try to fit in there while I was grieving, and to try to adjust to being far away from everything I'd known. I'd wanted to bury those memories so deep I'd never have to think about them again, so I could understand why Asher had never wanted to speak about any of this.

"I blame Four-Finger-Frankie for everything," said Asher. "Him and all his associates. They all deserve to be punished." He held my gaze, his voice as hard as his eyes. "Every single one of them."

"What did you do after she died?" I asked, my mind still skimming over all my own painful memories.

"My brothers and I went back to San Dante. We finished our schooling and life went on. But I've always had a thing about falling."

"We're not going on the trapeze." My voice was firm. "Neither of us."

He stared at me a moment longer, then let out a slow breath. Some of the muscles in his face relaxed a little, as though telling me about his past had been a difficult chore he was relieved to have completed. "We are. We'll do it together."

"No way." I shook my head. "There are plenty of other fun things we can try. I've always wanted to learn to juggle. We can do that instead."

"Fear is just a chemical reaction that developed in our brains to make cavemen run from lions."

"That doesn't mean you should ignore it."

A muscle twitched in his jaw. "If I hadn't learned to control my emotions in Mexico, I wouldn't have been able to perform the cup and ball trick perfectly every time, day after day. I wouldn't have been able to deal with Mom's changeable moods, or hold it together when she locked us in the apartment. This is no different. I need to control my fear, not let it control me."

A woman appeared from the back of the tent. It was the slightly built trapeze artist I'd watched perform last time we were here. As she headed toward us, Asher eased his hand out of the python grip I had on it so he could stand up.

I stood too. "Lions have fangs. Sometimes it's smart to run away from them."

"Circuses have safety nets."

"Yes, but—"

"Here we are." The trapeze artist had a strong Australian accent. "Sorry for the wait."

Her face was free of makeup, and she wore a simple leotard and tights instead of a sparkling costume. She barely came up to my shoulder, and though I was normally comfortable in my own body, she was so lithe and graceful that I couldn't help but feel big and clumsy in comparison.

She told us her name was Kasia, and led the way to the ladder while she assured us by the end of our lesson we'd both be able to swing upside down... and to fall safely into the big net that suddenly looked extremely flimsy.

"Are you sure you want to do this?" I muttered to Asher.

"I'm sure." Weirdly, the tension in his voice eased my worry a little. The stronger his emotions were, the less likely he was to show them.

Kasia strapped us both into harnesses attached to elastic lines, explaining the lines would make us fall slowly instead of quickly.

"Is falling slowly supposed to be better?" I hissed to Asher, my stomach filling with excited butterflies. "Or will that just give us more time to be scared?"

His eyes softened on mine, and he leaned in to steal a kiss. After what he'd told me about his childhood, I couldn't help but kiss him back with more intensity than was appropriate, given Kasia was watching. He felt and tasted so good, my world narrowed to the warmth of his mouth, his hand in my hair, the passion of his lips, his body close to mine.

But he let me go too soon. I tried to cling for a moment, my head swimming, but he was drawing away.

"For luck," he murmured.

Which is when it occurred to me that being dizzy

might not be the best state for climbing thirty-foot ladders.

"Ready?" Kasia wore a wide smile, watching us with open approval. "Follow me now, and let's climb."

Asher got straight onto the ladder with no hesitation and climbed so fast I had to hurry after him, too dazed by his kiss to be as nervous as I should be.

Asher paused about halfway up and glanced back at me. He paled as his eyes went past me to the ground, but then he focused on me and when he spoke, he sounded calm. "Are you okay, Iola?"

"Are you?" I was keeping up with him so closely that I put my hand on each rung as his foot left it.

He didn't answer, and I suspected it was because he didn't want to lie and say he was fine when he wasn't. I could respect that.

"Hey," I said. "I want you to know this is the first time I've accepted an invitation to swing. I'm not usually that type of girl."

He chuckled, which I counted as a win even though it sounded strained.

"I'd apply for a job as a trapeze artist," I added. "Only I'm afraid of being let go." For the rest of the climb, I told circus jokes, trying to take his mind off how high we were. Finally Asher reached the platform and stepped onto it. I was right behind him, and when I joined him I noticed he wasn't looking down. Probably a good thing. The ground was scarily far away, and the net was hard to see. It didn't seem like it could save us if—when—we fell.

I squeezed Asher's forearm. "You're doing great," I murmured.

He rewarded me with a tiny hint of a smile in return, an impressive feat considering what he'd been through. No wonder he'd been able to build a successful construction company. With that kind of determination, he could do anything.

"No need to be nervous." Kasia faced us, seemingly unaware of the fact that the edge of the ledge was just a hair's breadth from the back of her heel. "We're perfectly safe." She grabbed the trapeze, releasing it from where it was hooked on. "I'll show you how to hold the bar, then you'll swing. First we'll just hold on with our hands. Then we'll try hooking our legs over it. If you're feeling confident at the end of the lesson, we'll try a simple catch. Okay?"

"Okay!" My excitement rose. Asher just gave a stiff nod.

"Who's going first?" asked Kasia.

"I will," I offered, guessing Asher might need a breather.

Kasia took me through some instructions, then I got to throw myself off the ledge, whooping as I flew through the air. I gripped the trapeze bar tightly, adrenaline making my heart race. The ground was a distant blur, and a combination of fear and exhilaration made me laugh out loud even as my heart felt like it might explode.

Reaching the apex of my swing, I flung my body up, lifting my legs for extra height, then swinging backward.

Kasia grabbed me when I reached the platform and pulled me back onto the ledge.

I let out a whoop. "That was so much fun!"

"Now it's your turn." Kasia handed the trapeze to Asher.

I wanted to tell him again that he didn't have to, but the determination etched into his face made the words die in my throat. His eyes were gray flint, hard and resolute. The force of his iron will took my breath away. His strength had been forged by all he'd been through.

If I'd had to jump from a high window as a teenager, there was no way I'd be up here. When Asher stepped off the ledge I could only watch in awe. I couldn't breathe as I watched him swing away, then back again. Only when he'd landed back onto the platform with more grace than I had, did I let out a cheer.

"You did it!"

I threw my arms around him, hugging him so tightly I was probably crushing him. My chest felt light enough to fly without the trapeze. Maybe it was crazy to feel proud, but his achievement made me even happier than my own.

"It wasn't so bad," he said against my hair, his voice amused.

"Was it almost fun?"

He chuckled. "I wouldn't go that far."

"Want to try it again?"

"Your turn first."

As we swung again and again, learning how to hook our knees over the bar and swing upside down, Asher visibly relaxed. When he finally smiled, I grinned back. I felt like my heart was soaring along with me, and I wished the lesson would last forever.

Finally, Kasia had us both swing upside down from platforms at either end of the big net, our knees over the bar and our arms stretched down.

"The next step isn't easy," she said to Asher when he swung back to our platform. "You'll meet in the middle and catch hands. We're almost out of time, so you'll only have time for one try. And if you fall, you'll just bounce in the net like I showed you, then make your way to the ground."

"Has it been two hours already?" I asked in disbelief. "It doesn't seem that long."

"Are you willing to try the catch?" Kasia's eyes darted between us.

"Yes!" I bit my lip, trying to contain my enthusiasm as I turned to Asher. "I mean, if you're up for it?"

He nodded. "Let's do this."

"Before we do, I just want to say this has been the best two hours I've ever spent. Thank you." I lowered my voice, suddenly remembering another great time I'd had with him. "I mean, apart from when we fooled around. But this is a close second."

He let out that rich, deep laugh of his that made me feel warm and tingly all over. Then he leaned in to murmur, "Let's try not to finish our lesson with screams, okay?"

My grin was so wide it hurt my face. "It's a deal."

"Ready?" asked Kasia. "You need to link hands very tightly." She looked at me. "You have to trust him so you can take a deep breath and release your legs from the bar."

"Do you trust me?" asked Asher.

"With my life. Only do me a favor and don't take that literally, okay?"

He nodded seriously. "I won't let you go."

We got into position, and together we launched ourselves from our platforms like a couple of seasoned trapeze artists. We both hooked our knees over our bars, stretching our hands out, searching for each other.

Then I spotted him hurtling toward me and grabbed for him. I wrapped my hands around his wrists and felt his strong fingers circle mine. Extending my legs, I let the bar slip out from under my knees.

I soared breathlessly through the air with nothing holding me up but Asher.

His gray eyes were determined and his hands were sure, his grip reassuringly tight. I was flying, both completely free and totally safe. Asher would never drop me.

I grinned up at him, and when an answering smile lit his face, I felt a warmth and certainty unlike anything I'd ever experienced. If only this perfect moment could last forever.

Which is when a thought flashed through my mind that was far scarier than the threat of falling.

Could this be what it felt like to fall in love?

# Chapter Nineteen

## Asher

One good thing about facing my fear of falling was the rush of adrenaline and endorphins produced by my brain, which left me feeling exhilarated throughout the journey home.

Considering I'd decided to divulge my secrets, my heart shouldn't be so light. But stealing glances at Iola as I drove, I was absorbed by her smile and sparkling eyes, the way she sat with one knee pulled up, how she swayed in time with the song playing on the radio, and the grace of her fingers as she used her hands to punctuate her speech. I laughed when she joked that a trapeze date would be the most unsubtle way possible to dump an unwanted girlfriend, and agreed when she said our first lesson had gone so well, Kasia must have been tempted to offer us a part in their show.

Her excitement and enthusiasm were so contagious,

even if I hadn't been riding an adrenaline high, she would have made me feel that way. I was just thinking how strange it was to feel so good before I had to do something that could bring it all crashing down, when Iola glanced over at me with a warm, satisfied look.

"Hey," she said. "I love seeing you look so happy."

The observation should have made me uncomfortable. I was revealing more of myself to Iola than I ever let anyone but my brothers see. And even with Kade and Mason, I held back when I needed to. Living with Mom's irrational moods had given me a caution that had served me well, and given me the skills that had made me strong. But I found myself smiling at Iola. Even if I wanted to hide my real feelings from her, I wasn't sure I'd be able to. She seemed to be able to read me easily; a skill she must have developed from all she'd been through.

It took a special type of person to have survived such a dark past and come out not just strong, but kind, caring, and insightful. She'd been betrayed and abused by the men who should have cherished her, and the fact she was brave enough to still be vulnerable put my own defenses to shame.

"You make me happy," I said simply. And the sheer beauty of her smile gave me a rush of endorphins even stronger than a safe landing after the most dizzying flight at the top of the circus tent.

The drive home with her felt too short and even after we arrived at Iola's house, the sea air seemed crisper than it had before, the ocean bluer, and the waves more impressive. Most of those perceptions were illusionary, but I couldn't deny what I knew was real. Iola had flung herself from a high bar with an almost-transparent net below her, trusting me to catch her. The fact she was willing to trust me that much filled me with awe.

But now Benedict had gone, I couldn't keep the truth from her. She needed to know her father had supplied the drugs that had killed my mother. Now she understood why I'd done it, maybe she'd be able to forgive me for arranging his arrest. And I couldn't afford to think about how bad I'd feel if she couldn't forgive me and walked away forever. I'd already put this off long enough. It was time to come clean.

Leaving my car in my driveway, I walked with her to her front door.

"I need to talk to you about something." I thought my voice sounded like a death knell, but it can't have come out that way because Iola's smile was unsuspecting.

"Sure. Let me just tell Gloria we're here. She probably wants to take off."

She opened her front door and called inside. A moment later, Gloria appeared, carrying a novel.

"There you are." Gloria smiled, looking from Iola's face to mine. "I don't even need to ask if you had a good time. I can see you did."

"It was the best. Thanks for looking after Ruff for me. After all she's been through, I was worried about leaving her alone, even for a couple of hours." Iola peered around Gloria. "Where is she?"

"She was in the living room with me, keeping me company while I read. Now she's probably asleep."

Gloria went back down the hallway with Iola at her heels. I followed the two women inside, coming to a halt behind them as they stopped in the entrance to the living room.

Ruff was hunched down while Nemesis lay on her back in front of the dog, all four limbs stretched out and her eyes closed. Her mouth was slightly open, as though she was too blissed out to bother closing it. Ruff was licking my black cat all over, so intent on what she was doing, she didn't even glance up.

"Ruff!" Iola sounded so shocked, her dog's huge head jerked up. Ruff stared at her with guilty eyes, her monstrous jowls wobbling.

Nemesis lifted her head too, taking us in with annoyed yellow eyes. Slowly she got to her feet, stretched, then stalked past us, heading down the hallway toward the open front door. Her tail was high and I had the impression of a swagger in her walk. She disappeared outside without looking back.

Gloria laughed. "I should go too." She gave Iola a hug and me a wave before heading toward the door.

"Thank you for looking after Ruff."

"Anytime. She's a sweetheart."

Their voices grew muffled as Iola walked Gloria outside, but I heard a peal of laughter and Iola calling goodbye. The two women sounded like they'd become close. Then I heard Iola's phone go, and she spoke to someone for a while. Her voice rose with excitement, but I couldn't make out what she was saying. Ruff had slunk off to her bed by the couch. Though the dog already seemed to have fallen asleep, I was pretty sure she was pretending.

The front door closed and Iola came back into the living room. She was beaming, her eyes alight with excitement. "I got some great news! My lawyer called from London to tell me that Benedict signed the divorce papers."

Relief rushed through me. That meant Iola's ex really had been neutralized and she shouldn't be in any more danger from him. "Congratulations," I said with feeling.

"Benedict also had to sign off on my settlement, which means I'll have enough money for a house." Her face was glowing. "If Dad gets convicted and his house is sold, I'm going to buy it. I'll get to live here permanently!"

My chest tightened. I fought to keep my dismay off my face. Fortunately, Iola had turned toward the windows, so if my expression betrayed my shock, she didn't see it.

"I love it here, Asher. I love San Dante, I love the people I've met, and Dad's home is perfect. If I stay here, I'll be close enough to be able to keep visiting Dad in prison. I know he's made mistakes, but I'm still his daughter and after all these years, maybe we'll finally get to have some kind of relationship." She spun back to face me, her face shining with hope. "I had to grow up without a father, but maybe it's not too late. Anyway, isn't it worth trying?"

I dragged in a shallow breath filled with razor blades and braced myself for the damage I had to inflict.

"Iola, I need to tell you something." Swallowing, I

wrapped my fingers around a metaphorical band-aid, bracing myself to rip it off. "I've been planning to buy this house. I'm going to bid for it at the auction."

Her lips parted and her hopeful expression turned into confusion. "But you don't need the house. Your place is right next door. Why would you buy two houses?"

"Because it means I can join the two sites together. With a larger land area, I can build a taller building."

"You can build…?" She blinked rapidly. "Wait. Does that mean you want to tear the house down?"

I nodded, feeling even worse than I'd expected to. Of all the people in the world I'd never wanted to hurt, Iola was top of the list.

"I don't get it. If you want to build apartments, aren't there other places you can buy?"

"It needs to be here."

"Why does it?" Her eyes had clouded, and the bewilderment in them buried itself deep inside me and clenched a cruel fist around my heart. All I wanted was to pull her into my arms and tell her I'd changed my mind, that she should have the house for herself.

But as difficult as this was, my company was riding on this building project, and the jobs of all my employees. There was too much at stake to stop now.

"I didn't tell you before because I wasn't sure how you'd react," I said. "I had to make sure Benedict was taken care of before I complicated things."

Her frown deepened and she turned back to the windows. I could see she was thinking that through.

I'd promised myself I'd also tell her I'd gotten Santino

arrested, but first she needed a little time. If I could soften the information, give it to her one digestible chunk at a time, maybe she wouldn't hate me.

Or maybe I was just being a coward.

There was a sharp knock at the front door. Ruff lifted his head and barked, but didn't get up.

Iola's expression turned uncertain, and she pressed her hand to her chest as though trying to slow it down. "I'm not expecting anyone. And even though I know it can't be Benedict, it's probably going to take me a while to not feel nervous about opening the door to a stranger."

"I'll see who it is." Striding to the door, I flung it open.

The man looming on the step was huge, with wide shoulders and a face that bore a strong resemblance to mine.

"Mason!" I exclaimed. "What are you doing here?"

"Carlotta had to go to the theater to run a rehearsal. I'm picking her up afterward and seeing as I had a little time to kill, I thought I'd surprise you." My brother narrowed his eyes. "Only I was the one who was surprised. What are you doing in Santino's house, Asher? It's the last place I'd expect to see you."

"Iola moved into this house a few weeks ago." I looked back at her, and she came down the hall toward us and stopped in the doorway. "Iola, this is my brother, Mason," I said.

From the front step, my brother offered his hand to Iola. "Pleasure to meet you."

I imagined how he must look to her. Bigger than most men, with nasty scars on his neck and arm. Shaking his hand would be like having hers wrapped in a warm meat slab. If we'd been alone, I would have reassured her he wasn't dangerous, at least not for anyone who stayed on the right side of the law. Mason had an overdeveloped sense of right and wrong, despite the fact he'd had to steal food and money when we were in Mexico. Or, more accurately, *because* of what he'd been forced to do.

"Hello, Mason." She let his hand swallow hers. By the way she blinked up at him, I could tell she was a little intimated by his size. I didn't blame her. Most people were.

"How did you know I was here?" I asked my brother.

"You didn't answer my knock at your place." He glanced next door. "I assumed you'd gone out, but I let myself in anyway, thinking I'd grab a drink in your kitchen and give you a call. Imagine my surprise when I spotted you through the window." Mason lifted his eyebrows. "I expected this house to be empty, but I guess it's been a while since that scumbag Santino was arrested. Do you know about this house's dirty history, Iola? If you're renting it through an agency they probably haven't told you who the owner is?"

Iola flinched, and I tried not to grimace. Mason meant well, but he had no idea he'd just barged into a minefield.

"Iola is Santino's daughter," I said.

Shock flashed over Mason's face, and it took him a moment to be able to swallow.

The warmth had gone out of Iola's eyes, and she drew her back up as though bracing herself against his judgement. "You clearly know my father's in jail," she said in a cool tone. "I was just telling Asher that I'd like to stay living here, in his house, so I'm planning to buy it."

I gave an inward sigh. If I could make her happy by giving her anything else in the world, I'd find a way to do it. But if buying the house was the one thing she wanted, it was also the one thing I couldn't afford to let her have.

Sometimes life really sucked.

"Hey, I'm sorry I said the wrong thing," Mason said. "I didn't mean to insult you." When he glanced at me, naked curiosity burned in his eyes.

"That's okay," said Iola, her posture still stiff. She gave us both a smile that didn't reach her eyes. "But I hope you don't mind if I excuse myself. It's been a long day and I need to feed my dog."

She clearly wanted some time to herself, but I hesitated, hating to leave Iola with so much between us still unresolved.

"It was nice to meet you, Mason," she said.

"You, too." Mason gave her a nod.

"I'll see you later, Asher." Her voice had turned crisp. Before I could protest, she stepped back and shut the door, leaving my brother and I on the front step.

Mason tapped my upper arm with his meaty hand. "Hey, what's going on?"

"Come next door." I led the way to my house, trying to shake my urge to barge back into Iola's and demand we talk things through. Although I'd explained why my brothers and I had good reason to hate drug dealers and everyone associated with them, I hadn't directly accused her father, and she clearly hadn't made the connection on her own. Her reaction to Mason calling her father a scumbag was proof that the groundwork I'd laid was nowhere near enough, and she wasn't much closer to seeing things my way than before I'd started telling her about my past.

We were barely in the door of my house before Mason said, "You're not dating Santino's daughter, are you? Does she know I was on the team that arrested her father? Does she know Carlotta was conned into *working* for that piece of shit?"

I dragged in a deep breath and let it out again in a sigh. "I'm going to tell Iola everything. In the meantime, don't tell Carlotta about Iola's connection to Santino, okay?"

Frowning, he clenched his jaw. "Asher, what are you—?"

"Iola knows we watched her father get arrested. I'm working up to telling her the rest, but she doesn't know what her father's really like. She didn't have much contact with him growing up, and she wants to believe the best of him. It's going to hurt when she realizes the truth."

The irony was that Mason didn't know all my secrets either. I hadn't told him that to buy the house next to Santino, I'd had to put my business on the line. He wouldn't understand the risk I'd taken. My brother was far too honorable, and his strong views on right and wrong weren't flexible.

I'd been so hungry to take down Santino and Frankie,

I'd been willing to gamble with my employee's livelihoods. He'd find it hard to accept what I'd done.

"You'd better tell Iola the truth about her father and what we did to him before she finds out from someone else," Mason growled.

I nodded wordlessly. He was right. But there *must* be a way I could soften the blow.

Mason let out a slow breath, his expression softening. Though I used to be good at hiding what I felt, his expression suggested he could see the desperation that had to be showing on my face.

"I'm sorry I called her father a scumbag." He sounded contrite.

"Her father *is* a scumbag. It's only that she hasn't had enough contact with him to be able to see that for herself. She's been wishing for a family most of her life, so she's desperate to be able to forgive him."

"I guess that's understandable," he said gruffly. "Family is family. I'd forgive you and Kade just about anything." He snapped his fingers. "Which reminds me, Kade and Natalie are coming to San Dante for a couple of days so Natalie can see her father. They'll get here tomorrow."

I stared at him a moment, shocked that I'd forgotten about Kade's imminent arrival. I'd been so wrapped up in plotting Benedict's downfall and spending time with Iola, I'd neglected everything else. Not just my family, but my business too. But Kade couldn't be arriving at a better time. This could be the answer I'd been looking for.

"We should have a family dinner at Dad's place," I

said. "I'll convince Iola to come, and she can get to know you all better." Maybe if she could see for herself how important my brothers were to me, she'd get why I'd done everything I could to get justice for what they'd suffered.

Mason gave me a sideways look. "You think that'll help?"

"It has to," I said grimly. "It's the only chance I've got."

# Chapter Twenty

## Iola

My prison visitation had finally been approved. I was going to get to see Dad again, and I couldn't wait.

The only reason I wasn't happier was the fight I'd had with Asher. Well, it hadn't been a fight, exactly, but it had been a shock when his brother had insulted my father. And I was upset Asher hadn't talked with me earlier about wanting to buy my father's house. He was used to playing things close to his chest and I understood he found it hard to open up, but it had still hurt.

At least working on a painting was a distraction from my thoughts. I was focusing on finishing the latest one off when there was a knock on my door. A moment later, I heard Asher call out.

"Iola? It's me."

Setting my palette down, I wiped my hands on a rag

and tried to get my emotions under control. After yesterday, should I really be so happy to hear his voice? The answer was no, but try telling my feet that. They were practically skipping their way to the door.

When I opened the door, Asher didn't exactly smile, but his eyes brightened and the tension left his expression. It was an Asher-style smile, and I could tell he was glad to see me.

My heart lifted without my permission. Even after he'd upset me, there was little I could do about feeling like my world was brighter with him in it.

"Hi," he said. "I'm sorry about yesterday."

I folded my arms, not ready to let him off the hook. "You should have told me you wanted to buy Dad's house."

"You're right. I should have."

"Are you still planning to bid for it if it goes to auction?"

He nodded. "I've been planning to buy it for a while and I'm financially committed. So yes, I'm still going ahead with the purchase. If I could let you buy it instead, I would."

"We'll just have to see who bids higher at the auction then, won't we?" I held his gaze, silently daring him to argue. If I'd been having this conversation with Benedict, he would have threatened me with petty acts of revenge by now. His favorites had seemed ridiculous at first, but over the years they'd worn me down. He'd tell his chef to serve me nothing but boiled cabbage, have all my clothes sent out for 'cleaning', or throw away my art supplies. And with him in control of our bank accounts, I hadn't been able to spend any money without his approval.

"You're determined to bid against me?" Asher's expression changed in the subtle way that told me he wasn't happy about the idea, but the tone of his voice stayed matter-of-fact, with no hint of anger.

"I am."

He nodded slowly, as though accepting my decision. "I won't enjoy outbidding you, but I'll still have to do it. I need the house."

I lifted my chin. "Then we'll have to see who wins on the day."

"That's fair." He gave another short nod as though the matter was settled. "Anyway, I'm having dinner with my family tonight, and I'd like you to come. Will you?"

I blinked, surprised he'd accepted my decision so easily. "Um," I said. "Dinner? I don't think..." I trailed off, unsure what to say.

"Please come."

"Why?"

"Because I enjoy spending time with you, and I'd like you to get to know my family."

I shouldn't have been surprised by the directness of his answer, but he still took my breath away. Even after admitting I was going to try to outbid him, he wasn't upset.

Squaring my shoulders, I tried to put our disagreement behind us as quickly as Asher seemed to have done.

"I'm not sure it's a good idea to crash your family dinner at the last minute," I said.

"You're not crashing, I'm inviting you."

"But I'm nervous of your family. What if they don't like me? What if I can't stop telling jokes?"

"They'll love you, Iola. How could they not? And if you tell jokes, they're sure to enjoy them as much as I do." He gave me one of his Pied Piper smiles, the one I was completely powerless to resist. "Okay if I pick you up at six thirty?"

"Okay," I found myself saying.

"Good. I'll see you tonight."

I watched Asher walk away before closing the door. I felt strangely befuddled.

Asher had made it seem like it was okay for us not to agree, and that it wouldn't change things between us. Bidding against each other at the auction would still be difficult, but Asher was so level-headed, I had a feeling we'd get through it. When I outbid him and bought the house, I was pretty sure he wouldn't hold a grudge.

Still, after hearing his brother's opinion of Dad, I'd held back the news I was going to visit my father tomorrow. It was probably better not to tell Asher anyway, until I'd had a chance to see Dad after so many years of being apart. Maybe tomorrow I'd find out for sure that he'd never be the real father I'd always longed for. Perhaps my visit would confirm that trying to forge a connection was wishful thinking. Or perhaps I'd discover a man who was finally ready to accept responsibility for his actions and be the person I needed him to be.

Either way, after seeing Dad tomorrow, I'd know whether Asher was right about him or not.

If one of us didn't change our opinion about Dad, Asher and I would probably keep arguing about it, which wouldn't be good for our relationship. If that was even the right word to describe what was happening between us.

Which brought up another sticking point. Did I even want to be in a relationship? How could I, when I was still dancing on the corpse of my marriage?

Whatever my feelings for Asher, he'd been right when he said we should take things cautiously. I had to hold myself back from leaping into something I might not be ready for.

Only I couldn't stop thinking about Asher's expression of pure determination as he leapt off the trapeze platform, and how his courage had made me brave. He made me feel like I could do anything, and that feeling was so addictive, I didn't want it to stop.

I spent way too much of the day deciding what to wear to dinner, wishing I'd asked Asher if the rest of his family would be dressed formally or casually. Finally I hedged my bets, and met him out front in a fitted red dress that Benedict had only ever let me wear with a jacket buttoned over it, with my hair carefully styled, and matching red lipstick for luck.

When Asher saw me, he went completely still. His gaze raked down my body, then returned to my face. His eyes glinted, and when he slowly licked his lower lip as though he were deciding whether to eat me now or later, I decided he approved of how I looked.

Still, I asked, "Is this okay?" because I'd spent so long dithering over different outfits, I wanted to be sure I'd made the right choice.

"You're stunning." His voice was low and grumbly. When he stepped forward to tuck a curl behind my ear, he looked possessive. His expression made a warm, tingly feeling grow low in my stomach, and I couldn't help smiling at him.

He dropped his face to the side of my head and murmured, "You smell as good as you look."

I thought he was going to kiss me, but at the last minute he drew back and just grabbed my hand for the walk to the car. He probably didn't want to smudge my red lipstick, I told myself, but I still had to swallow a few times because my disappointment made my throat feel thick.

With any other guy, I'd suspect he was holding a grudge because I wanted to bid against him to buy Dad's house. But if that was what had upset Asher, I was pretty sure he'd be direct with me. No, something else had to be wrong. But as much as I simultaneously dreaded and needed to know what it was, I didn't want to think about it on the way to see his family. I was nervous enough already.

His father's house was only a few streets away, and last time I was there, seagulls had been doing their best horror movie impression. Now it was quiet. As Asher escorted me to the door and rung the bell, my stomach was churning. What if I made a fool of myself?

Asher took my hand and squeezed it. "Don't be nervous."

I licked my dry lips. "Never go to war against an octopus. It's too well armed."

"They'll love you. I promise."

I caught a whiff of a scent that made my mouth water. Someone was cooking something that smelled delicious.

"Two snowmen next to each other," I muttered. "One turns to the other and asks, do you smell carrots?"

The door opened.

The man I'd met yesterday filled the doorway. Asher's older brother Mason. He towered over me, and his shoulders were wide enough for two men. He had scars on his neck and arm, like he'd been carved up with a knife.

"Hey," he said. "Nice to see you again, Iola."

"You too." I swallowed nervously as he stepped forward and offered his hand. "It's a big pleasure." I had to let go of Asher's hand to take Mason's. "Really, a giant-sized pleasure," I added as his huge hand enveloped mine. "I hope I haven't muscled my way in here. The only part of me that's ever worked out is my push-up bra, but I guess you hit the gym pretty regularly, huh Mason?"

Asher's brother gave me a bemused smile. He was looking at me like I was odd, but at least it didn't seem like he was sizing me up for a straitjacket. At least, not yet.

"Mason's harmless," muttered Asher in my ear. "Big, but friendly."

"Hi there," called a woman from behind Mason. He took up so much of the hallway, I could barely see more than a glimpse of blonde hair and a wide smile. "Mason honey, why don't you make us some drinks?"

Mason retreated down the hallway, letting Asher and I come in, while the woman squeezed past him. She was so pretty, I was glad I'd worn a nice dress and taken some extra time with my makeup.

"I'm Carlotta." Instead of shaking my hand, the woman hugged me. "It's lovely to meet you, Iola."

"You remember seeing Dad's neighbor, Trixie?" Asher asked. "Carlotta's her daughter."

I frowned, thinking of the small woman with the wild gray hair. "Trixie with the water gun?"

"You've met my mother?" Carlotta raised her eyebrows, looking from me to Asher.

"Not exactly," said Asher. "We watched from the car while she fought with Dad."

Carlotta groaned. "When is their war going to end?"

"Iola!" Another gorgeous man crowded into the hallway, this one grabbing me in a hug. "There you are! I've missed you!"

I squeaked as he squeezed me, overwhelmed at being hugged by the handsome celebrity I'd only met briefly on the beach when he'd set me up with his brother. "Hi Kade."

"That's enough, Kade." Asher's tone changed. "Put Iola down," he ordered. "Stop manhandling her. That's something you should never do without permission."

"Relax, bro." Kade let me go with a wink. "Iola and I are old friends. I met her first, remember?" It was obvious he was baiting his brother, but his smile seemed to be inviting me in on the prank and with his dimples on full display, it was impossible not to be charmed by him.

"Kade, stop it." Asher's voice was a growl, but I knew him well enough now to recognize there was no anger in it. I couldn't believe the twins would ever get seriously angry with each other.

Still, when Asher put his arm around my shoulders, claiming me as his while making shooing motions at his brother, I couldn't help but laugh. He was more relaxed and animated around his brothers than I'd ever seen him. Hopefully during the course of the evening, I'd be treated to at least one of his devastating smiles.

"Iola, I want you to meet Natalie," said Kade. "Nat? Where are you?"

Another woman shouldered her way into the crowded hallway, shaking her head with disapproval. She had long brown hair tied back in a messy ponytail and was wearing glasses. "Do we have to make all the introductions in such a crowded space?" she complained, slapping Kade's arm with such an affectionate look, she had to be his girlfriend. "Let the poor woman come in and sit down." Eyes twinkling, she turned to me and stuck out her hand. "Hallway or not, it's a pleasure to meet you, Iola. I'm Natalie."

I shook her hand, a little overwhelmed by the enthusiastic welcome from Asher's family. But they all seemed so nice. If I'd been lucky enough to have brothers and sisters, this was what I would have wanted them to be like.

"Where's Mason gone?" Kade started down the hallway away from us. "He'd better not have snuck back into the kitchen to eat the ingredients for our dessert."

"Uh-oh. I sense trouble." Natalie rolled her eyes at me with a smile before dashing after Kade.

"Come and meet Dad." Asher led me to where the man with enormous hairy eyebrows I'd last seen with a water gun was sitting at a dining table. It was a combined living and dining room, with couches and a large bookcase full of books. The only thing separating the dining table from the kitchen was a wide counter. In the small kitchen, Kade and Mason jostled each other as they argued playfully. Carlotta and Natalie were with them, laughing together over their antics.

"Dad, this is Iola," said Asher. "Iola, my father, Edward."

Asher's father stood up. "Welcome." He raised his giant eyebrows. "Would you mind stepping out onto the back porch with me, please?"

"Um. Ex-squeeze me?" I swallowed, looking around nervously. The four people in the kitchen were too busy bickering over some chocolate that had mysteriously vanished to have heard Edward's strange request.

Asher frowned. "What are you up to, Dad?"

"Don't worry, son. I just want to have a quick word with her alone." His father took my arm. "Come on, Iola. We'll be back before you know it."

"Um." I let Asher's father lead me out the back door onto a small porch. The skin around Asher's eyes had tightened, but the fact he didn't try to stop us was vaguely comforting. Though my anxiety level was ratcheting up and a million bad jokes were fighting to get out, I managed to clamp my lips shut.

As soon as the door closed behind us, Asher's father asked, "May I borrow your cellphone?"

"Um," I said again. There were so many jokes bubbling up, they were tangled in my throat. Wordlessly, I pulled my phone out of my bag and handed it over.

He dialed a number. Faintly, I heard a woman answer.

"Mrs. Watson?" Asher's father asked. "This is your proctologist. After scanning your rectum, we found where you left your head."

"You think that's funny, you speckle-brained dinosaur?" The woman on the other end of the phone was yelling loud enough that I could hear every word. "My ancestors on the *Mayflower* were bored with that joke. Rotten fish stink less than that joke. You're so unoriginal you should—"

Edward hooted with laughter, disconnecting while she was mid-rant. "Trixie has caller id and won't answer if it's a number she recognizes. Can you imagine how mad she is that I tricked her into picking up the call?" His grin was triumphant. "Hopefully she'll come outside so I can see her face."

Sure enough, Trixie flew out of the house next door.

The small gray-haired woman hung over the rail of her back porch, shaking her fist at Asher's father. "You wooly-headed mammoth herder!"

"Quit your bellyaching. I outsmarted you fair and square!" Edward all but deafened me with his bellow.

"You couldn't outsmart a crayon!"

Asher opened the door. "Hello Mrs. Watson," he called.

"Hmmph!"

"Come inside now, Dad." Asher's voice was perfectly calm, his expression placid. It was almost impossible to detect his exasperated amusement, except for one softly quivering muscle near the corner of his mouth. He held the door open for his father, and I followed Edward inside.

Carlotta and Mason had taken seats at the dining table. Kade was at the stove stirring a large saucepan. Natalie was next to him, carefully chopping vegetables with such concentration, it seemed like something she wasn't used to doing.

"Don't look at me like that," Edward said to Asher, sitting back down at the table. "I had to do it. I owed Trixie one after she used my name to report a Bigfoot sighting. Did you know there's a Bigfoot Society that keeps an official register of sightings? Now my name's on their list!"

"Maybe Bigfoot really is running around San Dante," said Kade.

Natalie wrinkled her nose. "Actually, I'm pretty sure

I once served him in the diner. The guy was the splitting image."

"Wouldn't it'd be funny if we all corroborated the sighting?" Carlotta's eyes lit up. "San Dante could become the Bigfoot capital of America. Like Roswell, only all the shops will be stocked with big, hairy feet souvenirs instead of plastic aliens." She grabbed Mason's arm, her voice rising with excitement. "It'd be hilarious. We have to do this!"

"Cute." Mason patted her hand. "But I have two brothers, remember? I've seen more than my fair share of oversized, hairy feet."

"Bigfoot doesn't have the same appeal as Roswell," Natalie said. "I like the idea of little green men crash-landing in the desert. Probably some teenaged aliens who snuck off with their dad's saucer."

"What happened at Roswell was real," Asher's dad announced. He sat back, his arms folded, clearly waiting for someone to disagree.

"It's just a conspiracy theory," Asher muttered in a resigned tone, as though they'd had this conversation before.

Carlotta directed her smile at me. "Everyone should be free to believe whatever they want. Don't you think, Iola?"

I could tell she was just trying to make sure I felt included, but being singled out made me sweat even more. As nice as they all were, they were all obviously very close, and I felt overwhelmed to be the only outsider.

"Three conspiracy theorists walked into a bar," I blurted. "You think that was a coincidence? No way!"

Asher chuckled, getting the joke right away. The others stared blankly at me. Kade had been stirring a saucepan of the delicious-smelling food, but his hand was frozen as he craned his neck to look at me. Natalie paused her chopping and pushed her glasses up her nose with the back of the hand that held the knife, her blue eyes wide.

They all had to think I was a freak. Even worse, Asher's father might think I was making fun of him. Oh lord, why had I made such a stupid joke?

Then Kade let out a laugh, Mason guffawed, Natalie chuckled, and Carlotta's eyes danced with mirth. Even Asher's father smiled.

"Iola, you're hilarious." Kade went back to stirring his pan.

"I love funny people," agreed Natalie. "Asher, get her a drink, for heaven's sake."

"Do you like curry, Iola?" Kade asked, sprinkling salt into the saucepan.

"I've had naan for a long time, but I'll happily tikka chance on it. I'd like to spice up my life."

Asher moved next to me, smile lines crinkling the corners of his eyes. But the others exchanged glances, and I groaned inwardly, wishing I wasn't so nervous. So far, the only things out of my mouth had been stupid puns, and Asher's family had to think I was a total weirdo. What the hell was wrong with me? They were all so kind, and I was making the worst impression possible.

Asher lightly bumped his arm against my shoulder. "I

ordered pelican curry once," he said. "It wasn't bad, but the bill was enormous."

"I must have gone to the same restaurant," said Carlotta without missing a beat. "I ordered the clownfish curry, but it tasted funny."

"I went there too," added Kade. "I had the pickle curry, and it was so good, I relished every bite."

Natalie held up one of the beans from her chopping board. "Um, isn't that restaurant a has-*bean*?" Her cheeks flushed and she gave a little laugh that was more of a groan. "Sorry, that was all I could think of."

"Is that restaurant on the moon?" asked Mason, his deep voice rumbling from his enormous chest. "Great place, but it had no atmosphere."

"What are you all talking about?" Edward frowned around at us. "Fish? Pickles? Beans? I don't want to eat any of those things."

Kade guffawed first, then a smile spread over my face, and Carlotta's laugh filled the room. I was so grateful, I could have kissed them all.

Kade sprinkled more spice into the pan. "Don't worry, Dad. I promise tonight's curry will be delicious."

"I don't know if I like curry," grumbled Edward. "What about steak, Kade? Or ribs. I like when you make ribs."

Asher put his arm around my shoulders and squeezed, giving me enough of his gorgeous smile to warm me inside and out. "Not nervous anymore?" he whispered in my ear.

"I love your family," I murmured back.

"Somebody's got to." Dropping his arm, he raised his voice to a regular level. "Dad, you can't just eat meat all the time."

His father scowled. "Don't tell me you're mixing in vegetables, Kade. I don't like them, remember?"

"I know, Dad. I won't feed you anything green." Kade shared a conspiratorial look with Natalie, then glanced at me and winked. On Natalie's chopping board, I could see beans, mushroom stems, carrot peel, and broccoli ends, but from Edward's seat at the table he clearly couldn't see over the big pots on the stove.

Asher poured me a glass of wine. "You'll have to excuse a little oddness from my strange family," he said. "But at least the food will be good."

It was the first time in my life anyone had ever apologized to *me* for weirdness instead of the other way around. A new experience. One that made me want to hug him.

"Dinner smells great," said Carlotta. "I'm starving." She bumped her shoulder against Mason's arm, and the enormous, slightly scary, scarred man gave her such a sweet smile, I had to look away. Their feelings for each other were so open, letting my gaze linger felt like an invasion of their privacy.

"Do you always cook on your day off?" I asked Kade, relieved I'd relaxed enough to ask a normal question.

"You think I'd let Asher or Mason make dinner?" He snorted, shaking his head. "You can thank your lucky stars I didn't."

"Asher's a good cook," I protested. "He made me

scrambled eggs the other morning, and they were the fluffiest eggs I've ever eaten."

"Did he?" Kade raised his eyebrows. "My brother cooked you breakfast?"

I blushed, realizing how that had sounded.

"Kade, stop it." Asher frowned at his twin. "You'll make Iola uncomfortable."

"But I like it when she's nervous. She knows some great jokes."

"So does Carlotta." Mason smiled at the woman by his side like she'd cured cancer. "She took the funniest photo for her Instagram the other day."

He launched into a description of what she'd done, and I gazed at Asher, taking the chance to admire his profile while he was focused on his brother. I loved the way they teased each other, with their love shining so brightly.

Asher was ridiculously lucky to have a family like his. No wonder he was so loyal. What wouldn't I give to have one person who loved me that much, let alone three?

My heart ached, because this was everything I'd always wanted. But this closeness didn't just happen by itself. They all valued each other for good reason. Whatever trials they'd been through, it had forged their bonds and made them genuinely good people. I couldn't remember having been anywhere I'd felt more welcome.

Asher must have felt me staring at him, because he turned to meet my gaze. His eyes crinkled, as warm as I'd ever seen them. He was so handsome, my heart decided to take a vacation from beating. But it wasn't his good looks that made me feel like I was glowing when he looked at me with such warmth.

I knew him now. I knew how clever he was, how kind and thoughtful. How tender and loyal, and surprising.

And there was one more thing I knew without a doubt.

I was falling in love with him.

# Chapter Twenty-One

## Asher

My family loved Iola. Well, of course they did. What wasn't to love?

More importantly, she liked them.

I'd taken a calculated risk by inviting her to dinner, betting that with my brothers aware of Iola's family connection, the conversation was unlikely to turn to Santino, and I was prepared to change the subject if it did. Now, as I watched her get over her nerves and start to relax, I was glad I'd taken the chance. I loved how she joked with everyone, and laughed at my brothers' good-natured wisecracks. I loved how she praised Kade's cooking, and how she'd read some of the books Dad had in his bookcase, and asked him for recommendations on others she might like. And how by the end of the night, she'd made plans with Carlotta and Natalie to visit an art gallery and have cocktails afterward.

And she was so stunning, I could barely drag my eyes away from her.

Her dress highlighted her spectacular figure. It was cut low enough to give more than a tantalizing glimpse of cleavage, and high enough that I could get an exact count of the number of freckles on her long legs.

Every time she smiled, I felt an ache in my chest, which meant it ached all evening. And the urge to touch her was so strong, resisting it brought me actual pain. My hands were clenched so tightly, they'd become sore. My spine was stiff, and my teeth practically ground to stubs.

By the time I drove her home, the awful truth had become terribly clear.

I was in love with her.

And nothing about my feelings was moderate, or measured, or controlled.

Now I understood why Mason had sacrificed his own safety for Carlotta, why Kade had been willing to give his heart back to Natalie after she'd already broken it when they were young, and why my father and Trixie seemed to spend every waking hour obsessed with each other.

I hadn't fallen for Iola softly, with restraint, or with caution. I was all too aware she could change her mind about me. She could easily crush my heart and inflict the kind of pain I hadn't felt since the day Mom had been in the grips of one of her drug-fueled rampages, and had screamed at me that she wished I'd never been born.

My feelings defied logic. How could I have let myself feel this way when I was about to confess the full truth of everything I'd done and drive Iola away?

Thinking about it, I was too quiet. As I walked her to her front door, she could tell all wasn't well. Her smile had turned into a puzzled frown, and instead of putting her key in the lock, she stopped and turned to me.

"What's wrong?" she asked.

I dragged in a breath, feeling moisture collecting on my palms and dreading her reaction. "I have to tell you something."

"Asher, are you okay?" It was just like her to be concerned for me rather than herself. Her heart was so big that in spite of all she'd been through with Benedict, she was only thinking about why I might be unhappy, and whether she could fix it.

"We need to talk," I said, steeling myself. "Let's go inside."

Ruff was lying in her dog bed, but she struggled to her feet to greet us, and when Iola took a seat on the couch, Ruff sat as close to her as she could get. Letting out a sigh, Ruff leaned heavily against her legs. Iola stroked her head, and I was very glad she'd gotten her back from Benedict. At least Ruff would be able to provide Iola with comfort, even if I couldn't.

I took the seat opposite Iola and sat stiffly, my mouth dry. "I told you about when we went to Mexico, and Mom dated Four-Finger-Frankie, the dealer who gave her the drugs that killed her. He's a small-time drug dealer with the Medea Cartel. Or rather, he *was* a drug dealer. He's currently in jail."

Iola frowned. "I've heard of that cartel. Didn't they arrest a lot of those guys a few months ago?"

I nodded, bracing myself to deliver my news, and made my voice as gentle as I could. "Both Frankie and your father were arrested together, here in this house. Your father was in the cartel as well."

Her jaw loosened and her hand froze on Ruff's head. She stared at me with wide eyes for a moment. Then she snapped her teeth back together, clenching her jaw and shaking her head. "Dad's made plenty of mistakes, but a drug cartel is organized crime. Bad men doing evil things. Dad wasn't part of a cartel. He'd never go that far. He ran an exporting business and supplemented his income with the occasional deal, that's all."

"You haven't seen your father for years and—"

"He's still my dad. I know what he would or wouldn't do." Her voice was now flat and sure, making my heart sink. She was going to be hard to convince.

"The cartel was responsible for Mom's death and a lot of the hardship my brothers and I went through."

"Responsible for your mom's death? You're trying to tell me that my father *killed* your mother?" She swallowed hard. Her face was going pale.

"Your father was Frankie's supplier." I held her gaze, every muscle tight with the effort of not reaching out to her. "After connecting him to Frankie, I invited a surveillance team into my house to watch him. I wanted the police to take him down. My goal was for every member of the cartel to go to jail. That included Santino."

The shock in her face made my chest ache, but I couldn't soften the blow.

"*You* had my father arrested?" Her voice had gone faint.

"I did."

"Why didn't you tell me?"

"I wanted to, but I didn't know how you'd take it."

She dragged her hands down her face. "The father I knew wouldn't hurt anyone." She leaned forward to hug the dog's big chest, turning her face to me so her cheek rested on the top of Ruff's head. "He can't have changed that much since I was a kid."

"He trafficked in drugs. That hurts people."

She lifted her face from Ruff, her brow crinkling. "I'll be seeing Dad tomorrow for the first time in years. And now I find out I've been kissing the guy who had him arrested?"

Her eyes were shimmering with emotion, her irises violently dark.

I flexed my hands on my jeans. "I understand this puts you in a difficult situation."

"I don't know what to think. This is a shock."

"I know. I'm sorry."

"You should go."

I nodded reluctantly and stood up, hating to leave things tense between us. But I had to give her space and let her come to terms with what she'd learned.

She walked behind me to the door and when I opened it, she said, "You've been drip-feeding me information. You didn't tell me you wanted to buy this house. Now you've added the fact you had my father arrested."

"I thought it would be easier if you didn't hear it all at once."

"I need to know everything, Asher. No more secrets. Is there anything else you're keeping from me?" She was in the doorway, her back ramrod straight, her jaw tight. She was holding the door, ready to shut it behind me.

Thrown by her direct question, I gazed into her beautiful, dark eyes. How could I answer? I'd plotted against her father. I'd done everything I could to make sure he went to jail for the rest of his life, and that his downfall would earn a huge profit for me and my family. Should I tell her about the twenty-five million dollars I'd make from tearing down his house?

Confessing it now, on top of all the shocks she'd already absorbed would be the wrong strategic move. My best chance for understanding, if not forgiveness, would come later, when she was less upset.

I relaxed my face, making sure my muscles wouldn't twitch so I wouldn't give anything away. "Nothing else." It was the first lie I'd told her, and as soon as I spoke, I regretted it.

"All right," she said stiffly. "Good night."

Then she closed the door, and it was too late.

## Chapter Twenty-Two

### Iola

Visiting the prison was another new experience, but a lot more intimidating than going to the circus.

There was a long list of instructions, an identification check, drug dogs, and x-ray scanners. Not to mention having to wear a bra without underwire so I wouldn't set off the metal detectors.

So maybe it wasn't surprising that when one of the stony-faced guards informed me I'd only be allowed limited contact with the inmate, I joked that if I went for full contact with my own father, I'd end up in the slammer myself. Yes, I'm ashamed to admit it was an incest joke. Bad taste, but fortunately the guard's blank stare told me he hadn't got it anyway.

If only the intimidating nature of the place didn't mean it was all but impossible for me to stop there. The guard's frown deepened when I added that it was a good thing that incest jokes in a prison weren't handled like bomb jokes at an airport, or I'd need to start prepping for a cavity search. And his stare grew flinty when I joked that in a place with so many bars, it should be easier to to get a cocktail. One that wasn't a Molotov.

That's when I saw him motion to another guard and I forced my lips to shut off any more babble before my cavities really did get examined.

Walking into the visitation room, my nervousness increased, turning into a cold, sweaty fear that made my clothes stick to me and my mouth feel dry. All my life, Dad had kept me at arm's length. He'd said it was safer for me to stay away from his business. Now all his crimes were in the open, and he didn't have to push me away anymore. Before my talk with Asher, I'd hoped we could wipe the slate clean and start over. But could Dad really be part of a drug cartel? And if he was, could I forgive him?

The visitation room was full of men in jumpsuits at tables surrounded by wives, girlfriends, relatives, and children. But the flinty-eyed guard directed me to where my father sat alone at a cold, metal table.

As soon as I saw him, my throat closed and I wanted to cry. Dad looked gaunt and sallow in his prison jumpsuit. His hair was grayer and a lot thinner than when I'd last seen him, and he was clearly weary, with dark shadows under his eyes.

I stumbled toward him with my arms up, and his smile was wide as he stood up and hugged me.

"It's good to see you, mija," he said as he squeezed.

I'd been trying to hold it together. But Dad's affectionate tone was too much. I pressed my face into his shoulder and let out a splutter of tears onto the rough fabric of his jumpsuit. Dad had always worn smart suits and smelled good, but not anymore. The cologne that always made me think of him was missing, and his jumpsuit was musty.

"Hush. It's okay." He squeezed me once more, then pulled back, glancing at the guards. That's right, we were only allowed a short hug of greeting and goodbye. So many rules, and I'd already forgotten most of them.

"I hate seeing you locked up." I dragged a wadded-up tissue from the pocket of my capri pants to wipe my eyes and nose.

"I don't like it either, but it is what it is." Dad sat down, and I sank onto the seat opposite him, relieved to take the pressure off my shaky legs.

"It's really good to see you," I said. "I mean, it's not good to see you in jail. But I'm glad to know you're okay after not having seen you for such a long time." I drew in a breath, steadying myself. "You *are* okay, aren't you?"

"Better for seeing you." He gave me a smile that looked as tired as he did, running his hand absently down the front of his jumpsuit as though he were smoothing the lapel of one of his suits. It was strange to see his fingers bare, when I'd only ever seen them covered with thick gold rings.

"You moved into my house?" he asked.

I nodded. "Thank you for arranging access. It was

exactly what I needed to get away from Benedict. Being able to live rent free for a few weeks has been a big help."

"You should have told me you weren't happy." He frowned. "Why didn't you say your husband wasn't treating you right? I would have done something sooner."

"I was angry with you." Maybe it was blunt to come right out with it considering Dad was stuck in jail, but I'd been furious when he'd dropped the bombshell about Mom's death being suspicious. If Asher was right about him being part of a drug cartel, it was harder than ever not to blame him for her death. And what about Asher's mother? Exactly how much blood did Dad have on his hands?

"I thought in England you'd be safe and happy." Dad put his hand on the table and clenched it into a fist, as though to show how angry it made him. "You were going to be royal, rich, and respectable. Everything I could have wanted for you. All the things I didn't have when I was growing up, and more. Most importantly, you'd be away from everything to do with my business."

"All I ever wanted was a father."

"That was the one thing I've never known how to do." Dad leaned forward, his forearms on the table, and dropped his voice so low that I had to lean in as well. "Listen, mija, this is important. My lawyer fought hard to get you access to my house for a reason. You need to knock down the walls in the big bedroom."

"What?" I blinked at him. "Why?"

"Just do it, okay. Humor your papa. I'll probably be in

here for a while, but there's one thing I have left to give you. At least this way, I'll know you'll be okay."

I swallowed, staring down at my hands. There had to be a good reason he wanted me to rip down the walls, and my best guess was that he'd hidden something inside them. Probably something he'd stolen. "I thought you didn't want me dragged into your business?"

"If you don't do what I say and they sell the house, we'll lose everything I worked for all those years. That can't happen."

"Dad, are you part of a drug cartel?"

His eyes flicked away for a moment. "It's nothing. It doesn't mean anything. Just connections."

Even though I'd expected his answer, my heart still contracted painfully. 'Connections' were what Benedict had, what he used against me. They weren't nothing. And I'd always believed cartels were made up of bad men doing evil things—I'd said as much to Asher. Did that mean Dad was evil?

"I'm sorry, Mija." His tone was gentle. "I know I've let you down, but it's not as bad as it sounds. Not like you see on TV."

"I'm going to try to buy the house," I said tightly, trying to keep my emotions in check. "That way I'll be around for your trial. I hate the things you've done, but you're still my father. This time, you can't send me away."

"Good. It makes sense for you to buy the house. It'll make things easier."

"Only I don't know if I'll be able to. I'll be bidding against Asher."

"Asher Lennox? He's still living next door? You talked to him?" Dad's voice rose.

I blinked at him, shocked by his sudden anger, and gave a reluctant nod.

"Ese hijo de puta!" His harsh tone made me flinch. "Lennox set up my arrest. He's the reason I'm here. I saw the surveillance pictures with the cops watching me from his house."

"He told me," I admitted in a small voice.

"He's on their witness list. He's going to testify against me at my trial."

I swallowed. Asher hadn't told me that part.

"He's said he's going to buy my house?" Dad growled.

"He's going to build an apartment building."

"An apartment building?" Dad's eyes widened. "That piece of shit! That's why he had me arrested. He did it to get his filthy hands on my house." Dad screwed up his face, looking to the side like he wanted to spit and was searching for a receptacle. "He bought his house so he could invite the cops in to spy on me, and now he's going to turn a big profit. He set this whole thing up to make money."

I sat back, my mind spinning. Asher had proven his talent for scheming, but I couldn't believe he'd have my father arrested just to make a profit.

"Don't let him get my house, mija. I'll die before I let him have it. And when they let me out of here, I'm going to rip his liver out and stuff it down his throat." Dad's fist unclenched and clenched again on the table and when he scowled, he looked a little scary.

"That's enough," announced a male voice from behind me.

I jumped. Though prison guards had been patrolling the room, I hadn't realized one had walked so close.

"Visit's over," said the guard. "Say goodbye."

I scrambled to my feet, my heart thumping so hard it was hurting my chest.

Dad got up too. "I love you, mija." He reached out to hug me.

"I love you too," I mumbled against his jumpsuit. Then I rushed for the door.

Once I was back in my car, tears banished, I sat in the driver's seat staring at my phone. I felt sick, like I'd eaten something bad, and the pounding of my heart was as heavy as a metronome.

I had to know the truth, but I was afraid of what I might find out.

Taking a deep breath and screwing up my courage, I called Asher.

"Hey." He sounded like he usually did, with his voice giving nothing away. But then he added, "I'm glad you called," and I heard his breath catch a little, like he was hopeful about what I might say back.

The sound made me ache. Part of me wanted to pretend everything was fine so badly, I had to talk myself into asking what I needed to know.

"Asher, did you plan all this from the start? I mean, did you have my father arrested knowing his house would be taken from him and you'd be able to buy it?"

He was silent for a long moment. Long enough for

my stomach to collapse in on itself and form its own black hole.

"We should talk about this in person, not over the phone," he said. "Where are you?"

My gaze went to the cold gray building in front of me. I was still in the prison parking lot, in the shadow of the concrete monolith. Somewhere inside it, my father was suffering.

"Tell me the truth, Asher. No more secrets."

He drew in an audible breath. "The truth is, when I discovered where your father was living, I bought the house next to him knowing it would be the perfect chance to get him and Frankie arrested. After moving in, I arranged for a surveillance team to watch him from my spare bedroom. I knew if they busted your father doing drug deals in the house, they'd be able to confiscate it. And I called my contact in the Justice Department to make sure they did."

I opened my mouth to say something, but nothing came out, and after a moment I closed it again. How had I not suspected it? All this time I'd been kidding myself I wasn't so naïve and trusting anymore, yet I'd let another man fool me.

"I told you what the drug cartel did to my family," said Asher. "That's why I planned to bring them down. The financial benefits were a bonus, but the main reason was because I needed to see Frankie punished. And Santino..." He paused. "Iola, your father's just as bad as Frankie. He hired Carlotta to work in his export company, then tricked her into carrying drugs across the border."

I couldn't say anything. Even if I hadn't known what Dad was capable of, my memories of him had always been precious. Now they were ruined.

"I'm happy I put your father behind bars," Asher said flatly. "He's not a good person. Prison is where he belongs."

My anger flared. Dad had always told me that he loved me, and that was more than I'd had from anyone else since Mom's death. "You're not the judge and the jury. You don't get to sentence him."

"Nobody forced Santino to break the law. I just made sure he was caught."

"And made a profit while you were doing it. How much money are you going to make, Asher? How much will you pocket from selling my dad out?" I was really asking how much money he stood to make by selling *me* out, but implying it was enough. Asher was a smart guy. He could read between the lines.

"Iola, please. We need to have this conversation face-to-face. Tell me where you are."

I stared at the thin, high vertical windows in the prison building that probably let in a meager amount of light while allowing no view to the outside world.

"How much?" I demanded.

"Twenty-five million dollars."

"Twenty...?" I trailed off, shocked into silence. Then I swallowed. Benedict would happily have sold his entire family into slavery for a fraction of that amount. "But it wasn't about the money?" My sarcasm came through loud and clear. "You're really trying to tell me twenty-five million bucks didn't factor into it?"

For seven years, I'd lived in a world where money and power ruled, and appearances were everything. I'd lived in a luxurious house, surrounded by expensive things, but the only things I'd really wanted were to have a husband who loved me, and to feel like I belonged. Instead, I'd been treated like Ruff. Trained and groomed, and brought out at parties to be shown off to Benedict's friends.

"I need the money, but it wasn't the driving force," he said. "It wasn't why I wanted Santino in jail."

"Benedict never let me have any cash of my own. He monitored my spending, and I could only buy what he wanted me to have. He controlled me with money, and good people don't *do* that, Asher."

"I would never—"

"Then why does it feel like you sold what we could have had?"

He didn't say anything for a moment. When he spoke, his voice was subdued. "That's not what I intended."

"You lied to me."

"I'm sorry, Iola. I shouldn't have done that."

Asher sounded wounded, but I was pretty sure he didn't feel as bad as I did. My heart was breaking. I'd fallen in love with him, and he had no idea.

"Was spending time with me part of your scheme?" I sounded as bitter as I felt.

"Iola, don't do this. You know it wasn't."

"How do I know? You're more cunning than I realized. There really is ice in your veins."

"Are you somewhere close? I'll come to—"

I rubbed the skin between my breasts, trying to ease the pain shooting through my chest. "No, I don't want to see you. I need to think things through."

He was silent for a long moment. When he spoke again, he sounded cautious. "That's all you need? Some time to think?"

My anger sparked again, its embers lighting up the blackness of my despair. "You don't get to pressure me. I've had enough of men telling me what to do."

"That wasn't what—"

"Goodbye, Asher."

I hung up and screwed my eyes shut, dropping my forehead onto the steering wheel. I felt like I'd just amputated a limb, sawing through my own flesh and bone. Even though the limb was going bad and had to be separated, the pain made me want to scream.

How did everything get so messed up?

# Chapter Twenty-Three

## Asher

Iola needed time. I accepted that. And it was underscored by the blinds she'd fastened over her windows to block my view into her house. As hard as it was for me to keep from calling her, from trying to convince her to forgive me, it was better to let her process what she'd found out.

But by Monday morning, I couldn't wait any longer. I'd given Iola two days to think things through, and they'd been the longest days of my life.

Now I needed to reach out to her, to tell her how I felt. But at the same time, I wanted to show I was respecting her wishes and giving her the time she'd asked for.

There was only one answer. Exchanging notes was how all this had started, so now I'd write the most important one of all.

But what should I write?

Sitting in my home office, I stared at a blank sheet of notepaper for so long, Nemesis eventually jumped onto my desk to see what I was doing. She sat down, her tail curled around her body, and gazed at me with unblinking yellow eyes as though waiting for me to start writing.

"Dear Iola," I said aloud, testing the words by sounding them out. "As you know, I've never wanted to fall in love."

I wrote the words down. My handwriting wasn't cursive and expressive like Iola's. It was neat and functional. We complimented each other perfectly, and somehow I needed to find a way to make her believe that.

"My mother was a victim of her addictions, and I couldn't trust her love. She was so unpredictable, I never felt safe around her."

Nemesis stared blankly at me as I spoke, clearly reserving judgment. I wrote down the words, then looked back at my cat while I thought of what I needed to say.

"Until I met you, I thought I'd never trust anyone but my brothers. The irony is, I'm the untrustworthy one. I'm the one who kept secrets. But I can't hide the way I feel anymore."

Nemesis examined one paw as I added the new paragraph. When I started talking again, she kept her gaze down as though filled with too much disdain to look at me.

"You've changed me, Iola. You've inspired me to let go. To laugh. To trust you despite how vulnerable it makes me feel, and to care about more than just protecting my family."

This time I wrote as I spoke. "Now I have no more secrets. No more schemes. You said you needed time, so I'll wait. I'll give you whatever you need. And even if you walk away, it won't change the way I've come to feel about you."

I dragged in a breath.

"I love you, Iola. I can't control it or contain it, and I've discovered I don't want to. I don't know if you can forgive me, but the last thing I want is to make you feel pressured like your ex-husband did. So what happens next is up to you."

I looked back up at Nemesis. The cat yawned, rolling her eyes toward the ceiling. Then she jumped off the desk. With her tail lifted and her butt swaying from side to side, she stalked outside.

"I accept your criticism," I told her as she disappeared. "But I'm still going to send it."

At the bottom of the letter, I sketched an anatomically correct heart, complete with muscles, arteries, and veins. Below it I wrote, *I have a heart-on for you*.

I considered pinning the note into a pair of my boxer briefs, and decided that could be a step too far. Instead, I folded the page into an envelope with Iola's name on the front. Taking it outside, I slipped it into Iola's mailbox. Surely she wouldn't see a letter as a violation of my promise to give her time. I could only hope it would convince her to call me.

I'd just gone back inside when my phone rang with an unknown number. I frowned at it. Could it be Ms. Lee from the U.S. Attorney's office calling about Santino's trial? I'd been on their witness list, until I'd decided that no matter what Santino had done, I couldn't testify against him in front of Iola. As eager as I'd been to see justice done, I no longer even wanted to attend the trial in case Iola misinterpreted my presence. When I'd notified Ms. Lee of my decision, she'd seemed to think my testimony wouldn't be necessary anyway, and their case was more than strong enough to convict him without me. Hopefully she hadn't changed her mind.

But when I answered the call, it wasn't a woman on the line, but a man.

"This is Doctor Greene," he said.

My heart lurched. "Doctor Greene? Has something happened to my father?" I'd met my father's doctor after Dad had heart problems last year, but Doctor Greene had never called me directly before.

"I asked your father if I could contact you. He came to see me with shortness of breath, and I thought you should know I've sent him to the hospital."

"What's wrong with him?"

"It could be nothing, but his ECG indicated a possible issue with his heart. They'll be able to tell you more at the hospital."

"I'm on my way."

Rushing to the hospital, I tried not to picture the worst possible outcome. To my relief, I found Dad lying awake and alone in a curtained-off bed, wired up to a heart monitor that was giving reassuring beeps.

"I hate this place," he growled in lieu of a greeting.

"I'm healthy as a jackrabbit. It's being here that makes me feel sick."

I let out a long breath, feeling my own accelerated heartbeat slow to a more normal level. "You had trouble breathing, Dad?"

He grunted. "Gave myself a scare. No need to overreact."

"You're okay now?"

"Course I am. And I can't wait to get out of here. Don't know what the fuss is about." He shifted irritably on the pillows that were piled up behind him. A crisp white hospital sheet was pulled up over his stomach, but his chest was bare, with several monitor patches stuck to it and cables snaking out to the machine.

For all his bluster, the way he clutched the bedclothes and the tight tension lines across his forehead told me he was more afraid than he was making out.

Sitting on the bed, I put my hand over one of his. "I'm glad you're okay," I said.

He made an impatient noise, huffing out his breath. "No need to get dramatic, son. I'm not about to die or anything." But he grabbed my hand and squeezed it surprisingly hard, like he didn't want to let go.

I gave him a half-smile. "You seem healthy enough. You might still have a few years left in you."

"That's what I've been telling the doctors. But do they listen?" He shook his head in disgust.

"I'll call Mason," I said.

"Don't need to worry him."

"He's going to find out anyway. Don't worry, I'll tell him you're a... what was it? A jackrabbit?"

Dad let out a smaller huff than before. "Fine. Call him."

I motioned to the No Cellphones sign next to the bed. "I'll need to go outside. I'll be right back." Giving his hand a last squeeze, I stood up.

"Get me a donut while you're at it," Dad said as I headed to the door. "Chocolate dipped."

I spun to face him. "What? Dad, you shouldn't—"

"I knew it! You and your brothers are going to nag me even more now." He narrowed his eyes. "That was a test. You failed."

"You're right, we'll still try to get you to eat good food. We don't want you coming back here."

"After all I've been through, I *deserve* a donut."

Shaking my head, I went out. And after finding a doctor to take me through my father's test results, I called Mason.

"Apparently Dad's tests are okay now," I assured my brother. "They have a few more to run, but they think it was a false alarm."

He told me he'd be there soon, and after hanging up, I went to the hospital's café on the ground floor to check their selection of food. The sign in front of a basket of apples made me smile.

*Today's Special: Buy one apple for the price of two and receive a second apple completely free!*

Iola would appreciate the joke. I even reached into my pocket to take my phone back out, thinking I'd send her a picture. Then I stopped myself. Dammit, I had to show her I respected her request to give her space.

"Two apples please," I said to the server.

When I went back to Dad's room and presented him with an apple, I expected him to refuse it with a caustic comment about it not being real food. Amazingly, he took it without more of a protest than an irritated grunt, and bit into it. I sat back down on the edge of his bed to eat the other apple without letting him know how surprised I was. The breathlessness that had put him in hospital had clearly shaken him a lot more than he was willing to say. Maybe donuts really would be off the menu, for a while at least.

Mason arrived a short time later. "Carlotta's sorry she couldn't be here," he said after greeting Dad and peppering him with questions about how he was feeling. "She's at the theater, in charge of a dozen kids."

Dad gave another irritated grunt. He was still acting suspicious of Carlotta, though I was sure he liked her more than he let on.

Mason eased his large frame into the visitor's car in the corner of the room. "Dad, I hope you don't mind me asking, but how's your insurance?" he asked.

Dad cast me a sideways look. Since he'd lost so much money to the scammers, I'd been covering a lot of his bills, but I'd asked him not to tell my brothers.

"Asher's been helping out with that," he said, counter to my instructions.

Mason raised his eyebrows at me. "You have been?" Then, to Dad, "I didn't know you were short of funds?"

"Don't worry about it," I said. "It's a small shortage, and I'm happy to cover it."

"Why didn't you say anything?" Mason gave me the kind of assessing stare that probably made criminals shake.

I stared right back. "No need. I've got it covered," I told him, though it wasn't strictly true. Not with my business on the line.

But Mason hadn't been back from Houston for long, and his jumpiness combined with the shadows under his eyes kept reminding me how difficult his last assignment must have been. Besides, all our money worries would be over for good once my plan came to fruition.

"Are you sure, Ash?" Mason asked.

I hesitated. Was the fact I was secretly paying Dad's bills and keeping it from my brothers a bad thing? I hadn't wanted to burden them with it. But I was still smarting from the fallout of lying to Iola. Should I reevaluate the importance of being honest with everyone in my life?

Before I could decide, Mason said, "We should call Kade and tell him Dad's in hospital."

"But the doctor said it was a false alarm. No point in making him come all the way from LA."

"Whether he comes or not is up to him. It wouldn't be fair to keep it from him." Mason pulled out his phone. "I'll call him."

Mason's answer cast more shade on my policy of only ever providing information on a need-to-know basis. He clearly didn't subscribe to the same view.

"You can't call him in here." I motioned to the No

Cellphones sign, and Mason stood up. "Back in a minute, Dad."

I watched him go out the door, then thought better of letting him decide what to tell Kade. "I'll be back in a minute as well," I said to Dad, and followed my brother out.

Mason was in the hallway, finding Kade's number on his phone.

"Make sure you tell him Dad's not in danger," I said.

"Of course. Have you called Iola?"

I wanted to call Iola. I'd spent every minute of the day wanting to call her. But I just shook my head.

Mason frowned, lowering the phone without dialing. "What's going on with you, Ash? And don't say it's nothing, because I can tell something's up. You don't always have to keep everything to yourself."

I let out a slow breath. "Iola's upset with me, so I'm giving her some time."

His expression softened. "Hey. I'm sorry. Let me know if there's anything I can do."

"Thanks."

"It's your fault, I take it?"

"That would be a fair assessment."

"You finally told her the truth about her father?" When I nodded, he added, "Should have been honest with her from the start."

"That could have made things worse. She might not have let me help her if she'd known the truth."

"Sometimes you have to trust people. Let them in,

show them the real you. Then you'll know that whatever happens, you did the right thing."

I blinked at him. This was the advice from my undercover DEA operative brother whose life had depended on nobody knowing who he really was?

"You've changed," I said.

He grinned. "Trying to. And so can you."

I cocked my head, studying my older brother. I had to admit he seemed to be recovering more quickly from his last assignment than I'd expected, throwing off the darkness that had threatened to swallow him. We probably had Carlotta to thank for that.

"Mason, do I seem like I value money more than people?" I asked.

"Why? Was it something Iola said?" He narrowed his eyes at me. "What exactly did you do? Sounds like you must really have fucked things up with her."

"Never mind," I muttered. "Are you going to call Kade, or what?"

# Chapter Twenty-Four

## Iola

I was in my bedroom pulling on the tailored capri trousers I was going to wear to Dad's trial when I heard a soft thump in the hallway.

Ruff heard the sound too. She'd been lying on the floor watching me dress, but she scrambled to her feet and lumbered into the hall.

I yanked the trousers up, my nerves jumping. Though I knew Benedict was thousands of miles away, my first thought was still that he might have come back and broken in.

But when I stuck my head out of the door with my capris still unbuttoned, I saw Ruff's tail wagging furiously as she sniffed Nemesis. The hall window was open, and the thump must have been the cat jumping off the windowsill.

Nemesis had something in her mouth. It looked like an envelope.

"What's that?" I asked, fumbling with my buttons, trying to do them up. Nemesis was holding the envelope face down, so I couldn't see if it was addressed to me.

Nemesis stalked past me and Ruff, slipping into my bedroom.

"Oh no you don't." I followed her. "No more panties for you." With everything that had happened between Asher and me, the last thing I needed was for his cat to present him with any more of my underwear.

Nemesis evaded me easily, vanishing under the bed.

Instead of trying to get her out of there, I went to the dresser. "I don't have time for your thievery today, Nemesis." Yanking open the second drawer, I pulled out all my t-shirts and dumped them onto the bed. Then I transferred my underwear from the broken drawer into my t-shirt drawer, and slammed it shut. "There. Problem finally solved."

Going to the bed, I peered under it. Nemesis was sitting just out of reach with the envelope still in her mouth. She studied me impassively with her intense yellow eyes.

"You may as well leave. My underwear is secure."

Slinking out from the other side of the bed, Nemesis leapt on top of the dresser.

"Fine, see for yourself. Go ahead and check the drawer. It's empty."

The walls of the house were still intact as well. After everything that had happened with Asher, I'd been feeling emotionally fragile. I wasn't ready to face whatever Dad might have hidden, or have any more unpleasant surprises, or make any hard decisions.

Nemesis swung her head to the wall and let the envelope go. It dropped into the crack between the dresser and the wall.

"That was petty. I don't have time to get it out now, so it had better be junk mail and not something urgent." I waved toward the door. "Time for you to leave."

Keeping her gaze fixed on mine, Nemesis curled her tail around her body.

"Ruff, will you help me get her out of here?"

With her tail between her legs, Ruff looked from me to Nemesis and back again. She gave a little whine, her eyes sagging apologetically.

I threw up my hands. "Fine. Go ahead and take her side. I've got to go. Don't let Nemesis convince you to carry out all our stuff for her while I'm not here."

I only just made it to the courthouse in time. When I arrived, Dad's trial was about to begin. Two guards led Dad into the dock, waiting on each side of him as he sat down. He looked dignified in a suit, and the sight was reassuring. He looked a lot better in normal clothes than a prison jumpsuit. My father didn't look like a criminal and though I knew he was one, I'd always found it hard to think of him that way.

I scanned the courtroom, but thankfully couldn't see Asher. I hadn't been sure what I'd say to him, and this way I didn't have to decide.

The jury were already sitting in their places, and I

was trying to catch Dad's eye in the crowded courtroom when the judge strode in. He was a tall man with metal glasses perched on his craggy nose, his brows creased into a v-shape. His black robes swished around him and the courtroom stood while the judge took his seat, then the list of charges against my father was read aloud.

My heart sank as the list went on. It was a lot longer than I'd expected. Though I watched the part of Dad's face I could see, he showed no emotion as the charges were read out.

Then the prosecutor stood up and outlined the case against Dad. It was far more damning than his lawyer had suggested over the phone. Dad had been regularly transporting large quantities of drugs across the border. Years ago, when we'd fought about what he did, he'd made it sound as though he'd only done the occasional illegal job, just to keep his legitimate business running and his creditors off his back. Explaining it, he'd made it seem like something he'd been forced into. Truth was, Dad had been running a major operation. And his so-called legitimate business now seemed like little more than a front for money laundering.

As the prosecutor went into detail about what Dad had done, all my precious illusions were shattering. I started feeling sick. My stomach was turning over.

I shifted uncomfortably in my seat, and Dad turned and saw me. His eyes were sunken and sad. His expression fell, and he mouthed something that looked like, "Lo siento."

But if it was an apology, it was hollow. He was all the

family I had left, and I'd so badly wanted to have a father, I'd been blind to what he really was. Just like my marriage to Benedict, when I'd spent the first year or two trying everything I could to make things better, believing that if I could make my husband happy, he'd be nicer to me. I'd hoped to turn the abusive, controlling shit-show we'd had into the loving relationship I'd so desperately wanted it to be. I'd even magnified every feather-light morsel of affection he'd shown me, enlarging it in my mind until I could almost manage to convince myself it outweighed the giant pile of contempt he'd heaped on with a shovel.

The prosecutor kept talking, and my ears rang with the truth I hadn't wanted to believe. As the case against my dad grew ever more terrible, my breaths grew more painful, as though something heavy was crushing my chest. The only way I could bear it was by digging my fingernails into the soft flesh of my palms.

Dad turned his head again and his imploring eyes met mine. Even now, my heart ached for him. Even now, I wanted to forgive him.

I couldn't listen anymore.

Scrambling to my feet, I stumbled out of the courtroom, all but running as I burst through the doors to take big, gasping gulps of fresh air.

How many times did I have to keep learning the same hard lesson? Over and over, my own desperation for family, for a *connection*, kept leading to deception and heartbreak. How often did it need to happen before I stopped blindly handing my heart to people, wanting to trust them, each time hoping they wouldn't let me down?

I made it to my car and sat in the driver's seat for a long time, waiting until I was in a calm enough state to drive. Finally I was able to start the car and make it home.

When I got there, I found Ruff asleep on my bed. Collapsing beside her, I threw an arm over her and buried my face in her neck. "Am I stupid, Ruff? With all that's happened, am I a total fool to want to trust people?"

Ruff whined, turning her head to bump it against mine.

I hugged her tighter, letting my tears soak into her fur. Remembering how Asher had said he could never trust anyone enough to fall in love with them, and how he'd seemed to think I'd feel the same way.

"No," I whispered. "I won't let myself become like him. I *want* to trust. I *want* to be able to love."

Dragging in a shuddering breath, I lifted my head and wiped my eyes with the heel of my palms. "No man gets to destroy my heart. Not Benedict, not Dad, not Asher. I won't let them change me, Ruff. I won't let them turn me into someone I don't want to be."

Ruff tried to lick my face. I pulled back, not wanting her to slobber on me. She drooled anyway, and I realized her saliva was dripping onto the pile of clean t-shirts I'd left on the bed. Now they were covered in drool, and I'd only put them on the bed because of Asher's kleptomaniac cat, and that stupid broken dresser drawer.

A hot spark of anger burned through me, and I grabbed hold of it like I was drowning. Rage was better than heartbreak. I'd rather smash something than cry.

Scrambling off the bed, I grabbed hold of the drawer

and yanked it out of the dresser so hard, it hit the wall with a crash. I dropped it, drawing in a ragged breath. There was a crack in the dry wall where the corner of the drawer had punched into it. Come to think of it, Dad had told me to break into the bedroom walls. Right now it was an activity that seemed perfect for my mood.

Picking the drawer back up, I angled it to pound the corner into the wall a few more times. When I'd made enough of a hole, I grabbed the edge of a piece of paper that was poking through the hole and tugged it free.

It was a fifty-dollar bill.

Behind it, still in the wall cavity, were more bills. I used the drawer to enlarge the hole. When it was big enough I could fit my hands through, I discarded the drawer and used brute force, ripping the drywall away with satisfying cracks.

Dust filled the air, making me cough, and packets of fifty-dollar bills tumbled out onto the floor. Thousands and thousands of dollars.

Dad's drug money.

This was the sum total of everything my father had done, all the crimes he'd committed. This money was the reason he'd spend the rest of his life in jail. He'd hurt people to get it. He'd wanted me to have it, to use it to start my new life. And if I didn't keep it, he'd thrown his life away for nothing.

The crushing weight I'd felt in the courtroom came flooding back, the pressure on my lungs so intense it was hard to breathe. My legs weakened.

I wanted to stay furious, to smash the entire house to

pieces. But the hurt and sorrow I'd been trying so hard to push away were too strong. I crumpled to the ground. Lying on my bedroom floor, I buried my head in my arms and wailed.

After a while, I felt Ruff pressing against me. She curled her body around me as best she could, trying to push her nose under the hands covering my face. Putting my arms around her neck, I leaned into her and let myself keep sobbing.

It wasn't until a long time later that I finally ran out of tears. I was still on the floor and the house was dark and silent. I was empty of everything. My chest was hollow and my nose had long since stopped running. But for the first time that day, I felt calm and my mind had gone clear. I finally knew what I needed to do.

Standing up, I switched on the light, dragged my suitcase out of the closet and started throwing all the money into it. Ruff lifted her head and let out a whine.

"That's right, girl, we're getting out of here." My voice was hoarse and my throat was raw. I wiped my eyes again, but they were dry. "It's just you and me now. We may be alone, but we're going to be okay. For the first time in our lives, we can go anywhere we want and there's nothing..." I stopped to correct myself. "There's *nobody* to stop us."

I piled all my belongings into the trunk and back seat of my car, leaving nothing behind. But it wasn't until I was driving away that I remembered the letter Nemesis had dropped down the back of the dresser.

Had to be junk mail. If not, I guess I'd never know.

*No Fooling Around*

I dragged my eyes away from the rear-view mirror, not letting myself watch the house grow smaller, and refusing to think about how happy I'd felt living there.

"There's no going back," I whispered to Ruff. "Somewhere we'll find another place to call home."

# Chapter Twenty-Five

## Asher

Iola was gone. She hadn't even stayed in town to watch her father get convicted.

Apparently, she'd gone to the San Dante police station to turn in a suitcase full of cash before she'd disappeared. Then the house next door had been filled with police teams for several days while they searched it from top to bottom, knocking holes in the walls and pulling up the floorboards. Since then, it had been empty for another four long weeks.

Luke, a friend who happened to head up one of the police teams, returned the letter I'd written to Iola. They'd found it in the house, so I had to assume she'd opened it, read it, and decided to leave it behind.

I tried calling her anyway, but when she didn't answer her phone, I understood that she hadn't responded because she still wanted to be left alone, and to keep calling against her wishes would probably do more harm than good.

But I wasn't the only one who felt the emptiness of the house next door like a pit in my stomach. Nemesis hadn't brought home a single trophy in the last few weeks, and had taken to spending her days sleeping on my pillow. She was clearly moping, missing Ruff.

As for me, I was trying not to think about the fact I might have lost Iola forever. But the idea she could disappear from my life was a raw, gnawing hole in my gut. It seemed to consume every minute of my day. It was the last thing I thought of before I slept, and the first thing I thought of when I woke.

I spent a ridiculous amount of time staring into Iola's empty house, hoping against reason and logic that she might reappear, while cursing my so-called brilliant plan that had somehow turned into the biggest mistake of my life. If only I could make things right with Iola. But if she'd read my letter and walked away, what else could I do but respect her decision?

Work was the only thing that took my mind off my troubles. As the auction day for Santino's house got closer, I got busier. The building materials needed to be ordered well in advance to prevent delays in starting work on my new apartment building. As I was already financially committed to the project, there was nothing else to do but go all-in. A construction site of that scale took a huge amount of planning, money, and time to organize, and with my entire company riding on it, I couldn't afford to drop the ball.

The day before the auction, I went to the project office to meet with Brenda, and found her in an annoyingly cheerful mood. When she took her hard hat off and sat on the chair opposite my desk, she wore what could only be called a beaming smile.

"This is the crew's last day on this job," she said, putting her hard hat on the floor in front of her chair and unzipping the front of her high-vis construction jacket. "And this week's been a killer. We've all been working long hours to get it wrapped up. Thank heavens we'll all get to take a break before starting on this new project of yours."

"Yeah," I said.

Brenda blinked her blue eyes at me. "What's wrong with your face, boss?"

"What do you mean?"

She pointed an accusing finger. "You just sighed. And now your forehead's wrinkling. If I hadn't known you for years and never seen you give anything away, I'd be tempted to call it a frown. Are you feeling okay?"

"I'm fine," I lied. "I need to go over the projections for the new project with you and lock in the timeline so you can schedule the staff."

"Okay boss." She glanced at her watch. "But our shindig starts in two hours, and the entire crew's going. Think we can wrap it up by then?"

"That's tonight?" I'd forgotten about her party to celebrate the successful end of the project we'd been working on.

She leaned back and propped her heavy, steel-capped

boots on her hard hat, crossing one leg over the other. "Starts at four. And I know you're an island, but it's not too late to change your mind. Even though we're planning to have fun, don't let that stop you."

I raised an irritated eyebrow. "I'm an island?"

Her grin told me she was teasing. "Whoever came up with the saying that no man is an island had clearly never met you, boss."

"Fine. I'll come to the party," I said grumpily.

She jerked forward. Her boots dropped off the hard hat, clunking onto the floor. "What?"

"It's about time I learned the names of the people who work for me."

Her smile had disappeared. "What's going on? Is this a prank?"

"I've never told you I appreciate all the work you do for me, have I?" I was pretty sure I hadn't. "You're the reason the company's so successful. I should have given you a bigger raise. You deserve it."

Brenda's eyes widened. "Oh my lord," she whispered. "Have you been diagnosed with something terminal? Tell me the truth, boss. You're dying, aren't you?"

"I'm not dying," I growled.

"Then what's wrong with you?"

"I don't want you to think money's more important to me than people. I don't want anyone thinking that." I ran an impatient hand through my hair, hating everything about this interaction, but needing to say it anyway. "I'm willing to get to know my employees." My voice dropped to a mutter. "If that's what it takes."

Brenda blinked several times, then shook her head. She reached to the floor to pick up her hard hat and stood up. "I don't understand, but if you're willing to come to the party tonight, I'm not going to argue." She put her hard hat on and zipped up her jacket. "I've got to tell the crew. And place some bets. Nobody's going to believe this, and I could make a stack of cash."

"We have scheduling to do, remember?"

"Oh. Right." She sat back down. "Do you have any more surprises to spring on me? It's been a crazy week, and now you're coming to the party? I think I might need a whiskey already."

"Here's a schedule of materials that shows when everything will be arriving on site." I handed her a printed list that was several pages long. "These are the trades we'll need." I handed her another list.

"Okay. Good." She squared her shoulders and started studying what I'd given her, focusing on what was important. Just like I needed to do.

My phone buzzed with a message.

*Mason: We need to talk. Can you meet me at Dad's?*

I glanced at Brenda. She was staring at the list, but her eyes were glazed as though she was picturing sipping a glass of whiskey.

With an inward sigh, I stood up. "Go and place some bets," I told her. "I'll see you tonight."

I was parking my car outside Dad's house when my phone rang. Every time it happened, I felt a surge of hope, thinking it could be Iola. But when I grabbed my phone, my screen said it was Violet Eaves. The sight gave me an irrational jolt of fear. I'd had to pay in advance for some of the construction materials. If anything went wrong now, it'd be difficult not to default on my next interest payment.

"Hi Violet," I said evenly. "The auction's still on, isn't it?"

"Of course it is. I'm calling to check that you're coming. Are you still interested in bidding on the house?"

I let out a relieved breath. "That's right. Are you expecting many other bidders?" I didn't really care about other bidders. I'd outbid them all no matter what, seeing as the house was worth far more to me than to anyone else. None of them had twenty-five million dollars to gain, and a company to lose.

What I really wanted to know was whether Iola would be at the auction. She'd said she wanted to buy the house. I had no idea if that was still her intention.

"Asher, you know I can't tell you about other potential bidders. That'd be a violation of ethics. I'll see you tomorrow, okay?"

"I'll be there."

If Iola came to the auction, I'd at least get a chance to speak to her. But it would also mean I'd need to bid against her.

Would it be worse to outbid her for the house she wanted, or if she didn't turn up?

If she didn't go, that didn't mean I would never see her again. No matter where she went, she'd still need to sell her paintings, so I'd be able to track her down. The only question would be whether that would be a bad thing to do. I'd hate for her to feel like I was pressuring her into seeing me if she didn't want to.

I was deep in thought as I knocked on Dad's front door. When it swung open, Mason was standing in Dad's hallway instead of my father, his muscular body filling the narrow space.

"Hey," said Mason. "Glad you're here. We need to talk."

That sounded ominous, and my brother's expression didn't make me feel any better. "Is it Dad?" I followed him in. "Did something happen?"

Mason motioned me into the living room with a scowl. There was no sign of Dad anywhere.

"Dad told me about being scammed." My brother planted his feet in the middle of the living room, crossing his arms. "He said you didn't want us to know?"

I nodded. "Because I'm handling it, so why worry you?"

"That's stupid, Ash." Mason let out an exasperated huff. "You've been paying Dad's bills and following up with the police by yourself? We could have helped."

"I didn't need help."

His frown deepened. "Do you realize how this makes me feel?"

"What do you mean?"

"We're supposed to look out for each other. That's what we *do*." He stalked to the far side of the living room, then swung back to face me. "Why did you keep it a secret? Does Kade know?"

"You were in Houston when it happened, and Kade

was in LA. Besides, after I win a property auction tomorrow, none of us will need to worry about money again."

"Look, Asher—"

"No." My usual calm tone suddenly deserted me, and the word came out so forcefully, I surprised myself. "Take a look at yourself, Mason. You have scars all over your body. You put your life on the line and sacrificed everything to take down the drug cartel. That was dangerous work, and it was just as important to me as it was to you. I wasn't about to distract you with some small bills when you were in the middle of it. Seriously. I had it handled."

He hesitated, and some of the anger left his voice. "But that doesn't mean—"

"My job is to make the money for us." I didn't realize how strongly I felt about it until I heard myself saying the words. "We *are* a team, Mason, and we look out for each other. That means you do what you're good at, and I do what I'm good at." Though I didn't like letting my emotions show, I couldn't keep my voice from rising.

Mason's expression softened. "We're not a team if you keep secrets."

I snorted a laugh, startled out of anger by genuine amusement. "That's funny coming from an undercover agent."

"I never hid anything from *you*."

Moving to Dad's couch, Mason sank down onto it. Though it was a normal-sized couch, his bulk made it seem small. And when he leaned back, I heard it creak.

"Listen," he said. "Mexico messed with all of us. We had to adapt to survive, and without the money you and

Kade made, we would have been in real trouble. But I have plenty of money now, and so does Kade. We don't need you to look after Dad on your own. We need you to talk to us and let us know what's going on so we can tackle things together."

I moved to sit on the chair opposite him, temporarily lost for words, because what he said sounded so reasonable, I couldn't argue against it.

Settling into the chair, I drew in a breath and looked up at the ceiling. I'd thought I'd been doing the right thing to make sure the people I loved were safe, but now I wasn't so sure.

"As much as I hate to give you credit, maybe you're right," I admitted.

Mason leaned back to tug his phone out of his jeans pocket. "Wait, I need to record that. Say it again, Asher, this time a little louder."

"Enough." I narrowed my eyes at him.

Mason laughed. "Seriously, now you've admitted the error of your ways, how about you start opening up a little more? You mentioned a property auction you're going to win?"

I blew out a resigned breath. "Fine. The truth is, I'm going to buy Santino's house when it goes up for auction tomorrow."

"*Santino's* house?" He gaped at me for a moment, then firmed his jaw and gave me a nod. "Okay, then I'll go with you."

"You don't need to do that."

"You're my brother, and now you're finally letting me

in on one of your secrets, I want to support you. Call it a symbolic gesture. Whatever." He waved a hand. "If you're going to buy that scumbag's house, I'll be by your side cheering you on."

"All right. Thanks, Mason."

"Don't mention it, bro."

"But there's a problem. Iola might also bid for the house. She could be at the auction." I looked away, because I didn't want my brother to see I was both desperate to see her, and dreading it. I couldn't explain feeling both things at once. It made no logical sense.

"You don't know if she'll be there? You two still aren't talking?"

I let out a sigh. "It would have made things a whole lot simpler if I could have stopped myself falling for her."

"Falling... in love?" My brother's eyebrows shot up.

"I should have known better."

"Hey, that's great news. Congrats!" Mason beamed at me as though being in love was something to celebrate. The poor, deluded fool.

"Where's Dad?" I changed the subject. "Why isn't he here?"

"He went outside." Mason nodded toward the front door. "Said he'd be back in a moment."

"Outside? I didn't see him anywhere out there."

"He's probably playing one of his pranks on Trixie."

I got up and went to the door to look up and down the street. There was no sign of him. I was about to go back inside when the front door of the neighboring house swung open. Trixie's house. Seeing as Trixie was Dad's arch-nemesis, it was the last house in the world I would have thought he'd go into. Only he strolled out of Trixie's front door as though it was normal.

Blinking, I double-checked what I was seeing. Yes, that was my father. With his enormously bushy eyebrows, pot belly, and dubious fashion sense, there was no mistaking him, especially as he was wearing one of his favorite mustard-colored shirts. I glimpsed Trixie's face at the window, watching him leave, so he hadn't murdered her. He must have been invited in.

"Mason." My voice sounded strangled.

"Yeah?" My brother came up behind me.

"Why is Dad coming out of Trixie Watson's house?"

"He's what?" Mason stood next to me as Dad made his way back to us. My brother looked as full of questions as I was. Neither of us spoke as Dad approached.

"Hi Asher," Dad said to me as though he hadn't noticed our stunned expressions. He went around us, into the house.

Mason and I gazed wordlessly at each other for several long, silent seconds. Then we followed him into the living room.

"Dad," I said. "What were you doing next door?"

Our father flopped onto his living room couch and stretched out his legs. "Fixing a broken faucet."

"What?" I managed to ask. Not the most eloquent of questions, but then again, the fact I could form words at all was cause for self-congratulation.

"I heard Trixie making a ruckus and went to see what

was wrong. Water was gushing from a broken faucet, and I could fix it. So I did."

"You fixed her faucet," I repeated dumbly. "You *helped* her?"

"Does that mean your war's over?" Mason asked. "Are you and Trixie friends?"

Dad smirked. Lifting one arm, he extended his clenched fist toward us. Then he opened it. He was holding two long plastic bolts and wing nuts. "These are the bolts that held on Trixie's toilet seat. Next time she sits on it, she'll go flying."

My brother let out a pained-sounding sigh. "You fixed her faucet, then sabotaged her toilet?"

"Fixing her faucet was the ruse that got me into her house." Dad chuckled. "Clever, huh?"

"He still fixed the faucet," I muttered to Mason. "It's progress."

Mason nodded. Just a few weeks ago, Dad would probably only have set foot in Trixie's house with a can of gasoline in one hand and a lit match in the other.

As much as Dad might pretend today's actions were normal, they had to be a sign his relationship with Trixie was slowly changing. If he was willing to go into her house to fix a faucet, who knew what might happen next?

A piercing scream came from next door. Then a door slammed, and a shout floated to us. "Edward Lennox, you obnoxious swine-fiddler! Give my bolts back!"

"Which bolts?" Dad bellowed back from the couch, almost deafening me. "The bolts on your neck that hold on your head?"

"You know which bolts!"

Mason plucked them from Dad's hand. "I've got this." With a long-suffering sigh, he headed outside.

"You told Mason about being scammed?" I asked.

Dad nodded. "I had to tell him. Wasn't right to keep it a secret from your brothers."

"It wasn't," I agreed. "I won't make that mistake again."

Besides, I couldn't be the only man in our family who wasn't capable of change.

# Chapter Twenty-Six

## Iola

"You look nice," said Gloria.

"Thanks." I smoothed down my dress and turned away from the mirror to face her.

We were at Gloria's place. Or rather, at Mavis's enormous, run-down, ramshackle beachfront mansion. Mavis wasn't just a ViaGranny, she was one of the gang's founding members. Now she was too frail to get out much, and Gloria had been living with her, taking care of her, for the last few years.

Mavis spent all her time downstairs, taking long naps in an imposing master bedroom and watching a lot of daytime television. Gloria's bedroom and living area were on the second floor, up a set of stairs Mavis could no longer navigate. Gloria had scattered artful decorations to make the place pretty in spite of its curling wallpaper and ancient paint, and it had an incredible view of the ocean.

After driving around several states, staying at campsites and using the time to think about what I wanted my new life to look like, I'd decided to come back to San Dante. Gloria had graciously offered me a bed, and Ruff and I had been sleeping in one of the upstairs spare rooms for the last few nights. That meant slipping into a bed that was usually already occupied by at least one cat and occasionally a giant rabbit, but I was enjoying getting to hang out with Gloria. And I was grateful that she'd set aside a small area in the back room of the community center where I could paint.

"So you'll definitely see Asher at the auction?" asked Gloria. "How do you feel about that?"

She was lying on my bed, stomach down, propped up on her elbows with her knees bent and her feet in the air, chatting to me while I got dressed. Ruff was asleep next to her, her big body taking up most of the bed, so Gloria was almost falling off the edge.

"Nervous. Afraid. Angry. Hopeful." I tapped my cheek, examining my feelings to see if I'd missed any out. "It's an emotional stew, with a bit of everything thrown in. And it's been simmering for weeks."

"You haven't spoken to him at all?"

I shook my head. "If Asher wanted to talk, he would have tried harder than one missed call. He didn't even bother to leave a message."

I was afraid my obsession with Asher was becoming annoying, so I kept my tone light. In England, Benedict had prevented me from making any close female friends, and I'd probably been taking advantage of Gloria a little too much. She'd heard me talk about Asher so often since I'd come back, it was amazing she was still willing to listen.

"Does it help if I vouch for Asher? Even if he doesn't show his feelings, I know he has a good heart." Gloria screwed up her nose. "Did I tell you I used to want to marry all three Lennox brothers? I thought the four of us could live in a big house together, and life would be perfect."

"Aww, that's cute. How old were you?"

"Oh, that was all through my twenties." She grinned, and I let out a laugh despite my nerves. "But seriously," she said. "He's a good guy. Every time I've asked him to help with raffles and community events, he always chips in."

"He told me he never wants to fall in love, and I have to accept that. I'm not sure we're even friends anymore. If we were, he would have called and tried to patch things up."

"The question is, have you forgiven him?" Gloria asked.

I looked around for my sandals. "I'm still mad at him for not being honest with me, but I'm not sure I need to forgive him for anything else. When he came up with a plan to get Ruff back, I was happy he had a devious mind. So how can I stay angry at him for plotting against my father before he even knew me?"

The other thing I'd been thinking about was what it must have been like for Asher and his brothers to have been locked in an apartment for three days, worrying about their mother, not knowing if she'd abandoned them. Three starving teenagers left without food, and Asher was the only one who'd fit through the window. Sacrificing himself to save his brothers was an experience that would stay with him for life. So no wonder he was always scheming and figuring out ways to make money. In his mind he was probably still carrying the weight of that responsibility. If his brothers needed saving again, he was going to be ready.

"He should have been honest with you," said Gloria.

I nodded agreement. "When Benedict was threatening me, I can understand why Asher stalled. Afterward, he had no excuse not to come clean." I spotted my sandals under a discarded t-shirt. "I've been trying so hard to get over him. I keep hoping maybe I didn't really fall in love with him, but with the way he made me feel."

Gloria rested her chin on her hands, her brow furrowed. "What do you mean?"

"I married Benedict because I wanted a place in the world. So I could be Mrs. Appleby. Maybe with Asher I was falling into the same trap, making the same mistake again."

"Looking for somewhere to fit in, you mean?"

"This sounds dumb, but when I was with Asher, I kept feeling like I wanted to belong to him." Doing my sandal up, I let out an embarrassed laugh. "Not, like, in the slavery sense. I'm not explaining it very well. But I know he'd never let anything happen to me, and that felt really nice, you know?"

She blinked at me, her eyebrows high. "That sounds like love."

"Does it? Or am I still looking for something I lost when my mother died and Dad sent me away?"

"Isn't that what love is, though? Two people knowing they belong to each other? Making each other feel safe?"

I frowned, because I'd been obsessing over it, trying to decide whether my longing for family had been blinding me to reality and making me yearn for a doomed relationship that Asher didn't even want. But what Gloria was saying made a lot of sense.

"Anyway, none of it matters." I huffed out a frustrated breath. "I've tied myself in knots over something that's never going to happen. He never wants to fall in love, so it's all irrelevant."

"At least you'll get to talk to him at the auction."

I nodded, searching the room for my phone. "I'll thank him for everything he did for me and say goodbye. Then maybe I'll be able to walk away."

I found my phone under a pile of clothes and when I glanced at the screen, my heart dived. "Oh crap, I'm going to be late!"

Gloria got up from the bed, and Ruff gave a little sigh before her snores started again. "You're sure you don't want me to come? I can see if Mavis won't mind having a late lunch, and—"

"Thank you, but Mavis will probably mind, and you have to get ready for your art class."

"Have you decided whether you're going to buy your father's house?"

I paused on my way to the door. For the last few weeks, I'd been weighing pros and cons. With the divorce papers signed, my bank accounts had been unfrozen and my lawyer had transferred a shockingly large settlement to me. When I'd questioned the amount, he'd told me almost angrily that it was only what was rightfully mine, the proceeds from my paintings and my portion of the marital assets, and after the way Benedict had treated me it had pained him not to fight for more.

I didn't care what Benedict had been left with, I was just pleased I could afford to buy a house. The question was whether I should buy Dad's place. And the only reason I was considering it was because of the joy it had given me. Walking in for the first time, I'd already been relieved beyond words that Ruff and I were finally free from Benedict. When I'd seen the photo of my father on the mantel, I'd burst into tears. It had felt like something precious I'd lost a long time ago was finally back within reach.

Even now, I still wanted to visit my father in jail, to try to have some kind of relationship with him, even if it was a cautious one. Maybe I was a fool, trying to cling to something that had only ever existed in my wishful imagination, but I wasn't ready to give up on him yet.

"I only lived in the house a few weeks, but they were the happiest weeks of my life," I said.

"Then you should buy the place and live there forever."

"But Asher wants it."

"You still haven't decided, have you?"

"I'll decide when I get there," I said as I left.

"Good luck!" she yelled after me.

I'd wanted to get to the auction room early to have a chance to talk to Asher. But when I arrived, all the buyers were seated in rows of chairs, and there were a surprising number of people holding paddles. The auctioneer was stepping up to the podium on the small stage, his gavel in hand, and Violet Eaves was moving between different bidders, offering words of encouragement. When she saw me, she hurried over.

"There you are!" Violet handed me a paddle with a number on it. "Just in time, we're about to start. If you want to make a bid, hold up your paddle, and if you'd like some help, let me know. That's what I'm here for!"

I mumbled something, but my attention was focused on the two men I'd spotted in the back row.

Mason was with Asher. Their heads were together, and they were talking quietly. I wasn't surprised they were both there, seeing as they always looked out for each other.

My throat closed up as I gazed at Asher's profile. Most of the time I'd stopped thinking about how good looking he was because so many more things about him were more important. But it felt like I was seeing him again for the first time, my heart flipping over as I gazed at the sweep of eyelashes from his gunmetal gray eyes, and the sharp angle of his jaw.

Then he looked up and his gaze burned into mine.

"Welcome everyone," said the auctioneer from the

stage, but I could hardly hear him over the pounding of my heart.

I'd spent the last few weeks arguing with myself, uncertain about everything. It felt like I'd been throwing so many colors onto the canvas in my head, it had become a muddy mess I couldn't make sense of. But at that moment, staring into his eyes, the picture became clear.

I loved Asher.

I wanted to be with him.

Even if he didn't feel the same way, I couldn't buy the house next to him, because he wanted it, and therefore I wanted him to have it.

Besides, he'd made it clear he didn't share my feelings, which probably meant I'd need to move away from San Dante. The only way I'd ever have a chance of getting over him was if I didn't have the fear of accidentally running into him when I wasn't braced for the impact.

Coming to the auction had been a mistake. The room was crowded, the auctioneer was already speaking into the microphone, and this was no place to talk.

Asher said something to his brother before standing up. Mason gave me a wave as Asher made his way over to me. I tried to wave back but my limbs felt stiff and awkward.

The auctioneer was talking about the house but Asher ignored him, striding toward me with his paddle in one hand. His expression was more worried than I'd ever seen it, his brow furrowed and his eyes dark.

I took a step back, glancing toward the door. The

bidding was about to start, and my presence was clearly distracting Asher.

"Iola." He caught my arm with his free hand and his proximity made me dizzy. "I'm glad you came."

"We should talk," I said. "But not now. We can sort things out later."

"I'm sorry for not telling you the whole truth earlier." His voice was low and urgent. "And you should know the house isn't as important to me as you are. If you want to buy it, I won't bid against you."

"Who wants to start the bidding?" asked the auctioneer. Someone raised their paddle and he pointed to them. "Thank you, sir. Your opening bid is one million, six hundred thousand dollars. Do I hear six fifty?"

My head was spinning and if my throat wasn't so tight, I'd ask Asher to repeat what he'd just said. Could he really be telling me he was willing to hand over a house that would make him twenty-five million dollars?

But there wasn't time for questions. The auctioneer was taking another bid from a woman in the front row. "We can talk later," I croaked. "The auction's started and you need to buy the house." I tried to pull my arm from his grip.

"Iola, don't disappear. Please." His usually calm voice was thick with emotion. "I can't let you go."

"But it's twenty-five million dollars. If you don't bid, you'll lose all that money. I don't want the house. I'm not going to buy it." To prove it, I dropped the paddle Violet had given me onto the floor.

"Like I said, the money doesn't matter as much as you do."

My heart expanded, filling with so much hope it all but stopped beating. All I wanted was to ask if he could really be saying what I thought he was. But he was wrong about one thing: the money did matter. If he didn't buy the house because of me, the cost would be too high to contemplate. I couldn't let that get between us.

"Do I hear one million and ninety thousand?" asked the auctioneer.

The woman in the front row raised her paddle again.

"Thank you, ma'am. Now, who's going to make it one ninety-five?"

"Asher, please let me go."

He released me, but he still hadn't so much as glanced at the auctioneer. His paddle dangled, forgotten from one hand. If I stayed in the room, he wouldn't focus on what was important, and I needed him to do his financial deal so we could move on.

"Buy the house," I told him with all the force I could muster. Then I turned and fled for the door.

# Chapter Twenty-Seven

## Asher

I called after Iola as she ran out of the auction room. It felt like she was taking part of me with her. All I cared about was making things right with her. If I let her go, anything might happen. She could leave the country. I might never find her again.

"Asher, what are you doing?" Mason had joined me at the back of the room, but I couldn't listen to him any more than I could listen to the auctioneer who was about to sell Santino's house to someone else.

After all the planning I'd done, the financial risks I'd taken, and all the work I'd put into it, I couldn't stay and buy the house.

I didn't care anymore about the twenty-five-million-dollar profit I would have made. I could swallow my pride and ask my brothers for help to keep my company afloat.

One way or another I'd find a way to keep my employees working. But if I let Iola go now, I may never get her back.

My mind was clear, my priority certain. There was only one thing I couldn't afford to lose, and she'd just walked out the door.

Mason grabbed my shoulder, but I slipped from his grasp, dropping my paddle next to Iola's. I strode from the auction room without a backward glance.

Iola was already on the other side of the lobby, disappearing into the elevator.

"Iola!" I yelled.

She looked around at me and her eyes widened. The elevator doors started to close, and she shot out a hand to stop them.

"Did you buy it already?" she asked as I reached her.

"Don't worry about the house."

Her eyes were big and wild, and she stepped out of the elevator. "But, Asher, you need to get back in that room and buy—"

"We need to talk."

"I'll wait. Do the deal, Asher."

"But I need you to know—"

She huffed with impatience and I realized I was doing more harm by not listening to her than if I stopped arguing and obeyed.

"You'll wait for me?" I asked. "You won't leave before we've talked?"

"I'll wait right here. Now go!"

Reluctantly, I headed back toward the auction room. But I hadn't even reached the door before I heard the hard thwack of the auctioneer's gavel coming down. "Sold!" A round of muffled applause followed the announcement.

When I turned back to Iola, her face had gone pale.

"You didn't get the house." Her voice was a shocked whisper.

I moved to her in quick strides. "The house doesn't matter. You're more important."

"I'm the woman who just cost you twenty-five million dollars."

It hurt my heart to see her so upset, so I made myself smile. "Worth every penny."

Her eyes searched mine as though she was looking for traces of regret or anger or resentment. I held her gaze, diving into the warm, dark brown of her eyes, feeling nothing but relief that she hadn't disappeared and I had a chance to make things up to her.

There were so many things I hadn't told her or shown her. Like how much she'd come to mean to me. Putting it in a letter had been a bad idea, and I couldn't blame her for not replying. This was my chance to tell her how much I loved her, and to keep telling her until she believed me and forgave me for my mistakes.

"I'm sorry you didn't get to buy the house either," I said.

"No, that's okay. I loved living there, but finding Dad's drug money hidden in the walls soured it for me. Now I don't feel the same attachment toward it." She frowned. "You said not buying the house would hurt you financially. Will you be okay?"

I slid my grip down her arms and took hold of both her hands. I needed to touch her, to reassure myself she was really there. And even though I didn't like the answer to her question, I'd never lie to her again. So I looked her in the eye and told her the whole truth.

"My business is in danger of going bankrupt because I put everything on the line. But I can fix this. First I'll talk to the bank and try to negotiate my way out of my loan contract. If all else fails, I'll ask my brothers for help." I swallowed, because despite my resolution to be more open with them, I still hated the thought of having to admit everything I'd done. I'd always tried to support them and ease their burdens. Accepting help in return would never come easily.

And because I'd resolved to tell Iola the entire, unvarnished truth, I added, "I'm afraid you'll think less of me now that you know I've risked everything."

"I don't care whether you have money or not. If you were penniless, it wouldn't change anything."

My lips tugged up. For a man in serious financial trouble, I felt surprisingly happy. "Good to know."

She squeezed my hands. "Are you really okay?"

I found myself smiling even wider. "As long as I have you, apparently nothing can bother me."

She bit her lip, and the movement drew my eyes. I'd spent the last few weeks missing her lips. My need to kiss them was a force impossible to resist.

"I have to tell you something," she said.

"Yes?" I knew I should look back into her eyes, but I couldn't drag my gaze from her mouth.

"I love you."

The words were simple, but the reaction they caused were anything but. My heart tried to escape from my chest, which squeezed tightly around it to keep it from getting free. My head swam. I simultaneously wanted to let out an exclamation of relief, a demand for her to repeat the sentiment, and a declaration of my own feelings. Fortunately, a jumbled, Frankenstein's-monster version of all the things I wanted to say didn't emerge at once. I was too busy bending my head to claim her perfect lips.

As I kissed her, she softened against me. I put my arms around her, drawing her closer, needing to fill my senses with her.

After weeks of not seeing her, talking to her, or touching her, finally having her in my arms filled me with a joy so intense it was overwhelming. It was quickly becoming clear just how essential to me she was.

Though we were in a public building, with casual bystanders likely to go past, I couldn't hold back my hunger for her. And though my kiss was almost savage in its intensity, she kissed me back the same way, pressing herself so hard against me, I couldn't control my body's reaction.

I needed to feel her skin against mine. To kiss her everywhere, and make her moan with pleasure.

I needed all of her.

And if the elevator hadn't dinged as it arrived on our floor, who knows what might have happened?

I pulled back a little, reluctantly loosening my arms to

create a little space between us. Some people got out of the elevator, their shoes clacking on the floor as they went past, but I was ensnared by the beauty of Iola's eyes and couldn't spare them a glance.

"I love you," I whispered.

Her smile was the most stunning thing I'd ever seen in my life.

"But you didn't want to fall in love," she whispered back.

"There's no taking it back now." I lifted my hand to the side of her face, caressing her cheek. "You want to get out of here? My car's in the basement." Then I remembered my brother. "Actually, let's take your car and Mason can take mine. Then he can pay for the parking." Not even the realization I probably couldn't afford to pay for it myself anymore could dim the warmth in my chest.

# Chapter Twenty-Eight

## Iola

I figured we might be at Asher's place for a while, so I asked him to stop at Gloria's place on the way so I could pick up Ruff. While I was there, I grabbed her dog bed and toys. And I packed an overnight bag for myself. You know, just in case.

When we got to Asher's beachfront house, I saw the *For Sale* sign was still in front of the house next door. The *Sold* sticker hadn't been added yet, but it wouldn't be long. It was a sad thought. In spite of my father's crimes, living there had made me happier than I could have dreamed.

"You okay?" asked Asher gently, as perceptive as always.

"Definitely." I gave him a smile as we got out of his car. "It's been great staying at Gloria's but I don't want to wear out my welcome. Maybe I'll get myself an apartment. I could look for a place with a view of the water and some outdoor space for Ruff."

Asher was carrying my bag, and he caught my hand with his free one as we went inside, Ruff lumbering ahead of us. His skin on mine felt so good, I couldn't keep from smiling at him.

"I hope you're not planning on going anywhere anytime soon." He had a sexy growl in his voice. "After not seeing you for so long, I don't want to let you out of my sight for days. Hopefully weeks. Longer, if you'll agree to stay."

"Fine by me. But are you sure it's okay for Ruff to stay here too? Nemesis won't be put out?"

"You tell me," he said as we went into the living room.

I stopped, staring at Ruff. She'd raced in ahead of us, dropped onto the floor, and was rolling on her back with her legs in the air. Her giant jowls flopped to one side as she gazed beseechingly at Nemesis with her head upside down.

The black cat was next to Ruff's head, giving her a haughty stare. She flicked her tail before extending one paw for Ruff to lick.

"For heaven's sake, Ruff, have a little self-respect."

My dog ignored me, her rapt attention fixed on the small black cat.

Asher put down my bag and stepped close. "I missed you," he murmured.

"I missed you, too."

Lifting my hands to his chest, I rested them against his pecs, loving their hardness. I could imagine him working out at precise intervals. He probably knew exactly how many bicep curls and pushups would keep him at peak fitness. And if that meant I got to run my hands over his gorgeous muscles, I was all for it. I'd even be willing to hold his dumbbells.

"I love you," he whispered. His eyes were soft and deep, the color of the smoke from a warm fire on a rainy day.

And the word 'kiss' didn't begin to describe what he did to me next. No mere kiss had ever been that hot. His mouth demanded everything I had to give, and his hands moved down my body, igniting me everywhere they touched. I slid my hands around his waist, pressing harder against him. Lifting onto my toes, I tried to position his hardness lower.

He obliged by sliding his hands to my butt and pulling me up, so I was lifted off my feet and could wrap my legs around his waist.

Or at least, that would have happened if I hadn't jerked with surprise as I felt the floor disappear, causing me to slide clumsily back down his body.

A picture of a stripper falling off a pole flashed through my mind, and as I landed back on the floor, I started to giggle.

Asher raised an eyebrow. "What's so funny?"

"Working in a strip club may never be a career option for me." I struggled to regain a straight face. "Do you have a bedroom, by any chance? One with a big, safe bed I can't accidentally fall out of?"

"This way."

Taking my hand, he led me to a bedroom at the back of the house, with windows facing the sea. Asher's room was so spotlessly clean it would almost have been too tidy, except for the pile of books on the nightstand. The room's high ceilings made it feel airy, and it smelled faintly of Asher's cologne, a scent I couldn't get enough of. His furniture was dark, with sharp, clean lines. Modern and slightly masculine. It was the perfect room for him. I instantly wanted to live in it forever. Especially because there was a large monochromatic painting of the sea on the wall above his bed, and the painting suited the room beautifully.

"Who painted that?" I asked.

"I did."

I swung to face him, open-mouthed. "You did?"

Asher took my upper arms and gazed into my eyes, his expression serious. "Iola, please tell me the truth. Are you worried you won't make enough money to get by?"

I blinked in surprise. "Excuse me?"

"Because you need to know I'll always look after you." He stroked his hands down my arms. "I don't want you to worry about anything. I may have just lost everything, but I have a plan to get back on my feet. And no matter what happens, I've got your back. Always."

It should have been funny, him worrying I might seriously be considering working in a strip club to make ends meet. But my throat felt suddenly thick with emotion. Not at his words, but the way he was looking at me. His face was open, his expression raw. He wasn't hiding from me or putting up any shields. I could see his resolve to take care of me. His unshakeable commitment.

Looking into his eyes, everything finally felt right.

Home wasn't the house next door, and it wasn't an apartment with yard space for Ruff. Asher was my family, and my home was in his arms. When he said, 'Always', I could trust he'd always be there for me, ready to catch me from whichever platform I wanted to leap from.

And if I told him I wanted to fly, he'd probably come up with an intricate scheme to break into heaven and steal me a pair of wings.

I blinked, fighting sudden tears, and his frown deepened, his levels of worry rising.

"Asher, there's something I need to tell you," I whispered around the lump in my throat. "I need us to be totally honest with each other, and there's something big you don't know."

He ran his hands up and down my arms. "You can tell me anything. I don't care what it is, nothing could ever change the way I feel about you."

"You don't have to worry about me needing to take my clothes off for money."

His frown turned into puzzlement. "Okay."

"My divorce settlement from Benedict was a little over four million dollars."

His jaw dropped.

Asher Lennox, the man previously renowned for being an emotionless humanoid android, actually gaped at me.

And the pure, beautiful satisfaction of that moment made all my throat lumps and eye prickles magically disappear.

I leaned into him, bumping my body against his as I slipped my arms back around his waist. "Now, where were we?" I pretended to ponder the question. "Oh yes. I think you were about to strip for me. I have some dollar bills in my bag."

His reluctant smile grew as he dropped his head to lean his forehead against mine. "I love you."

"You're just saying that because I'm rich."

"Actually, I'm saying it because I'm hoping to get you naked. You think it's going to work?"

"I will if you will." I was already tugging at his shirt, struggling to pull it off and toss it aside. His body was so beautiful it should be hanging in an art gallery. I ran my hands over his ridged muscles appreciatively, following the trails where they led.

He unbuttoned my dress and let it fall. Drawing back, his eyes devoured me for a moment, then with a growl of appreciation, he bent to kiss my neck. At the same time, his hands slid behind me to unhook my bra.

I went to work on his jeans, fumbling the buttons undone and pushing them and his boxer briefs down together. He kicked the tangle of clothes off impatiently, dragging my panties off with the same rushed urgency. Then he sank onto the bed, pulling me down with him, so I was straddling him.

The curtains were open, the sun pouring in. And seeing as his bedroom looked out onto the popular white sands of San Dante beach, the fact that I was sitting stark naked on top of an equally naked man should have made me feel exposed. But if any of the sunbathers or swimmers on the beach could see me, I didn't care. The only thing that mattered were his eyes, lingering over my body with a powerful intensity behind them, as though he was mapping and memorizing me.

Though he'd already seen me naked, last time we'd done anything like this, he'd kept his clothes on. Now that I could see him, I thought I should start some sort of petition to make that illegal. Asher's body was so perfect, he should never be allowed to wear clothes again.

I bent to kiss his chest, to nip at his nipples and then lick my way down his body. I wanted to touch and taste every bit of him. I loved how his lean, muscular body felt under my hands and mouth. He had a little hair on his chest, surprisingly defined calf muscles, and a ticklish spot under his arm—when I touched it, he jumped a little and then laughed with me. As gorgeous as he was, I was determined not just to admire him, but to find all the places that made him groan.

When I reached his hard, beautiful length, he let me explore that too. I licked him, then took him into my mouth. When he started to protest that he needed to be able to kiss me, I let him have a turn exploring me, kissing me all over, and licking between my legs like he had before. The way he did it felt so good, I never wanted him to stop. But I was still panting with eagerness, pressing myself harder against his mouth when he pulled himself back up my body.

"I want you." His voice was as rough as sandpaper. "I need to be inside you." Holding himself over me, he pressed his nose against mine, his breath ragged. "We were apart for five whole weeks and it felt like five years to me."

"Five decades," I agreed. "No, five centuries."

"Five millennia." Easing off me, he reached over to the nightstand, opened a drawer, and fumbled in it for a moment before pulling out a condom.

I opened my mouth to say, "Five times infinity," but when I propped myself up on my elbow, the words died in my throat. He just looked so magnificent rolling on a condom, his muscled back to the window, that my throat went dry. All the love scenes I'd read or watched, all the imaginary heroes I'd sighed over, they were nothing compared to the man in front of me.

I loved every one of his hard, square lines, I loved his darkness, and the simmering intensity he never let out, the hidden passion most people never saw. He was a secret I wanted to hug close forever. To cherish, and protect, and guard.

If he was mine, that made me the luckiest woman alive. The thought made sudden unwanted tears prick at my eyes again, because I wanted him to be mine so much that it scared me.

He moved over me again, his elbows on either side of me. His brow drew down into a worried line and his eyes were the softest shade of graphite.

"Are you okay?" he asked. "What's wrong?"

"Asher, will you paint a picture for me?"

There was a flicker of surprise in his eyes. "I'm not an artist."

"I disagree."

His eyes crinkled. "We can paint something together if you like."

"Yes, please."

He kissed my nose. "You look like you have something else to say."

"Just that I love you." I could feel the words carving themselves deeper into my soul every time I said them. They were a part of me now, the truth of the words a simple fact that was shaping me into someone new.

"And I love you." He said it back to me just the same way, and I kissed him with everything I was, pulling him onto me and into me.

Then we moved together, two becoming one.

He tangled his hands in my hair and his limbs with mine. His lips found the sensitive place under my ear, and he groaned my name. I arched into him, wrapping myself around him, making noises that weren't quite words as he lifted me into orbit.

It was sometime after I'd exploded into a million points of light and drifted slowly back to earth, remaking myself into someone who was panting, dazed, and ecstatically happy on the way, that I knew it for sure.

He was mine and I was his.

And together, we were perfect.

# Chapter Twenty-Nine

## Asher

The next morning, I watched Iola come out of the bathroom wrapped in a towel. Her hair was wet, her eyes held a deep, satisfied contentment, and her face was glowing.

Her lips lifted and I had to smile back at her. In fact, I might never stop smiling. She was going to ruin my reputation for being inscrutable, but who cared? When she was in a towel, fresh from the shower and looking sexier than ever, nothing mattered more than exploring the deliciousness that happened to be wrapped in so very little.

"Stop right there." She narrowed her eyes at me even as her smile grew wider. "You have to let me put some clothes on. I let you shower and dress without molesting you, even though I was sorely tempted."

"You're stronger than I am." I drew her close, not

caring her towel was damp. If I had my way, she wouldn't be wearing it for much longer anyway.

"I need sustenance," she objected, laughing. "After yesterday and this morning, there can't be a drop of moisture left in my body."

"I'll get you a glass of water." I pushed a tendril of hair from her shoulder and kissed the wet spot left behind. Then I moved my lips up to her neck, nipping at the place I knew would send shivers over her skin.

"Mmm." She angled her head to grant me better access. "You'd better make it a big glass."

There was a loud, insistent knocking at the front door. Ruff barked, and I reluctantly lifted my lips from Iola's body.

"That had better not be Mason," I growled. "I told him I needed to talk to him, but not until this afternoon."

"It *is* afternoon. Well, almost." She tilted her head back to focus her gorgeous dark eyes on me. "You're going to tell him everything?"

We'd been lying in bed talking this morning, and I'd been wrapped in a spectacularly contented haze, which I now blamed for an uncontrollable urge to be completely truthful and transparent with everyone in my life forever more. I'd decided to start by telling my family about the imminent failure of my business, and messaged Mason to tell him I needed to talk to him.

But that conversation could wait.

I had far more important things to do first.

"I'm going to tell him to go away," I said, giving her forehead a kiss and heading to the door. "He can come back after lunch, like I told him to do in the first place." Ruff lumbered behind me to the door.

"No, Mason should stay. You need to talk." Iola moved into the bedroom, shutting the door behind her. "I'll put some clothes on."

I wanted to object, but she was right. Iola and I would have plenty of time to spend in bed.

That thought made me smile to myself, and feel a whole lot better about the difficult conversation I was about to have with my brother.

Mason called impatiently as he knocked again. "Asher! You there? Open up."

I counted to ten to give Iola more time to dress, then I opened the door. "Why didn't you use your key?" I started to ask.

But it wasn't just Mason standing outside. Kade was beside him, grinning at me. They both held a coffee in each hand, four coffees in all, and Mason thrust one at me as he charged inside.

"I didn't want to let myself in if you and Iola were both here. Who knows what you'd be doing or where you'd be doing it?" Mason clapped me on the back as he went past, his swing so hard I almost dropped my coffee. "Hey, what is this animal? Is it a horse or a dinosaur?" He stopped to pet Ruff's head.

"What are you doing here?" I asked Kade.

"Nice to see you too." Kade shouldered past me as well, following Mason into my living room and petting the dog as he went by.

"I take it Iola's here?" asked Mason.

"In the bedroom."

Mason shot Kade a smirk. "Told you."

Kade grinned and clapped me on the back in the exact spot that was still sore from Mason's enthusiastic welcome. "Congrats, Ash. You finally got something right for a change."

The bedroom door opened, and Iola emerged wearing jeans and a t-shirt, with her hair still wet. Her face was glowing and she looked fresh and gorgeous, even with her hair leaving wet marks on her shirt.

"Hi Iola," said Kade. "Got you a coffee, but we weren't sure whether you took cream or sugar, so it's black."

She took the cup from him, her eyes wide with surprise. "Thanks. Black is great. How did you know I was here?"

"Last I saw Asher, he was running after you," said Mason. "I was hoping he managed to catch up, and didn't mess things up again."

"I thought you were going to be in LA for a few more weeks," I said to Kade.

"Yeah," my brother agreed. "Funny story as to why I'm here. But first, we both want to know what you wanted to tell Mason. That message you sent him this morning didn't sound like you at all. You're going to let him in on what's going on? Color me intrigued." He dropped his car keys onto the coffee table and flopped onto the couch, waving at the other living room chairs. "Sit down. Let's talk. I can't wait to hear what you have to say."

Mason moved to sit next to him, and Iola chose one of the single chairs, sinking onto the edge with her back straight and her coffee in both hands, as though she was still a little nervous around my brothers. I took the chair next to her.

As I sat, I glimpsed movement from underneath the coffee table next to the couch. One black paw slowly extended from beneath the table. A claw soundlessly hooked the car keys Kade had put down, drawing them off the edge. Nobody else seemed to notice the keys disappearing under the table.

Nobody but Ruff. She lowered herself onto the floor. Dropping her head mournfully onto her paws, she gazed longingly at Nemesis. The cat slunk away, the keys dangling from her mouth as she headed for the hallway.

Ruff let out a heavy sigh and closed her eyes.

Seeing as I'd promised to be one hundred percent honest with everyone from now on, I should tell Kade-the-prankster his keys were vanishing. I opened my mouth...

Then I closed it again, hiding my smile. Ninety-nine percent honest would be close enough.

Mason leaned back, spreading out on the couch, and fixed me with a forceful look. "So, Asher. You wanted to tell me something?"

Iola shifted in her seat. "Maybe I should make like a prom dress and take off. This should be a family meeting."

"Stay," I said. "You're family."

A smile spread over her face, making her luminous

eyes shine. Her expression was everything I'd hoped for, and I only wished I could have put my arms around her and kissed her. My brothers should have let us take the couch.

"Welcome to the family." Kade flashed his dimples at her.

Mason frowned impatiently. "Talk, Asher. What do you have to say?"

I gave an inward sigh and paused to take a steadying sip of coffee, because telling my brothers about the mess I'd made went against every instinct I had.

"I signed a contract with the bank to borrow a large amount of money." I sounded stiff, and the words were reluctant, but at least they were coming out, and meeting Iola's steady gaze gave me the resolution I needed to keep going. "The money was to pay for my house and Santino's. Unfortunately, because it's a high-risk loan, the interest rate is twice what it would normally be, and I had to use my business as collateral."

"You borrowed money you're not going to use?" asked Kade. "Now you can just pay it back."

I shook my head. "The details are complicated, but I had to take a fixed position. I was counting on buying Santino's house and getting the land revalued. With increased collateral I'd have had more flexibility. But now I'm stuck with a large loan, and interest payments so high, they'll eat through the money in no time."

"What exactly are you saying?" asked Mason.

"Unless I come up with a plan to fix this, my business will fail, and my employees will lose their jobs."

Kade raised his eyebrows. "I thought your business was going well?"

"It is."

Mason's frown deepened. "So, you bet everything on being able to buy Santino's house? Wasn't that reckless?" My brothers weren't making it easy for me.

"It was reckless," I agreed. "I gambled and lost."

Kade leaned back, resting his arm across the back of the couch. "Let me make sure I understand. You're in big financial trouble now, all because you didn't buy a house? Have I got that right?"

"That's right." I let a little irritation leak into my voice, because though he sounded sympathetic, his body language was telling a different story. Could my brother be stifling a *grin*?

Kade and Mason exchanged a look I couldn't read.

"Sounds like you got yourself into some seriously hot water." Mason didn't seem upset either.

"Are you *happy* about this?" I stared from one to the other.

"Don't get riled up." A smug smile spread over Kade's face. "The only thing we're happy about is that we bought the house for you."

"What?"

"Kade and I bought it." Mason looked just as smug as my twin.

"Mason called me from the auction," said Kade. "The auctioneer was hustling for the last bids, and I had to make a split-second decision to partner with him in order to buy the house."

"Two million, one hundred and forty-three thousand dollars," added Mason. "Way too much for me to cover, even with the big bonuses I've put away. I needed Kade's help or I could never have done it."

Kade nodded. "It was the strangest phone call I've ever had. Mason was babbling something unintelligible, and I could hear the auctioneer in the background. I didn't even have time to talk it over with Nat, and said yes without really knowing what I was buying. So after I spent way more money than I've ever spent on anything, I thought I'd better hustle my ass down here to find out what was going on."

My brain had kicked back into gear, but all the gears were spinning at once. I had too many thoughts rushing through my head, which was almost as bad as not having any.

"You had no idea why I wanted the house," I said stupidly. "Why'd you take such a big risk and buy it?"

Kade shrugged. "Because it seemed important to you and we knew there had to be a good reason, not that you like to share any of your plans."

"He's already getting better at that," Iola said with a smile. "That's why he called you."

"Seeing as Kade and I don't want the house for ourselves, we'd like you to buy it from us." Mason leaned forward, frowning. "You can do that, right? Because if you say you don't want it anymore and we're stuck with it, Carlotta's not going to be pleased with me."

Kade held up one hand, his grin growing mischievous. "Hold on a moment, Mason. I like that house, and

Nat and I have been looking for a place to move into. Maybe I don't want to give the house up."

Mason glowered at him. "That's not funny, Kade."

The cogs were slowly clicking into place in my brain, and my thoughts were starting to regain some kind of traction. After the auction, it hadn't been easy to adjust to the idea of being broke. Now I was adjusting to the idea I was going to be wealthy again. It should have been easier, but it was taking a few minutes for my mind to realign.

"You're going to buy the house from us?" Mason raised his eyebrows, waiting for my answer.

I tapped my cheek, trying to focus. "Of course, but maybe there's a way we can avoid paying the closing costs twice."

Iola cleared her throat. "I'm no expert, but may I throw in a suggestion? What if you two kept ownership of the house, and the three of you became business partners so you all had a share in the deal?"

Kade and Mason turned their frowns onto her, and I realized I still hadn't explained to them what an exceptional financial windfall it was going to be.

By buying the house, they'd made sure our futures would be bright. The leap of faith they'd taken had been huge, but I should have guessed my brothers would have my back. Iola was right. It was only fitting they should share the rewards.

"A brilliant idea." I smiled at Iola, happy I'd be able to show her how much I appreciated her genius as soon as we were alone. "My company will build the apartments. The work is fully costed, the plans are approved, and the construction materials have been ordered. Completing the building works will take a year, but we'll pre-sell the apartments so we can walk away with guaranteed money in our pockets. And if we're partners, we'll split the profits equally."

Kade pushed his lips to one side. Mason frowned, tapping his fingers on his coffee cup. They looked at each other for a long moment, then at me.

"I'll have to run it by Carlotta," said Mason. "As long as she's okay with it, I'm in."

"And I need to talk to Nat, but I already know what she'll say." Kade waved his hand as though it was a done deal. "Have you named the new building yet? Because *The Kade Lennox Enormous Erection* has a ring to it." He shot Iola an apologetic glance. "Sorry, Iola. Please excuse my crude joke. I'm a little excited."

"Stop it, Kade." Mason turned back to me. "How much profit do you think the building will make?"

Iola made a muffled sound, clearly trying to suppress a delighted laugh. "You really don't know? Neither of you?" Her eyes were shining, her face alight. She was so stunning, my heart expanded, and the air in my lungs felt lighter than helium.

I was the luckiest man alive.

Leaning forward, she shot me an eager grin. "May I tell them? Please?"

I smiled back, well aware that I probably looked as besotted as I felt. Nobody had ever been as happy as I was at that moment, with the woman I loved about to tell my brothers they'd made the best decision of their lives. I couldn't wait to see the expressions on their faces when they found out we'd all just become twenty-five million dollars richer. Judging by the wideness of Iola's smile, neither could she.

"Go ahead," I said. Then I sat back to enjoy it.

# Epilogue

## Asher

Kade and Natalie held their wedding reception in the penthouse of our brand-new apartment building, the one I'd built on the site where Santino's house and my house used to be.

The building was a credit to my team, who'd worked hard on it for a year. The other apartments had all been pre-sold, but with the enthusiastic approval of my brothers, Iola and I had decided to keep the penthouse for ourselves. We hadn't moved into it yet, though. Our wedding present to Kade and Natalie had been to fit the space out especially for their wedding reception. Even filled with wedding guests, the apartment felt large and airy, with high ceilings and a large balcony overlooking the ocean. We'd converted the living room into a big dance floor, with the band playing on a makeshift stage. And the room that would be Iola's art studio currently held a bar, where two bartenders had been kept very busy mixing cocktails.

Iola and I couldn't wait for next week when we'd move in, after all the festivities were over and Kade and Natalie had left for their honeymoon. Tonight, though, we'd been dancing for hours, and it was almost midnight by the time we decided to take a break.

Hand-in-hand, we strolled into what would become our master bedroom when Iola and I moved in. Carlotta's friend Willow ran an events business and we'd worked with her to convert this room into a sitting area for the reception, with several plush couches and chairs grouped together in cozy circles. Willow had done an exceptional job with the decorations. The room was lit with twinkling party lights, and dozens of glowing paper lanterns. The way the lanterns seemed to float could only be described as ethereal.

With most of the guests still on the dance floor, I was pleased to see Iola and I had the sitting room to ourselves. We sank onto one of the couches, Iola kicked off her shoes, and I dragged her legs onto my lap to rub her calves.

She sighed with pleasure. "That feels so good. My legs ache from all that dancing."

I pushed her dress up to her knees, enjoying the feel of her skin under my fingers. I never got enough of touching her, talking to her, or laughing with her. And her legs were shapely. They were too sexy to be hidden by her long, red bridesmaid's dress, though I approved of the way its silky fabric clung to her curves. If I had my way, her dress would be short enough that I could count every freckle on her legs, but as we could see the dance floor from where we were sitting, I resisted the urge to push the fabric any higher.

"You're beautiful," I told her, though I'd already said it at least three times that night already. For some reason, I couldn't stop saying it. Perhaps because I'd thought the words so often that they kept slipping out.

Iola smiled at me, then looked over to the dance floor where Kade and Natalie were swaying together. "What about the bride? Isn't she radiant?"

"She looks happy," I agreed. "I suppose she's almost as beautiful as you are."

"You're not exactly an impartial judge." Despite her admonishing tone, Iola's cheeks were flushed with pleasure and her eyes shone. "Wait, I think Kade and Nat are going to come over here."

Sure enough, my twin and his new wife joined us, sitting down on the couch next to ours. Natalie was wearing an ivory wedding gown, and her hair was curled up on her head in a complicated design. She wasn't wearing her glasses, and I guessed she'd probably decided to wear contact lenses for the event. Though her glasses suited her, I had to admit she also looked very nice without them.

"My feet hurt," she said, toeing off her shoes. "I'm not used to heels. You've got the right idea, Iola."

"Put your legs up here," Kade patted his thighs. Natalie put her legs up as he'd suggested, hitching the trailing end of her gown to one side, and the two of them mimicked our position, with Kade massaging Natalie's calves.

"Oh yes." Natalie let out a happy sigh. "Thanks. That feels good."

The next song finished, and Mason and Carlotta emerged from the crowd of dancers. Carlotta moved toward the direction of the bathroom, while Mason strolled toward us. A smile still lingered on his lips, and he looked blissfully happy. In fact, both my brothers did. Looking at them enhanced my own pleasure at being here with Iola.

It had been a very special day. The only day that would beat it would be when I married Iola. I'd been waiting until after Kade's wedding to propose, not wanting to take the focus off my twin. But it would soon be my turn.

Mason squeezed his big frame into an armchair next to us, then leaned over to talk to Natalie.

"I read the romance book you wrote," he said.

"You did?" She lifted her legs off Kade's lap to sit up straight. Her eyes looked a little worried. "What did you think?"

"Before I answer, I have a question. The hero was supposed to be Kade, right?"

"Of course her hero is based on me." Kade looked smug. "Only there weren't nearly enough sex scenes for it to be true to life. There should have been a whole lot more."

"I loved your book, Nat," exclaimed Iola. "I've read it twice!"

Surprised, I blinked at her. "You've read it?"

"Of course. Haven't you?"

"Not yet," I admitted, making a mental note to read it as soon as possible. Though I'd known Natalie had been taking a break from her successful murder mysteries to write a romance novel, I hadn't been aware my brother had a starring role.

"I had to skip the sex parts." Mason wrinkled his nose, tugging at his tie to loosen it. "Knowing you could have used my brother for inspiration made me feel ill. Sorry, Nat."

Kade shook his head, pretending to be disappointed. "You shouldn't have skipped those pages. You might have learned a thing or two from me, the Love Master." He lifted his hands to his chest, put one fist into his other palm, and bowed his head as though he was a martial arts sensei.

Mason whipped a cushion from behind his back and threw it at Kade, who dodged his head sideways to avoid the missile. Natalie grabbed the cushion as it bounced and lobbed it back, laughing.

Carlotta came into the room, crossing to Mason. She sank onto the arm of his chair, then let out a laugh as he reached up and tugged her into his lap. Her bridesmaid's dress was the same as Iola's, red and silky. Somewhere on the dance floor, their friend Gloria was wearing a matching dress, but the floor was so crowded with people enjoying themselves, I couldn't spot her.

"Where's your father?" Carlotta asked Natalie. "Did he leave already?

Natalie nodded. "Dad left after eating two slices of wedding cake. He said he needed his beauty sleep to look his best. Ever since Kade's agent promised him his own TV show, he's been quite the diva." Laughing, she rolled her eyes. But I could tell she was pleased by her father's new-found success. Natalie and her father had always been close, and when she'd been forced to sell her father's beloved café, she'd been afraid he may not recover from the loss. Instead, he seemed to be thoroughly enjoying his new life in the limelight.

"Look over there." Jolting up in Mason's lap, Carlotta pointed at the still-crowded dance floor. "My mom and your dad are dancing together."

I jerked my face to look. Sure enough, Trixie Watson and Dad were doing an old-fashioned waltz. Trixie was wearing a gown with a full, hooped skirt, like something that had probably been the height of fashion at the turn of the nineteenth century. And I had to admit, Dad looked rather dapper in his suit. He'd even combed his eyebrows, because they weren't as wild as normal. Their hands were clasped together, and Dad had his other hand looped around Trixie's waist, resting on her lower back. He seemed to be holding her as closely as her full skirt would allow.

"Is that some kind of illusion?" asked Natalie, her eyes wide. "Or is it really happening?"

Kade shook his head. "I wouldn't have believed it, but love really must be in the air."

Mason was frowning. "Is there something slippery on the floor? A bucket in the rafters he's planning to tip over her? He must have an angle, right? This has to be a prank."

"I don't think so," I said. "They don't look unhappy to be dancing together."

Iola turned into me, kissing my neck before resting her face on my shoulder. "This has been such a lovely wedding," she murmured.

I moved my mouth to her ear, nuzzling her earlobe until she shivered. "This is nice enough," I murmured back. "But our wedding will be better."

She pulled back a little to raise her eyebrows at me, her grin wide. "Our wedding? That's not a proposal, is it?"

"Not yet. When I propose, I'm planning to sweep you off your feet."

She moved closer to kiss me. "You already have," she whispered. "Thank you for making me part of your family. I've never been happier."

I lifted a hand to touch the face of the woman I loved more than words could ever describe. "We could have a family of our own, if you'd like." I held my breath for her answer, a sudden vision of her cradling a baby making my heart expand with hope.

Her face lit up in response, the glow in her eyes giving her excitement away. "I'd like that." She laughed a little. "I'd really like that."

"Me, too." I kissed her for a long time, my kiss a promise of all we had ahead of us. The family we'd create together, the life we'd share, and the memories we'd treasure.

Finally, with a sigh, Iola nestled against me. Carlotta was still in Mason's lap, watching her mother dance with our father with a look of puzzled amazement, and Kade was whispering something to Natalie that was making her blush. I put both arms around Iola, smiling at my brothers.

They smiled back at me, both looking as content as I'd ever seen them.

Whatever trials or challenges life might bring, there was one thing I knew for sure. All three of us Lennox brothers were exceptionally lucky in love.

# Author's Note

Thank you for reading Asher and Iola's story.

Want more light-hearted romance? The other books in the Lennox Brothers series are No Funny Business and No Laughing Matter. Or try the first book in the Lantana Island series, Boss With Benefits. It's set on a tropical island and is guaranteed to make you smile.

To get updates on new books, and to be notified when I have sales or special deals, head to my website: www.taliahunter.com

# Also by Talia Hunter

## THE LENNOX BROTHERS ROMANTIC COMEDY SERIES

**No Funny Business**
**No Laughing Matter**
**No Fooling Around**

## THE LANTANA ISLAND SERIES

**Boss With Benefits**
**The Engagement Game**
**The Devil She Knew**

# About the Author

Bestselling romance author Talia Hunter likes to include her three favorite things in her novels: toe-curling romance, snort-laughs, and heart-warming friendships.

She recently moved to Australia, where she's constantly amazed and not at all freaked out by the weird and wonderful critters. When she's not writing, you can usually find her with a glass of wine, a good book, and a jumbo-sized can of bug spray.

She loves to laugh, and if you feel the same way you can keep up with her new releases and special deals by visiting her website.

www.taliahunter.com

Copyright © 2021 by Talia Hunter

All rights reserved.

No part of this book may be reproduced in any form or by any electronic or mechanical means, including information storage and retrieval systems, without written permission from the author, except for the use of brief quotations in a book review.

Printed in Poland
by Amazon Fulfillment
Poland Sp. z o.o., Wrocław